KNOCKING

ON HEAVEN'S

DOOR

KNOCKING
ON HEAVEN'S
DOOR

A NOVEL

SHARMAN APT RUSSELL

YUCCA

Yucca Publishing books may be purchased in bulk at special discounts for sales promotion, corporate gifts, fund-raising, or educational purposes. Special editions can also be created to specifications. For details, contact the Special Sales Department, Yucca Publishing, 307 West 36th Street, 11th Floor, New York, NY 10018 or yucca@skyhorsepublishing.com.

Yucca Publishing® is an imprint of Skyhorse Publishing, Inc.®, a Delaware corporation.

Visit our website at www.yuccapub.com.

10 9 8 7 6 5 4 3 2 1

Library of Congress Cataloging-in-Publication Data is available on file.

Cover design and cover illustration by Ivan Zanchetta

Print ISBN: 978-1-63158-068-0
Ebook ISBN: 978-1-63158-077-2

Printed in the United States of America

To all writing teachers past, present, and future

KNOCKING
ON HEAVEN'S
DOOR

PART ONE

Brad understood why The Return had become sacred to the tribes. One hundred fifty years ago, the supervirus had wiped out almost every human being on the planet. In response—combining the power of the worldwide web with the psychic comfort of hunting and gathering—the survivors had recreated a Paleoterrific lifestyle, a stable and flourishing culture. Humans lived peacefully now among the resurrected Paleos. They beat their little drums and sang their heritage songs and decorated their camel skin tents. Moreover, the latest discoveries in physics only confirmed their cultural animism. Utopia! They had already forgotten the lesson they were supposed to learn.

CHAPTER ONE

CLARE

Clare breathed in the smell of blood. Sharp, metallic, in the air, on her skin. She slipped her knife into the space between the joint and bone of the mare's hip—a small young female but still too much meat, more than enough for their next few days of hunting. Tonight she and Jon would feast on the rump with garlic and onion, some saltbush leaves, perhaps a mint paste. If they followed the stream east, they might find watercress. Clare felt happy thinking about her dinner. She felt . . . lust. A fervent yearning. Her mouth filled with saliva. A violent tenderness. Her heart expanded, blossomed, pressed against her ribcage so that she mewled without sound, kittenish. She slunk forward, barely in control, through the grass . . .

No, no, these were not her thoughts.

"Cat! Cat!" Clare yelled and stood, dropping the knife, picking up her spear from the bloodied ground. Her hunting companion rushed to join her, his spear also in his hand.

"Where?" Jon asked.

On the rock ledge above them. Of course, a perfect place for sleeping and drowsing and waiting for prey. Clare and Jon would never have lingered near such a ledge if that weren't where the mare had been, their own chosen prey, the foolish young female separated from her herd and resting in the shade. Clare pointed and began backing away, always facing the low rock cliff. Jon understood and fanned off to the side.

Muck-a-luck. Clare's hands were wet with blood. She took the time to dry her palms on her leather shirt. The saber-toothed cat was still slinking, still seconds away, his presence betrayed by that telepathic, reckless yearning. No one knew why these hunters and scavengers lusted for human flesh the way they did. Some receivers in the tribe claimed this was more than hunger and more like love, a desire to be *with* humans, *bonded* with humans, *inside* each other. Clare found herself muttering, "You'd like me to be inside you, would you?" as she pushed down her fear and gathered up her anger. This was her mare, not his, her life, not his. He could have the mare when she was done. She had a tasty dinner planned. She was on a hunting trip with a friend. She had worked hard and deserved this.

Clare estimated the distance, backed up some steps, and tightened her grip on the spear. When the cat leaped from the ledge, landed, and raced toward her, she would have to strike in one of two places.

There. That thump on the ground, heavy body, paws on dirt. Clare shifted to a slightly different angle. The blur of movement running. Her own rush of terror. I-adore-you, the big cat spoke clearly in her mind. I-love-you. I-want-you. Clare aimed for that thought— thought that could travel in waves—and threw hard into a liquid eye. Jon's spear drove hard, too, slipping between ribs and slicing lung, so that the blurred form jerked, stabbed on two sides and seemingly pinned to the air. Motionless before toppling over, unconscious, and then dead.

4

"Are there more?" Jon panted. Saber-tooths often hunted in family groups.

Clare shook her head. Her hands were trembling now, and she sat on the ground. But Jon's release was different, an adrenaline kick of energy as he stretched out the saber-toothed cat to measure the length, 170 centimeters, looking at the teeth, 25 centimeters, estimating weight, 200 kilograms. An adolescent male, Jon proclaimed. Not particularly big. Most likely chased away by one of the other males in his family. Not thin or ill but inexperienced. Lonely and stupid.

Clare already knew this from listening to the cat's thoughts. She sometimes forgot that Jon was a mute. That didn't prevent him from being a good hunter. Paleos were not nearly as common as the modern natives—deer, elk, antelope, buffalo—or the imported species—horses, camels, African lions. In any case, no one hunted the Paleolithic animals. How could you hunt someone you could talk to?

Jon sang the butcher's song and finished carving out the mare's choice parts, wrapping the meat in her own skin, filling their packs. There was no question of disturbing or skinning the saber-toothed cat. Clare let the fear echo and fade somewhere in her chest as she stood and took her turn as guard. Before leaving, they looked back at the bodies, much of the mare still intact, opened and welcoming to the scavengers waiting for their share, the direwolf in the scrub brush, the teratorns circling above. The saber-toothed cat could have fed on this meal, too, roaring to scare away the other animals, gulping the still-warm flesh, his long canine teeth too fragile to break bone. But he had chosen another path, perhaps for something that resembled love. The big cats were a mystery.

The rest of the trip was uneventful, although Clare would have reason later to remember the last day's hike back to their summer camp.

Of the two omens, the first was ordinary—a flock of crows blocking the light. Jon heard the cries *ka-ka-kroack* and sound of wings and turned to look behind him, pointing to the black belt undulating in the blue sky, bearing down on the sun like some mythical monster. Muck-a-luck, Clare thought again. Crows overhead, the world growing dark, crow sound, crow humor, crow feather, crow shit.

Jon raised his arms and began to scream. He specialized in crows and ravens, magpies and jays. Once Clare had watched him scold a bird trying to steal meat from the drying rack. "*Knocka-knocka-knocka,*" Jon's shoulders had hunched in the effort of a liquid gurgle while the child whose job it was to guard the rack watched intently. "*Ka-skreet!*" Jon scolded, and the unrepentant raven dove in the middle of his response, the meat dangling from its beak, the child hopping up and down. Now Jon was also hopping up and down, a strong full-grown man carrying a pack, throwing back his head and shrieking happily, "*Ka-skreeeet-ka-skreeet!*" joining in the crow-river-storm.

The light was dimming fast. They would have to stop walking now and wait out the flight of birds, which might take hours. *Ka-ka-kroak!* The crows screamed. Jon screamed. Clare felt impatient. She had things to do in camp.

Then she shook her head, shaking out those thoughts. What would her students say? She lived in abundance, the best of times, the best of worlds. Jon was right to celebrate the crows gathering in flight, practice for their winter migration. Sour-smelling drops fell on Clare's hair as she stood on the trail and untied her pack and set it on the ground: ululating, joining the wind, the black river above yellow grass, the yellow grass mixed with verbena and phlox. Jon shouted encouragement. He said something Clare copied, mimicking his *ka-ka*, his joy in the existence of crows who came winged and wild like a sign—for Jon would surely see this as a sign, Clare knew, of something good or bad about to happen, something obvious they should do, like prepare for the journey to their own winter camp.

And he would be right. Something good or bad *would* surely happen. Someone would be injured. Someone would conceive. The tribe would move to a warmer valley in the east. Clare screamed with gratitude, throat muscles straining, feet lifting. People like Jon were always right. The world formed a pattern, interconnected, interdependent. She, he, saber-toothed cat, mare, crows, without separation.

She hopped and hoped even so that the birds would fly fast. After a week in the field, she longed to be in her tent, bathed and dressed in clean clothes. She was hungry for something other than mare. She had the story about the saber-toothed cat to tell around the camp-fire and a few things to tell her girlfriends (about Jon, yes) and she was eager—she had to admit—to get back to her other work, for the pure lighted screen of her solarcomp and orderly appearance of papers scrolling down, each paper turned in on time, each a gem of rhetoric and composition. Clare cawed. Not likely! But the assignment was an important one, especially in this anniversary year. The subject of The Return evoked the best and worst responses from her advanced writing group, students of all ages but mostly teenagers ready to move past the mandatory courses in literacy. The sooner she saw what María had managed to write after weeks of procrastination and whether Dimitri had written anything at all, the better she would feel. She had a lot of grading to do. She wanted to get started.

And then it *was* hours before they were released from darkness, well spattered, Jon still smiling. Clare set a faster pace now—until close to the summer camp, when she stopped and held up her hand. She heard the baby cry, monotonously, whimpering with pain. Help-me, help-me, momma, momma. The mother groaned in anguish and anger. Monsoon rains had softened the soil of the can-yon's edge, soft soil that gave with the calf's weight, rocks slithering under padded feet, causing the calf to land awkwardly on his front leg, rolling, bruising, thudding to the bottom of the streambed. The fall was not far. The fall did not kill the baby. The mother groaned as she made her way down, half sliding, her hairy rump scouring the ground clear of pebbles and thorny plants. She ignored the discomfort, the recklessness—she was not a reckless animal! Not someone to hurry like this. She lifted her trunk as she rushed to stand and sway back and forth before the baby, his leg twisted beneath him, the bone exposed.

I-saw, I-saw, the baby cried, something-beautiful.

The vibration in Clare's head was so loud she almost swayed back and forth, too. Her head hummed unpleasantly. "A female mammoth," she said to Jon. "A kilometer away. Her calf . . . I don't know . . . saw something and went toward it, slipped down a canyon."

"Two mammoths," Jon repeated.

The baby wept. Clare felt the pain as an idea, not in her own body. Please-momma-please.

"So?" Jon shifted the pack on his back. Female mammoths were not dangerous, and they were not meat.

"If we . . ." Clare hesitated. The mother would guard her son from predators until he died from thirst. The mother would sway back and forth and murmur comforting sounds and touch the baby's face. The mother would not leave for any reason, not for her own thirst or hunger, not because of any danger—a pride of lion or shortfaced bear. The mother could not, of course, set the calf's bone. Nor would she let Clare do that. Mammoths didn't like human beings. Even if Clare could make the animal understand that she only wanted to help, that she could save the baby, even then the mammoth wouldn't want, wouldn't comprehend, this kind of help. If an injury did not heal on its own. If a tooth cracked. If a child was born weak or deformed . . . Clare felt the leather bag around her neck.

"He has only Thee," she quoted the Costa Rican Quakers.

"How does that apply?" Jon wondered.

"It doesn't," Clare said and continued walking.

8

This second omen was different, a genuine prognostic. But Clare did not recognize that at the time.

Her tentmates were out dancing. From inside the camel skins, Clare could hear the drums. *Whump-whump-whump.* She was too tired to read but sat cross-legged in bed, solarcomp on lap, and looked quickly at the first few papers. Some of her students had approached the assignment as a summary, describing the supervirus in such a matter-of-fact tone that the death of almost every human being on the planet became just one more world war or melting ice cap. A few had their facts wrong. "The Return," one student concluded, "was a natural result of the near extinction of the human race, a kind of silver lining in a stormy cloud since we have all gone back now to a better way of living harmoniously on the earth."

Clare exhaled. The Return was not a natural result at all. The Return had been sheer breathtaking serendipity. She skimmed through the topics the others had chosen to highlight: the over-heating of nuclear reactors, the compromise insisted on by the Los Alamos Three, the extraordinary decision to abandon guns and motor vehicles. Nothing she hadn't seen before. She paused at Jon's work on animism. Yes, he had included the latest TOE or Theory of Everything. Jon was a cultural animist, not a scientific one, but she was relieved to see he gave physics its due.

Powering down the solarcomp, Clare felt guilty. Should she feel guilty? Jon was not one of the younger students. No one could object to their having sex. She was a widow, after all. Okay, yes, Jon's wife was still alive . . . but everyone knew the marriage had failed and the woman was living with another man. And Jon was sweet, a good singer around the fire, a good hunter, even a good student. Clare thought of his paper, which had depended perhaps too much on figurative language. Still, he must have worked hard to have it ready before their trip.

She thought of Jon now at the campfire, bragging about the saber-toothed cat. The force of their spears. The sight of the cat stopped so suddenly, motionless in the air. Clare nestled into her bed, unkinking muscles, curling and uncurling toes. The drums were beginning to fade. One more slow dance. At the last unkink, she pinpointed her source of guilt: she felt as excited about Jon's paper as she had about anything in their new love affair.

Now she reached for the bearskin she used as a pillow, a scrawny black bear her husband had killed a decade ago when their daughter was born. Preparing for sleep, she searched among her favorite images of Elise, the one with the garland of flowers, the one by the river of shells. The bawling calf intruded into the scene. But there was nothing she could have done. Calves died. Daughters died. Clare touched the leather bag around her neck. Six years and the grief fading like the drums. The women in the tribe had said this would happen. They hadn't mentioned how much else would fade, too.

A Bed of Bone, a Sea of Ash, submitted by María Escobar

Our assignment is to write about The Return and I have thought a long time about this. I found it very hard to do this assignment and then I realized that it was because my mind keeps going round and round and round about what happened before The Return when almost everyone in the world had to die and there were billions of bodies lying in the streets and in their homes rotting and filling up with disease. Men, women, and children just dropped where they were and lay on the ground. People couldn't take care of each other because the supervirus struck them down so hard and so fast—like a bolt of lightning! No one knows where it came from. Maybe from a mutation in our viral-powered batteries and electrical stations since none of those things worked afterward. Or maybe it was made by someone who just hated the human race! Whatever the reason, all those people died and all those people were just like me with their own hopes and dreams, their special way of thinking about things. Maybe their lives weren't as good as mine because they lived in a polluted world with constant wars and not enough food and water for everyone but they were still people and the fact is that my life is so good now because they died and made room for me and for all the other animals and plants. They had to die so we could have The Return and live like we do on a planet in balance with the right number of people and with social institutions like the quest and the Council and the elders and the right way to do things. But still it seems sad that this had to happen and I sometimes think we are all standing on a big graveyard, that we all live on a bed of bones and a sea of ash. I know I am turning in this assignment late but I hope you will still read and count it as part of my work in your evaluation of me as a student. I do need to be positively evaluated so I can go on my long quest next year and so I am turning this in late even though I know it is really late.

The Founder Effect,
submitted by Alice Featherstone

Our assignment this week is to write about The Return, summarizing in four hundred words or less "the key elements that came together to create one of humanity's most singular and impressive achievements." Hah. That was an easy forty words.

In the late twenty-first century, scientists produced the first clones of extinct animals like the mastodon and glyptodont. The big surprise was that some of these Paleos were telepathic. The existence of thought that could move in waves sent physicists off in a new direction, with the dream of unifying quantum mechanics with the electrifying principles of panpsychism; at the same time, the idea of speaking to animals caught fire in the public imagination. Paleos were the latest and biggest cultural phenomena. More importantly for us today, Pleistocene Play Parks in North America and Mongolia expanded our understanding of the Paleolithic lifestyle, that grand period of almost two million years during which human beings evolved and flourished as hunters and gatherers.

In the early twenty-second century, when the super-virus hit the earth like a bolt of lightning, a conference of Pleistocene scholars at St. Petersburg, Russia hid for six months in an antique bunker readied for nuclear attack. These academics, people from all over the world, developed and pushed forward the idea of The Return. Meanwhile, a group of computer scientists in the southwestern United States lived for almost a year in a more sophisticated bunker prepared in case of biological warfare. These men and women were committed to maintaining the planetary wireless web which allowed the few survivors left to communicate with each other. At the same time, an extended family of Quakers in Costa Rica carried the exquisitely rare gene of immunity. These Friends relied on their civic beliefs; as Quakers, they insisted on consensus and worked around-the-muck sending out long-winded emails exhorting humanity to live harmoniously on the earth, forsaking the viral technology and intra-species violence that had crushed us like lice between your grandmother's fingers.

The Return was a result of this founder effect, three populations kept connected by radio signals and the solarcomps. Although other groups in Africa and elsewhere died out or disappeared from the worldwide web, those of us committed to The Return survived. The re-creation of a Paleoterrific lifestyle, innate to our species, is our "final utopia;" or as the Russian tribes say, "We are home."

Let me conclude, after 395 words, that we've reached the anniversary of our 150th year and we still can't stop talking about how great we are.

A Question, submitted by Carlos Salas

I wonder if you would send us a new picture of yourself? I have just had the honor of participating in the Council elections, which as you know can be lengthy among the Costa Rican Quakers and are quite unlike your elections by majority rule in the Los Alamos tribes. This was my first time in the silence since I have proven myself as a young adult and I would like to thank you for your guidance in helping me reach clearness through my writing. During this process, the posted photos of the Council members struck me as particularly useful for we are, of course, visual animals highly attuned to nuances of the face and body. And this made me think of you and the fact that we have not had a recent image of you in many years.

CHAPTER TWO

DOG

Dog thought of himself as a dog because that is how Luke thought of him, as the kind of loyal beloved pet that Luke had read about on his solarcomp when he was a child in the lab—the indomitable robot Trevor of the *Trevor* series published just before the supervirus, a motorized dog but still recognizably canine with lolling tongue and metallic bark; Lucy, the Staunch Standard Poodle, heroine of the urban penthouse; Günter, the German Shepherd, fighting crime and terrorism; and many other, older stories, Lassie the Border Country, Flipper the dolphin.

Dog reminded himself that dolphins were not dogs. Dolphins ruled the sea. Dog wasn't sure if that was his mistake or Luke's. As often as not, his thoughts became images tangled up with words and the words sometimes crossed meanings like two ants exchanging smells, each heading off in the opposite direction. Luke did that, exchanging *boy* for *girl* and *flipper* for *paw*, and since their minds were a bit too enmeshed, Dog suffered from Luke's confusions.

Like thinking he was a dog instead of a direwolf, a true Paleo altered slightly by a few mutations that affected him—to be honest— more than slightly. Dog began scratching the fur on his neck with his left hind-foot claws. Most direwolves had four claws on each foot while he had five. Most direwolves, like Dog himself, were heavy-muscled, wide-shouldered, big-jawed, sharp-teethed scavengers. But unlike him, most didn't have a mind that sometimes left its borders, Border Country Lassie! and so didn't have Luke and sometimes Lucia tangling in his head, wheelboarding through neural synapses (what was wheelboarding?) and flooding his dendrites with memories that didn't come from him, not from his hormones, not his receptors.

Dog scratched, releasing a cloud of fleas. Fleas, Dog thought without much interest. Their DNA was relatively simple: adenine, thymine, guanine, cytosine. The helix zipping and unzipping. Sending and receiving. Dog was obsessed with DNA, having first learned about this magnificent double molecule from Lucia and since that day making it entirely his own, calculating the genetic sequence of fleas and trees and bees and snow geese, species he stored away in a file (what was a file?) somewhere in his brain. Dog felt lucky that so much DNA filled the world, so many different kinds of flexible comb-like strands of nucleotides twisted about each other like snakes in a den fitting together, interlocking, sending out signals, receiving signals. The weak and the strong hydrogen bonds.

Lucia, the weak and the strong, spending years in her den at the lab studying DNA and then later, when she left the lab and became Luke, mourning the flaws in her biohologram, the lack of a penis where she felt there should be one, where she could imagine that fleshy tubular structure protruding so clearly that it seemed, voilà! there it was! (What was voilà?) Luke/Lucia were obsessed with their genitalia. Dog understood. Who wasn't?

But neither Luke nor Lucia had the ability to see DNA as Dog did, the alpha male of this obsession: a mental image of twisty ribbony codes, the teeth of the code always pairing the same way—complementary, protruding, nitrogenous bases—but varying, too, in their seemingly infinite electro arrangements. The helices appeared whenever Dog focused on a living creature, the focus usually triggered by smell, but sometimes—like this flea—by movement or color or even sound. A lion's cough in the night. Lion: thymine, adenine, cytosine, guanine. A water spider on the scum of a pond. Water spider: cytosine, guanine, cytosine, guanine.

The flea hopped from one hair to another hair on Dog's flank as Dog tilted his head and turned to sniff the cloud of insects. The DNA in this flea was a little different. An error in replication. This flea would live a little longer than other fleas and lay more eggs and breed more fleas, and some of them would live longer and lay more eggs and breed more fleas. Who would all live longer because of this change in a single gene.

Dog felt conflicted. He adored mutations! Still he snapped at the flea, hoping to crush it between his teeth.

Dog! He could hear Luke calling.

Luke, he answered, don't get your pants wet.

Inspired, Dog urinated on a patch of prickly pear. Luke would probably have rabbit for dinner. They ate rabbit almost every night.

Prickly pear: adenine, thymine. Dog inhaled the satisfying odor of himself: phenol, ammonia, steroids. He began to trot, half hurrying, half not, toward the campsite that Luke had set up for the night. The nights turning slightly colder now, the cold welcome, not a stranger.

Halfway home, skirting the edges of an eroded canyon, Dog saw the column of light three meters tall and thin, a stick of glow floating above the ground. The hairs on Dog's neck stood up. His head lowered. His eyes slitted. His ears lay flat. He was ready for an attack!

Although there was nothing to attack. Only a thin stick of glowing light.

But that light . . . Dog trembled. The stick of light disappeared. Dog whined. Superstitiously he backtracked, another longer way to Luke.

On seeing him, the crabby old man picked up a real stick as if to beat Dog for being late. Forget it, Dog said. He wasn't a pup anymore. The crabby old man grabbed Dog by the long guard hairs on his neck. Dog twisted and turned his head, trying to bite the man's arm, growling deep—a very satisfying growl after his pathetic whining just a short while ago—and managed to nip a little flesh. The old man yelled and shook harder, not letting go. Dog scrabbled with his feet and surprised the old man by lunging forward, hitting Luke's knees with his shoulders, bringing the human down with a thud. This was very *very* satisfying. Now the grip on Dog's neck loosened and Dog could reach the crabby old face. He bared his teeth, his long yellow fangs dripping saliva.

"No, no," Luke pleaded. Dog almost howled with pleasure. A surge of adrenaline. Dopamine! Oxytocin! "No," Luke commanded, but Dog began to lick his face, long swoops of tongue over leathery skin. "Get off me!" Luke said. "That's enough!"

Dog felt an intense surge of love, so that his penis stiffened.

Normally the crabby old man would give up now and roll on the ground to protect his eyes and mouth. But today Luke reached down to grab Dog's back feet, giving them a squeeze. Dog was startled and fell to the side as Luke came up, lifting paws from the ground. "Hah!" Luke struggled to a standing position, still holding Dog's back legs. The crabby old man had won this round. Payback, Dog warned him. Luke laughed out loud.

They ate rabbit that night, meat that Luke had snared and cooked over a fire. Dog leaned hard against Luke's leg as though wanting more food although in fact he was full. Rabbit: adenine, adenine, adenine. He just wanted to feel Luke's hard shin bone, and then he wanted Luke to rub down his fur with his long hand, and then he wanted Luke to cup his muzzle and shake it lightly back and forth, and then he wanted Luke to thump his hindquarters, and then he wanted Luke to remove the tick from his shoulder, and then he wanted Luke to flatten his fur again, all the way down his body with his long hard hand.

The moon shone yellow, round and full, a pregnant woman, a gourd full of seed. Luke felt nostalgic and became Lucia after dinner, the crabby old man as serene wise woman. Lucia's voice was higher and her pets softer, more gentle, and Dog liked them, too. He wanted to talk now about the glowing stick of light. Remembering, he saw it again. The stick had been a flower glowing, floating, vertical, a flower stem three meters long, topped by a composite of smaller flowers, each ovule fertilized and forming a seed. Sunflower: guanine, cytosine, adenine, thymine. But this glowing flower didn't have DNA. None at all. Nothing there. No there. Something was very wrong with this flower.

Dog couldn't explain any of this to Lucia/Luke. Their communication was limited, based on patterns, games they already knew. On not much new. Dog leaked out feelings. Lucia leaked out words. Dog grunted and leaned hard against her leg.

Tonight she was sleeping in a tree house made of woven grass and willow branches while Dog dug a hole under a nearby mesquite. Bushkies like Luke lived without the protection of the tribe or lab. They had to protect themselves from the saber-toothed cat who liked to eat humans, from the giant shortfaced bear who liked to kill humans. Lucia petted Dog good night and climbed up to her high safe nest. A sailor boy, Dog thought, a ship's mast. But no, that was wrong. Where did that come from? Dog circled three times and slept lightly as always. Until just before dawn when he drifted into something deep and dark, a beautiful extinction.

That's when they attacked. The male threw a yucca net over Dog's face, half blinding him. They must have been watching Luke/Lucia because they knew Dog was there, they knew where he slept, guarding her through the night. He couldn't understand why he hadn't caught their scent. Why he hadn't heard them? The female and boy began beating him with clubs as he floundered from under the dangling mesquite pods. The blows landed on his ribs and rump, on his head. He pawed and bit frantically at the spiky rope. Surging to his feet, he threw the netting aside.

The humans were covered in mud and leaves, their skin rubbed with skunk cabbage. Now he smelled them. Skunk cabbage: the double helix roiled, dipped, unzipped. They carried clubs and moved back, forming a half circle. They were not genetically related. Dog could smell that, too. The male radiated contempt, the female, fear. The boy was chaotic. There was no love between them, only craziness. Only the bushkies left the tribe, and hardly any could stand each other. Dog had never heard of three bushkies together.

Dog snarled.

"Scramscramscramscram!" the larger male yelled.

The boy threw a rock, which hit Dog in the shoulder. Another bruise. A bone could crack. He might lose an eye. Perhaps he should rush them, growling and biting? Dog shivered. He had teeth. He was stronger. He could scare them away. But he was a coward. That was the problem. Direwolves had that gene, the scavenger gene, sneaking through grass when an animal died, creeping and cunning when something was killed by another hunter. Not the hunter himself, not the killer himself, but sneakily, constantly prowling the edges. Scraps and remains. Marrow in the bones, tendons and joints. There was always something left when the lions were done. There was always something rotting somewhere in the grass. The direwolf snuck, snatched, escaped.

Dog couldn't help himself. Luke! he shouted in warning. Lucia! He howled. The boy picked up another stone. The female swung her club in the air. Dog bolted. He was built to run away.

CHAPTER THREE

BRAD

Brad sat in his office wishing he were famous. Centuries ago, he would have been famous, perhaps as famous as Einstein or Copernicus, although that level of fame was not really necessary. Brad's long legs stretched out, cramped under the wooden desk, as he brooded in his wooden chair, staring out at the sunflowers crowded up to the window, their yellow petals radiating power, the dark-brown centers bursting with seed. He wanted to be admired— he squinted at the flowers, over two meters high, as tall as he was. He wanted his name to light up someone's face, for his email to get that awed response: Brad! *You're* the guy . . .

People in the lab knew, of course. But they never spoke about it anymore and all the papers and emails sent out to the population centers in Russia and Costa Rica were strictly anonymous, in accord with the theory that science and ambition should not be encouraged. Achievements were dangerous. The desire for fame was dangerous. Brad's longing felt inchoate. But with a sharpness at the core. He had put it all together when he was in his twenties, a decade ago, the universe as a four-dimensional image formed of waves that were themselves formed by electromagnetic and quantum processes. The vast substratum, the consciousness of the universe—waves and frequencies—organizing and projecting what was experienced as the physical world. The holographic principle.

Brad's mood shifted. He felt himself relax. The holographic principle. Simple holograms were produced through interference, two or more waves passing through each other to create a pattern. The holograms of the twenty-first century had split a laser beam in two, bouncing one beam off an object and letting the beams collide to create an interference pattern on photographic film. By passing another light through that film, the original image reappeared in three dimensions. Later, scientists would discover the biohologram, the way DNA used frequencies and interferences to organize a three-dimensional body, the way the double helix acted as a radio sending and receiving, a holographic projector of electromagnetic information, organizing billions of cells in constant non-physical communication. Quantum non-locality. A complex electromagnetic field.

Then Brad had put it all together. Yes, *he* had done that! The sunflower outside his window existed on all levels of physics, very large (gravity) to very small (quantum mechanics), in three dimensions (matter/energy/consciousness), in four dimensions (time), and in five dimensions (consciousness/the holographic principle). TOE. The Theory of Everything. Five additional dimensions were relatively unimportant. The human mind could not make sense of them all. But math could. His math could.

"Still sulking?" A least favorite colleague bounced into the room. She looked at the bright side of things. She was that type.

Brad moved to keep her away from his computer, talking as a distraction. "I shouldn't have to do this. I could die."

"Maybe." Briefly his colleague smiled, as though that might be the bright side of things. "But most people don't. Everyone has to do this. You've avoided it for as long as anyone I know."

"I have bad eyesight."

"You're getting a guide. You'll have lots of help."

"I hate sleeping in trees."

"Well, that's the point, isn't it?" The least favorite colleague laughed outright. "You've become alienated from the cultural fabric, Brad, from who and what we are as a people—as a species. If ever there was a reason for the quest, you are that reason."

By now, Brad had effectively blocked her from his screen. Blah, blah, blah, he thought, rearranging her on his hierarchy of least favorite, putting her down even lower than before. This meant elevating certain others, which was problematic. "I'm sure you're wrong," he said smoothly.

"You'll come back a better person." His colleague was really grinning now. "That would be good for everyone."

Only a few remaining juniper, rough-barked giants, dotted the hills surrounding the lab. In the last two hundred years, most of northern New Mexico had returned to grassland, the forests burning and dying, the rustling yellow grass—blue grama and black grama, sideoats grama and hairy grama—flowing out like water dipping and rolling with wind and swells, punctuated by the occasional green tree and pink rock cliff, dominated by the bright blue sky. Brad felt a familiar ache in his rib cage. Nothing so pretty as this view.

Just behind the hills, the city of Los Alamos blighted the landscape. Scavenger parties went there reluctantly. No one liked the sad cities, and some receivers insisted they could feel the sadness, which had a color like smoke. Brad suspected they were simply projecting their emotions. He was a receiver himself and had been to Los Alamos more than once.

Walking slowly, carrying a leather pack, spear in hand, Brad turned to look back at the lab and its cluster of adobe buildings. He and the other lab rats lived full-time at the compound while the other half of their community, another hundred people or more, came from all over habitable North America. For a few months, they helped produce the solarcomps, monitoring the satellites that orbited the earth, keeping the balance, and then happy to leave and not return, back to their wandering tribes. Brad never understood that.

He adjusted his eyeglasses. The feel of nanoplastic against thumb. He wondered, not for the first time, if plastic was as conscious as wood. Scavenger material. Was there any difference between "natural" objects and those made by humans? Experiments in the late twenty-first century had indicated not.

Ahead of him, his guide seemed to pause, as if waiting. At their introduction this morning, he had felt her staring at his face. "Yes, they are called glasses." Brad had nodded pleasantly. "Taken from dead people."

No doubt she made everything herself, the deerskin tunic and pants decorated with plant dye, the spear carved from wood with an obsidian point, all the fetishes and artwork of The Return. She looked older than Brad felt himself to be or at least more weathered, sun bronzed, sun beaten, with those wrinkle lines around her mouth and eyes. Her braid was striking, however, that long thick brown hair. Those dark brown eyes. The mouth nicely shaped with lips that curved up in a slight bow. That was interesting. And her features were symmetrical.

As he followed the swinging brown braid, Brad thought now of amending himself: the glasses were not taken from dead people but from a specialized store with a drawer of eyeglasses kept as novelty items since people in the twenty-second century mostly had their eyes lasered, with the wealthy getting their genes changed, too. The glasses were an old-fashioned technology and would, someday, finally run out. Brad had already mentioned this to the Council, how the lab must eventually start grinding lenses. How Spinoza in the sixteenth century had been a lens grinder, telescope lenses and microscope lenses, the first Westerner to use a geometric proof to define God, define substance, define finite and infinite, showing by logic and definition that God was an infinite being composed of one substance who contained everything, everything created from that divine substance. Who had said, "We are all modes in the Body of Being." Energy mode, consciousness mode, matter mode. Nothing was outside the Body of Being. There could be no Creator outside Creation. It was not exactly TOE but the beginning of TOE as explored by Einstein and Bohm and all the great physicists to follow.

His guide waited more obviously now for him to catch up, her expression careful not to show impatience. Pleasantly, Brad nodded at her again. He recognized the stoic impassivity of the tribes, alternating with Dionysian celebration. He would have to insist on his right to think during the next few weeks. Her job was to watch out for him. His job was to think, despite what her elders said.

"Do you need to rest?" the woman asked.

Brad waved a magnanimous hand, and she led him away from the view, down one hill, up the next. He walked behind and huffed a little but still kept the pace, his stride longer than hers after all. Surreptitiously, he watched her bare legs, the rippling movement of calf muscle. He was in better physical shape than she or anyone else thought. He lifted weights in his office. He ran laps in the compound. He had even spent the last few months practicing with his spear. He hated sleeping in trees, and he was frightened, yes, of being eaten alive by a lion or giant shortfaced bear. Who wouldn't be? But avoiding the quest all these years had become more of a game than anything else, manipulating the Council, seeing how much he could get away with.

"When do we camp?" he called ahead, partly to slow the woman down. The afternoon light was already turning yellow, mid-October, and the days shorter.

"Maybe we'll walk through the night," she shot back. Brad felt a mild alarm. She was his guide, and she was in charge. She could make him walk through the night if she decided that this was part of his quest, something he needed to do to come back a better person. Every member of the human tribe—and he was a member, Brad admitted, even lab rats were members—had to go out into the world alone or with a guide for weeks at a time, every two years, every four years. Keeping the balance. Keeping humble, keeping alert, connected, unsafe. The principles of The Return.

He hadn't done this since he was fourteen years old.

Instead he had been busy discovering the secrets of the universe. Did she know that? Brad hurried to catch up. What was her name again? "We met so quickly before," he said, at her side. "When did you do your service in the lab?"

The woman seemed amused. "A long time ago, when I was a teenager. You were there. A teenager, too."

"I'm sorry I don't remember you," Brad said insincerely.

"You really don't want to be here, do you?" she asked and seemed genuinely curious, without judgment.

Brad shifted his pack, his shoulders already feeling the strain. How honest should he be?

"I don't either," the woman answered for him, and now she did slow down so they could talk. Her clothes were decorated with red spirals. Brad found himself counting the red dots. "Guides get information first, about who they are taking. You haven't ever done any serious hunting. You exercise some but not much. You wouldn't be able to walk comfortably through the night. You don't know much about the plants and animals in this area. You've spent your life in the lab. As my student, as a hunting partner, you could get me killed."

Her tone was neutral. Her eyes kept moving back and forth— scanning the grass, the bushes, the horizon. She was looking for something to eat or for something that might want to eat them.

Brad remembered walking like this beside his mother, listening to her explain how there were secrets everywhere. He had also watched her scan the horizon, and he had felt safe because he was with her, because he was a child walking this very hill perhaps, this blue sky, this yellow grass. His mother had been on his mind lately—the anniversary tomorrow, and he wouldn't be home, wouldn't light the candles or honor her spirit. He remembered his mother on her deathbed. The cancer had taken over, and she mumbled incoherently. Soon after, working through the night, he had written the equations that resolved the holographic principles of four different theories, starting with Einstein's. It was as though her death had liberated him, as though death were his inspiration.

"You're wrong about the plants and animals," he corrected the woman. "I know them pretty well."

"You've *read* about them?" she emphasized the verb.

Brad suddenly felt tired of her. "Do you have something against reading?"

The woman whose name he couldn't remember smiled. "No. Actually, I teach reading and writing. Mostly I work with students who probably do have something against it, against too much reading anyway, too much writing." She thought about that for a moment. "What they like is what we are doing now. This . . ." she gestured. They had reached the top of the next hill, a large valley opening below them. Grazing herds spread across the yellow grass, an extended family of camels, a large group of elk, another of horses, each group a careful distance from the other. There was plenty of grass for everyone, with only mild discomfort that they had to share. Flocks of birds swirled above the animals, dots of black rising and falling. A range of mountains seemed to fill the eastern sky.

Is that where we're going? Brad wondered. She was in charge. He hated that.

"This is what stirs them and me," the woman said. "We live in abundance, the best of times, the best of worlds. Thousands of years and billions of deaths to reach this beauty, this wealth, this diversity—to hold it in our hands. All of history has brought us to this moment, and if the burden is great and the cost high, then the prize—this moment—is even greater. If Thee cannot see that, what can Thee see or know or understand?"

The woman quoted the Costa Rican Quakers and looked at him sideways. Her tutelage was beginning. It wasn't only about survival.

And Brad found himself nodding. Of course, he understood why The Return had become sacred to the tribes. One hundred fifty years ago, the supervirus had wiped out almost every human being on the planet. In response—combining the power of the worldwide web with the psychic comfort of hunting and gathering—the survivors had recreated a Paleoterrific lifestyle, a stable and flourishing culture. Humans lived peacefully now among the resurrected Paleos. They beat their little drums and sang their heritage songs and decorated their camelskin tents. Moreover, the latest discoveries in physics only confirmed their cultural animism. Utopia! They had already forgotten the lesson they were supposed to learn.

Brad looked at his guide and wondered, frankly, at her ignorance. Oh, he had a hundred replies for her, all the ways their wonderful world balanced on a knife blade, about to fall and crash. Humpty Dumpty sat on a wall. He could quote the Quaker proverbs, too. He opened his mouth. She looked back at him and waited, her mouth curved slightly in a bow. The afternoon light colored the grass. He smelled something sweet and tangy, some herb crushed by their passing.

In that moment—and that's how things happened for him, a glimpse of something bright and luminous, a flash of inspiration followed by years of persistent effort—he felt his body lighten as though he had just taken off his pack. She was literate. She had soft round breasts. She had read the Quakers. He saw their sexual future. He would tell her about his work. She would listen admiringly and ask the right questions. They would spend hours together talking like this around the campfire, about life and history, about everything.

"How old are you?" he blurted. Could he possibly get this woman pregnant? Could she still have healthy children?

The woman led the way, silently now since he had made his interest too obvious. Brad was discouraged but not overly so. It had been a long time since he had felt something like this so strongly. He knew he had a difficult personality: arrogant, obnoxious, withholding, then demanding. He had gone through every possible relationship at the lab until they were all now his least and least favorites. But he had certain virtues, too. He went after what he wanted. And he didn't often fail.

Following her legs, those calf muscles working, Brad breathed more easily, going down a winding game trail to the valley below. He guessed they would be gone less than a month, not a long quest and not a short one. Someone had already calculated this. He needed enough time away from the lab to show his hunting-and-gathering prowess and to reweave himself into the fabric of their culture. One with the people. One with the species! His pack, he had been told, would feel heavier tomorrow and heavier still the day after that. But by the last day, it would be a part of his body, a weight he accepted like a leg or arm. Perhaps he would bring down an elk. Perhaps he would perform the camel dance. Perhaps his guide would sing the peyote song. Perhaps he would hallucinate, have a vision or two. Whatever was required, Brad decided now, he would oblige. He would work to please her.

The final part of their descent was through a rocky area, jagged thrusts of hardened lava and tuff, an anomaly in the undulating grass. Brad watched his feet in the scree and gravel, knowing he would feel these jolts tomorrow, the awkward angle of his back against gravity. Something brushed his ear, and he glanced to the right for no particular reason.

The tiniest of movements caught his eye, the play of shadow and light, a peripheral tease. Much later he would think that this glance aside had been the beginning. If something had not tickled his ear. If he had not stopped to peer more closely into dirt and rock. Later it comforted him to shape this into a story: the fate of the world, perhaps of the universe, hanging on a glance.

The small animal puzzled him at first. Its position was so odd. And what was the creature attached to? Brad stopped, squatted to see better, and exclaimed. Almost immediately, the guide was at his side.

Someone had stretched a white-collared lizard on its back. Someone had spread apart the lizard's front legs, lengthened out the back legs, and driven the limbs with sharpened thorns into a cross of wood as long as Brad's palm. Each leg, in addition, was wrapped with twine to prevent escape. Someone had crucified a lizard on a cross made of wood and yucca fiber. Then that someone had built a shrine, a circle of rocks that Brad saw now was a careful construction of walls dug into the ground, a miniature grotto, with the lizard propped against the larger back wall.

Brad knelt to peer into the grotto—was he mistaken somehow?— and had a dizzying twist of perspective, as if he were only as big as the lizard itself. The man-sized creature rose up in front of him, white throat pulsing, in the center of a glittering rock room, the walls embedded with silver mica and white quartz. The air smelled of dust and blood. The arms stretched out. He knelt before the sacrifice.

Brad blinked, back to his real size, kneeling on the ground. From that position, he jerked, the pack shifting so that he almost lost his balance. He yelped in pain as he put down his palm and felt skin tear against volcanic rock. The guide steadied him and then picked up the gruesome object, the lizard that was suddenly and clearly dead.

"A bushkie," the woman standing above him said. Brad got to his feet, and she handed him the cross and lizard.

He dropped them back into the grotto. "It's disgusting," he heard his voice jump too loudly. "You know who did this?"

"No, I've never seen anything like this before. But someone saw a bushkie at the other end of this valley. An old man."

"It's disgusting," Brad repeated. "How can people like that exist?'

His guide shook her head. "There aren't many of them."

"There shouldn't be any."

She stared at him. "What would you have us do?" she asked. "People are sometimes damaged. They are born that way. Should we kill them?"

Brad hesitated.

"Cage them?" the guide pressed.

Brad shook his head.

After that, they started looking and found six more tiny bodies stretched out and impaled with thorns, each enshrined by circles of rock. Some were older than the others, dried in the sun. Brad worked to keep his temper, to act like her, so calm and rational. Secretly he felt the presence of mental illness like pain in his stomach, bile in his mouth. Occasionally a man or woman left the comfort of the human tribe. Almost always they were chemically damaged. Schizophrenics. Delusional. Usually they didn't live long on their own. Their very smell attracted predators.

The guide—her name was Clare—said that the bushkie had done this over a period of months. The mummified lizards were likely from summer, the newest bodies from a week or two ago.

"You think this is some old man?" Brad confirmed.

"Yes, he's been seen," she said, leading them down into the valley to where Brad hoped was a safe place to camp. Perhaps a little shaken herself, Clare didn't insist that he hunt that evening. They ate jerky instead, cold food from her pack, and slept in a tree.

But Brad had to catch the next night's supper. He had expected this. He was already getting more help than others who went on a quest, already pampered with jerky for his first meal. For most of the day, getting supper proved harder than he had imagined, mainly because Clare was so aggravatingly cautious. She wouldn't let him approach a mare that had strayed from her group. "That herd is too close. The stallion will be here before you can bleed her," Clare said. "And he'll be angry." She insisted that camels were similarly dangerous. "Watch for antelope," she advised. "If you're good with the spear . . ." When Brad suggested snares for smaller game like rabbits and mice, Clare agreed they could do that in the evening—but too much trapping meant stopping early for camp, and she wanted to move on into the mountains.

Their luck turned when they saw the tracks of javelina. Brad led the way, grateful to be downwind, and got within thirty meters of a large family group. He hefted his spear, rose from a crouching position, adjusted his glasses, took time to aim, and launched the weapon. He missed the animal he was trying to kill. But got the one nearby!

Clare seemed impressed as the group took off, leaving an adolescent kicking on the ground. The small-tusked male showed its gums and teeth and tried to run, the air heavy with its odor. While Clare kept watch, Brad did the work of killing and butchering, remembering to remove the musk gland before cutting out enough meat for tonight and tomorrow.

"What now?" he had to ask afterward. Should he skin the javelina for its hide? How would they carry the bloody food?

His guide considered. "We'll go to the river," she decided, putting the meat back into the carcass of the animal and deftly tying its legs into a package of about forty kilos, which she attached to an outside loop on Brad's pack. The guts, gland, and offal were left in a pile. "It's not far," she assured him.

Brad felt pleased, despite the new strain on his back, and regaled Clare with plant lore for the next hour of walking. The different species of prickly pear and how to cook them. The astringent qualities of oak. The use of mullein for bladder problems.

They followed a game trail, a narrow path in the waist-high grass. The autumn sun was warm but not unpleasant. Eagles, vultures, and teratorns hunted in patterns across the blue sky. Quail whirled up like musical notes. Clare still kept watch, occasionally shushing him when she needed to listen.

"Say it," he said. "I know more than you thought I did. I know a lot about plants."

"Everyone knows a lot about plants," Clare said.

He told her how certain plants have the ability to take in toxic metals. Pennycress could store up to 25,000 parts per million of zinc. Sunflowers absorbed radioactive strontium. Sunflowers, in particular, were extraordinary. Their phytoremediation properties included . . .

Her mouth quirked further up. "I admit it!" she protested at last. She was a teacher. She appreciated research.

"Say it," he teased.

But "Here's the river. Be quiet now," she pleaded.

Rivers, Clare reminded him, had to be approached with care. Water was where predator and prey came together. Like most rivers in the American Southwest, this one was small and ephemeral, a few braided channels shaded by sycamore and cottonwood trees, lined with cattail and red-tipped willow, widened suddenly by the flood of a monsoon. Clare made the motion for silence as she led them through a tangle of underbrush and fallen trees, a new explosion of thorny seeds attaching themselves to their leather clothes and boots. The dead javelina caught on the branches of hackberry, and Brad wanted to complain but did not. The colors of the changing leaves took some of his attention: the sycamores rusty red, the cottonwoods yellow. People thought math was black and white, numbers on a page. But when he dreamed of equations, and sometimes when he wrote them, he saw color—not in the numbers but in the relationships between numbers. Colors on a continuum like these tree leaves, bright and beneficent.

At Clare's insistence, they cleaned the javelina meat quickly, lingering only to scrub their hands free of blood and fill up their leather bottles for the next day. Then they retraced their steps back into the grasslands. The waterways belonged to the lions at night, Clare said, part of the agreement between humans and lions, who knew how not to get in each other's way. When they did meet, both parties would back off slowly, the lionesses respectful although the males sometimes menaced to show their power. Since The Return, lions and humans had forged back their old relationship, as had wolves and humans. Other predators in the area could also be avoided, especially since Clare and Brad were both receivers and would sense any Paleos like the giant shortfaced bear or saber-toothed cat. Only hyenas might be a problem. Tonight, with so much wood nearby, they could put their belongings in a tree but sleep more comfortably on the ground, taking turns to keep the fire alive.

Around the campfire that evening, Brad tried to explain his ideas about color, about numbers, about red-leafed sycamores and math—a talk he had imagined and perfected in the last hour of walking.

But "I know of your work," Clare interrupted him. She tended to the roasting javelina meat, pushing it out of the direct flames. "A student of mine wrote a paper on animism." She paused. "You were mentioned."

Brad was distracted by the smell of fat in the air.

"Not directly," he said after another pause. "Not by name."

"No, of course not. But when I agreed to be your guide, I learned who you were. I don't pretend to understand your equations." Clare raised both palms to forestall more discussion on the subject. "But I appreciate what you've added to our . . . religious view."

Brad caught a certain tone and responded quickly. "You say *religious* as though you weren't religious yourself."

"I believe in the science." Clare turned the meat over.

Brad salivated.

"I understand the basic ideas," Clare went on, "an all-pervading consciousness, the vast substratum, the holographic principle. But, for me, it's abstract. Physics, not religion."

Brad acted shocked—and, in truth, he was. This was his guide? His spiritual leader? His own animism was deep and not at all abstract. Consciousness was everywhere, in everything, uniquely expressed. What, for example, was the unique consciousness of this oak behind him? He didn't know. But he would be interested in finding out. What had happened to the unique consciousness of the javelina he had killed? How was the consciousness of rock different from that of javelina? Javelina from human? It wasn't his field, and he regretted that. Math didn't work at this level.

"Don't misunderstand me . . ." Clare sat back on her haunches.

They were both salivating.

"You believe in psychology," Brad finished her thought. "Animism is good for our species. You believe in The Return."

"Don't you?" Clare asked, and although they stopped talking long enough to eat, she returned to the conversation as eagerly as he did. She didn't let him dominate, either, but had a number of strong if misguided opinions.

"Look at what we know about the Paleolithic cave paintings." Her lips gleamed, greasy in the firelight. "Their art had the same animals, the same style, the same perspective for over twenty thousand years. Twenty thousand years of a stable art and a stable culture. This is how we were meant to live."

"That's history. That's not the point," Brad informed her. "The question is if we *can* live this way. It's about change and flux. It's in my equations. We can't go back. We can't return . . ."

"Oh, muck-a-luck, that's an insult to the elders and the Council and even the Los Alamos Three. Everyone knows we can't return. You're avoiding a real debate by misinterpreting the other point of view. It's the either/or fallacy."

Brad realized his disadvantage, arguing with someone who taught writing. "I'm not saying . . ." he backtracked.

She accused him of circular reasoning. Of begging the question. Of false analogy. Concerning The Return, she stayed firmly on point—that three uniquely different populations connected only by solarcomps and the wireless web couldn't have stayed connected, couldn't have achieved and maintained a common culture, if they had not been grounded in something innate to the species. Then she took the last of the meat, and he stopped talking, shocked again. She hadn't even thanked him for their food. It had been his kill. Wasn't she supposed to thank him?

Suddenly and decisively, Clare said they had to sleep. Tomorrow they would be climbing into the mountains. "I'll take the first watch," she offered, unperturbed by their argument.

Brad closed his eyes, imagining color. Red sycamore. Bright yellow cottonwood. Not much of the day had been what he expected, and he rather liked that. Certainly, he had not thought he would spear an animal on his first try. What extraordinary luck.

CHAPTER FOUR

CLARE

A Second Paper, submitted by María Escobar

I've decided to turn in a second paper and if you think it is better you could disregard the first paper and just count this one? I found something really interesting while doing research for this assignment and that is the fact that Pleistocene scholars think that 70,000 years ago the human species dropped to as low as 2,000 people. Now we have many more people than 2,000 although we don't know for sure how many since we don't know who still lives in places like Africa and China and Australia but we are still very low compared to what we were before The Return and we still carry the burden of conscious-ness-made-conscious in the world. Of course the Paleos are conscious too but not like humans. They are more like ordinary animals thinking about their problems and not thinking much about the future or anything other than eating and sleeping and mating. They don't read or write, for example, which are two very important skills. It is just that we can hear what they think and feel and they can hear us which is why we don't hunt them because they are so hard to catch by surprise.

So it really comes back to us. Like the elders say, we are the universe reflecting on itself. We are consciousness-made-conscious of the earth. That's something we realized with The Return and now I wonder if we didn't also realize it a long time ago when we came close to going extinct or if it requires what we have now, our computers and radios so that we can talk to each other all the time? I think these are interesting questions that we could discuss in future papers. Another question I just thought of is why are the Pleistocene animals extinct if they were so hard to hunt?

This reminds me of one of the Quaker stories that is told all the time here around the fire and that really seems related to this idea. George Fox was the founder of the Quaker religion and he lived hundreds of years ago when there were many billions of people on the planet and prisons where they kept thousands and even millions of people even if these people had done nothing wrong. These prisons were horrible places of disease and suffering and even children were kept there, children who had hopes and dreams and special thoughts just like me and you. One day George Fox's wife saw a young boy hanged in the prison, strung up by a rope around his neck and choked to death. She was disgusted at this terrible cruelty and she went to her husband and said that he had to prove to her the existence of God's love. (This was when the Quakers thought God was an actual person.)

George Fox said he couldn't prove the existence of God's love. Only she could prove the existence of God's love. "How can God prove the existence of His love?" George Fox asked his wife. "Can He speak to us through the trees? Through the animals? Through the sky? No, He speaks to us through you. He proves his love through you. How can He prove His love? He has only Thee."

This story is meant to show that we are the consciousness-made-conscious of the earth and that we are the ones who can speak and think and read and write and prove the existence of love. It's a burden but it is also a gift and as the elders say, if the cost is high, so is the gift we get of this moment now.

In the morning, Clare and Brad returned to the river, where Clare found shoeprints in the sand, two males, she guessed, and two females, mingling with the tracks of other animals. From the erosion on the heels and overlapping of a fox, she thought the humans had been here yesterday. Clare noted what else had visited this spot since then—raccoon, crane, duck, heron, hare. No lions or hyenas. No camels or horses or antelope.

The nearness of other people required a decision. This far north, the tracks probably did not belong to her tribe. More likely, this group was ranging south from the Colorado region where she had friends and relatives: on her mother's side, her aunt and grandmother; on her father's side, three cousins and an uncle. When she mentioned some names, Brad nodded. He knew them, too. Like most adults, they had done their service in the lab.

Clare sat back on her heels to think. An encounter with another group was always valuable. They might know things she didn't—a good place to find honey, a bear's den, a quarry of chert or obsidian. They would have already emailed news of births and deaths, divorces and marriages. But emails were public, usually sent from elder to elder or teacher to student, open for everyone to read. Face to face, there would be more details and more gossip, secrets, and entertainments. Maybe they would want to drum and dance. Have a party.

None of that was about Brad's quest. And her responsibility was to him, or rather to the quest itself, its shape and outcome. She was not in charge exactly—or rather, she was not in charge, obviously. They might cross the path of a giant shortfaced bear or rattlesnake or glyptodont. As they moved away from the river, certain springs could be dry. They might need to travel east instead of west, across Humptoothed Mountain instead of Easy Pass. Brad's skills were not terrible. They would eat better than she had feared. But his thoughts wandered. He stared at the leaves. He might trip while climbing down, fall while climbing up. She might have an accident as well, Clare reminded herself. She was not in charge at all. She only facilitated.

How did drumming, a party, fit into that pattern? Clare pretended to study the tracks that ran across the sandy bank. The morning air was crisp. She breathed in the smell of river. Gossip might be good for Brad. He was a different kind of student, living outside the tribes. Perhaps his quest involved people as much as javelinas and cottonwoods. Perhaps he needed to hear the boasts of other hunters instead of only listening to his own. Naturally, she wanted to find these hunters for her own reasons. Brad, she guessed, would rather not—for his reasons.

"Let's follow them." Clare rose and nodded at the prints, with another nod to Brad that he should take the lead.

"Why?" the man asked. What a difficult personality, Clare thought. How different from anyone else she knew. His appearance was different as well, darker than the people in Clare's tribe, dark as a walnut tree against the winter sky. His face branched out, angular like that tree, with high cheekbones and a sharp nose sticking out from the eyeglasses. And he was tall, the long legs and arms of his African ancestry. Mostly the people in North America had inter-bred to a common brown skin, brown eyes, brown hair, even a common body shape. But genes still hid in odd places, and the rate of mutation caused surprises. Occasionally, you saw someone who was blonde or red-haired. Someone who had tightly curled black hair like this man, cut short in the fashion of lab rats.

She didn't bother to answer his question although she untied from his pack the remaining extra meat, the javelina package that she still wanted to use as a teaching lesson—what to do with the animal's brains and skull, the multiple uses of a foreleg bone. The snarling head would bounce on her back now, since they would have to go faster if they wanted to catch up. They would have to go much faster, and perhaps that was part of this quest's pattern, to push Brad harder. Already the decision had a consequence that seemed to be a good one.

The hunters did not make following them difficult. They walked slowly, first along the river and then out into the expanse of grass-land, meandering and not stalking prey. Brad seemed to realize he had to quicken his pace, and Clare was pleased she didn't have to tell him that.

This was going well, she thought, surprisingly well. No one in her group had wanted to take on this quest, and they had worked hard to flatter her into volunteering. It's a challenge, they had said around the fire. You're so good at this! Your students love you! Everyone was smiling. The ruse was so transparent. And every-one smiled more when she agreed—succumbed—because it *was* a challenge, partnering with someone who had avoided the quest for so long. And it was something different, too, the reverse of what she usually did, teaching students like María to read and write and think about the past when they would so obviously rather be out following tracks, alert in the present physical world. Here was a stu-dent who actually thought too much, read too much.

41

As they walked, Clare looked for a sign from the hunters, some-thing to announce who they were and what they saw. It was a habit only some people had, looping a willow branch into a circle, for example—the meaning clear: we are the Round River people. The placement of the circle might also tell where the group was going or what game they had seen. It was something to do, especially when you were outside your own hunting grounds. Clare's cousin was a person with this habit, and she had made those loops herself when she had traveled with him and a Round River group years ago. For an entire summer, she had stayed with her relatives in the Rocky Mountains to the north, a strenuous and exciting time full of tests and competitive mountain climbing, four, five, six thousand meters! And the wildflowers! Like drinking fermented prickly pear juice. She had felt as light-headed.

Clare looked and hoped for a loop of bundled grass. Her cous-ins were serious married men now, which would make them even more fun to tease, especially about that long-ago summer. They had all been camels then, all the young men and women, stupidly mis-chievous, playing tricks, testing, galumphing, knocking each other about in play. Too many jokes about gas and urination. Remember-ing, Clare almost laughed out loud. Perhaps a cousin would be with this group—why not? They were avid hunters. And if they were not these hunters, there might still be a way for her to send along a joke, something in code, something to amuse them.

She stopped to let Brad drink, knowing he would be thirsty and unused to this speed. She had filled two leather water bottles at the river and was carrying them both, something he hadn't noticed. Anyone else would have objected. It was a point of pride to carry your own weight. Clare felt more intrigued than annoyed. Did the lab rat not know the rules or just not care? Either way, how long could you live with other people like this? Did he get into many quarrels? Was he often eldered?

"Why are we doing this again?" Brad asked, his dark skin shiny.

Clare suppressed her irritation. "For one thing," she said, "we should tell them about the bushkie and the lizards."

And the man nodded, because this made sense to him. He had seemed especially disturbed by the lizards. Anyone hunting in the area should know about them. Everything, Clare understood, had to make sense to this student—and on his terms, not just because someone else said so. Because of this, he had questioned The Return so persistently last night, worried it like a hyena. He looked for places to attack, holes that needed filling. It was annoying and draining but—Clare took a mental step back—his argumentativeness also had value. In fact, she would use him as an example in her next lecture. It was important to question. Important to debate. Sometimes Clare wished her other students would worry at things more.

But not too much, she qualified. Too much independence and they would never turn in any of their assignments.

In a few hours, they began moving uphill. Brad was breathing hard and needed again to stop and drink. Clare had to wonder what these hunters were doing. The grazing animals were down below, not up here in this volcanic debris, these giant boulders thrown into the air millions of years ago. Humped rocks lay in a heap, melded together. Pillars of rock rose weirdly, eroded into mushrooms or phalluses. On the highest boulders, shelves of slickrock gave predators a place to lie and drowse on a warm surface. No deer or antelope would linger here long.

Yet here, apparently, was where the hunters had decided to make an early camp, for in the distance now Clare could hear voices. Brad had stopped and was also listening. He looked apprehensive, and Clare understood. These were strangers to him. He was the oddity. She moved around him to take the lead.

Brad surprised her by grabbing her arm. He made the sign for silence, touching his lip, and the sign for listening, cocking his head.

Clare listened again. Maybe, yes. The voices seemed unusually loud. Maybe one of them was angry. She shrugged and nodded at her student. His hearing was good. Like him, she didn't want to walk into a quarrel.

They moved closer to the noise, quietly, not calling out. Soon Clare could hear a female sobbing, a continuous wail that hardly contained space to breathe.

A man screamed. "Blahblahblahblahblahblah! Blahblahblah!"

The fierceness was wrong, completely wrong, and now Clare also felt apprehensive. She had seen people fight before. She had seen anger between men and women, often about sex but sometimes, too, over status or chores. In front of other people, in a society of thin-walled tents, most arguments stayed within prescribed bounds. No one wanted to suffer the consequences of upsetting the community, the long speeches and criticisms afterward, talking it out endlessly around the campfire. No one wanted to be everyone else's entertainment. So people were careful. They controlled their worst selves.

"Blahblahblahblahblahblah," the man gabbled.

Clare couldn't make out the words and motioned to Brad. She was going over there. Higher up. Her finger pointed: you stay here.

But Brad shook his head. He would not stay here. He would follow her.

Clare scowled. The tall dark man shook his head again. It wasn't the time to debate, and she took off her pack, waiting while he did the same. Then she went on with exaggerated movements—quiet, her spear in hand—hoping Brad could be quiet, too, climbing up and circling the voices for a place where she could see and not be seen.

When she found it, she bent low, crawling through the slickrock space between two high rocks. Brad crouched and crawled behind her.

The male voice got louder. There was another higher-pitched voice. The female had stopped crying. Clare and Brad were above a small natural clearing surrounded by pink-and-white cliffs. Clare stretched out on the ground and inched forward, scraping against pebbles, sticks, and thorns. Lifting her head slightly, she could see the scene below. Brad inched beside her, well hidden by a tuft of grass. Despite everything else, she noted her approval at his cautiousness.

Below, an old man knelt in a circle of stones built as a wall one meter high. The man was small and beardless, in leather tunic and pants, his gray hair loose about his face. The stone circle was five meters in diameter, and the man rested on his knees at its center, the earth around him swept bare. It took Clare a moment to understand why this man held his arms oddly. His hands were tied behind his back, his head down as though he were injured or tired. Just outside the stone wall, another man stood and screamed, his mouth a hole in a flowing brown beard. In one fist he held the hair of a female, who slumped against his leg. Clare scanned the area, back and forth, trying to take in everything. Another younger male sat on the ground, also outside the circle. There was the strong smell of skunk cabbage.

"Bushkies," Brad mouthed.

But four of them? Clare had never heard of bushkies coming together like this. They lived alone, almost by definition.

Abruptly, in mid-howl, the bearded man stopped screaming. He lifted the female, holding her against his waist with one arm, where she hung as though half-conscious. The old man in the circle of rock did not move. The young man outside the circle also did not move. The man holding the woman began to speak, normally now, although hoarsely. He had had a vision. He was going to save the female. He was going to save the world. He knew what to do. His voice deepened. He chanted.

Something about his speech was familiar to Clare. Briefly, she closed her eyes. She knew what the man was doing. She recognized the cadence. The repetitions. Even some of the words. This was what the tribe did when someone died. They had a ceremony before the circle of fire. They used certain phrases over and over, rhythms like a drum beat, familiar and comforting. They had done this for her husband, fallen from a cliff, a feather in his hand. They had done this for her father, gored by a stallion; for Esperanza, dead of old age; for Wren, deformed at birth; for Gregory, bitten by a rattlesnake; for Jon's father and mother, who hunted together and who had died together, their judgment clouded by dehydration. Clare thought for a moment, eyes closed, of the death chants she had heard.

They had done this for her daughter. The longing was like an attack, unexpected, inappropriate. It hollowed out her chest. She felt gutted. She wanted her daughter. She wanted her little girl. The warm hands patting her face. The weight of the body carried on her shoulder. The high voice prattling nonsense and singing, always singing. A sorrow shook Clare's body. The shock of loss all over again.

"Bushkies," Brad repeated sourly.

Social Problems: Assignment Four, submitted by Dimitri Wu

We have to deal with the problem of scavenging. How much should we scavenge from the cities and what should we scavenge? And who should do this?

Here in Russia and everywhere else, the survivors of the supervirus first kept away from cities and towns and villages because they thought the disease was still there, wherever people had once been. They thought the supervirus was still in those dead bodies and in buildings and in anything people had touched. I believe they were right to be so careful. Like most of us here, I don't think the supervirus came from any human source but from a mutation in the viral batteries. Those viruses were everywhere, grabbing conductive metals and lining them up into nanowires. By the twenty-second century, viral technology was the answer to every problem, from expensive energy to pollution and global warming. Everything was run with those cheap viral batteries.

After a long time, we realized that the supervirus was really gone and we could now enter these places safely. But did we want to? No! We had become happier with the things we made ourselves from the earth. We were happier living the life we were meant to live, the deep-down true life rediscovered by our great-great-great-great-grandmothers and our great-great-great-great-grandfathers. (I am myself descended from Li Kuo-fu Chao, specialist in the radio communication between Paleos and humans, and from Long Wu, specialist in Paleolithic tool-making. Of course, everyone in our tribes has ancestry among such scientists since these were the men and women who survived the supervirus by hiding for many months in their antique bunker. I know I am not extraordinary in my heritage but I am still proud of it, still respectful. Sometimes I think I inherited from these ancestors a certain knack for making spear points, since mine rarely break when I am flinting, as well as the ability to hear Paleos better than my friends. This is particularly true when it comes to mammoths. We have many mammoths here in Russia and Mongolia, unlike some other parts of the world, and I have found that I can hear them from a very far distance.)

But back to the social problem of scavenging. Of course, we have to scavenge some parts and supplies so we can have the computers decided on in the Great Compromise and so we can connect to the worldwide web and the satellites going above the earth. We don't want to lose the history of humanity, which is also why we still have to write papers. We have to scavenge what we need for radios, too, for communication in case the computers fail.

And the decision of who scavenges is also not such a difficult one. As it turns out, most of those people have to be mutes. In the beginning, when we sent receivers into the cities, they always came back lonely. They came back weeping, like my grandfather did when he had to go scavenging as a punishment when he was young. My grandfather went to bed and didn't stop sleeping for two days. He said he couldn't explain how he felt, only that I should avoid scavenging myself, and this I have done. My grandfather is a wise man and I listen to what he says.

In conclusion, scavenging is another social problem we have to deal with. We have to scavenge but we don't like to and we do it respectfully and without great joy.

Social Problems: Assignment Four, submitted by María Escobar

Animism is not really a social problem but it is a big part of our society and so I thought I would write about it. Animism is integral to who we are! Back in the twenty-first century when they cloned the first teratorn, the scientists got quite a shock when this large hungry scavenger bird started squawking for food and demanding meat. Some of the scientists realized that they were hearing this bird in their own heads! That they were receivers! But no one knew what receivers were then because no one thought that consciousness could exist outside the physical body. People didn't know much about electromagnetic fields or the holographic principle. They just believed in simple biology and nothing else.

Then people's brains began hearing the thoughts of the Paleos and they realized that they were wrong and that consciousness could exist outside a body and even more than that. Consciousness could travel. The consciousness of a teratorn can travel about two kilometers down from the sky where I can hear it when I am out in the jungle hunting with my friends. Probably the teratorn I was receiving yesterday sounds a lot like the one they first cloned, just squawking and squawking for meat whether it be fresh or rotten. Teratorns are not fussy.

Hearing the Paleos changed everything and scientists had to rethink a lot of things. They started thinking about consciousness and thoughts moving and mainly they thought in terms of waves, how waves are everywhere, radio waves, low frequency waves, high frequency waves, light waves, sound waves. Satellites in space already let us connect to the waves of the Internet on our computers and people were used to being "bathed in the web" as the proverb says, or "bathed in waves." The Paleos made us realize that people and animals could also receive and send out waves or at least humans could receive waves sent out by certain Paleos although humans can't send waves back to the Paleos very well and they can't send out or receive waves to each other. My friends and I try to do this all the time and we really can't.

The physicists started thinking more about waves and they started the idea of panpsychism which means there is a kind of constant wave going on everywhere that is a form of consciousness or at least it is something that consciousness can travel on and through. It is everywhere and in everything. This new idea meant that people started doing a lot of experiments with animals and plants and rocks and they had some very interesting results. Then came the supervirus and everyone died. Those of us who didn't die stopped doing any kind of experiments except for continuing to think and reflect about all of this which the Council and elders encourage us to do because we are the universe reflecting on itself and because animism is part of who we are and part of The Return as decided on by the Pleistocene scholars who lived in Russia and then agreed to by the Los Alamos Three and the Costa Rican Quakers.

Today we sometimes say panpsychism and sometimes animism and one way to understand that is to say that panpsychism is the scientific and technical term and includes the holographic principle, and animism is what most of us believe. We believe the world is alive and conscious and all the parts of the world are alive and conscious. There are many different ways of believing this. (I know I should end this paper soon because you have word counts and I respect that and I am almost done but for this last thought which I think is important in its way.) I have a tree I like to sit under and I talk to this tree and I think it hears me and I think being friends with this tree calms me down and helps me be a better hunter and gatherer. I'm a receiver but I can't really hear what this tree is saying because humans can only hear certain Paleos and nothing else. My friend Carlos doesn't believe in talking to trees or rocks or even animals that aren't Paleos because he follows more the Quaker beliefs that are very matter-of-fact and scientific. Even so this is not the kind of thing we argue about because we both believe in the fundamentals of physics and that's what's important whether we call it panpsychism or animism. We both have the same belief even though the details differ a little.

As I said before, this is not a social problem. It's more like a social achievement!

Re A Question, submitted by Carlos Salas

I hope you don't think I was being too personal when I asked for a recent picture. And thanks for your comments on my last paper. They were extensive and I learned a lot. You are really a great teacher. Thank you again.

CHAPTER FIVE

DOG

Dog shivered although he wasn't cold, and Dog watched. The part of him that was Luke felt bad, bad, bad. He had run away. He had run away from Luke who was hurt now, scared and tied up. Dog called out to Luke/Lucia but neither of them answered.

Dog had followed the bushkies and Luke to this camp and then to the river and then back to this camp. Along the way, Dog ate part of a dead skunk and a snake and an antelope already picked over by hyenas. He was hungry now but stayed hidden in the mesquite and brittlebush and watched the bushkies as they gathered around the rock wall. The circle had taken a day to build because the younger male was clumsy and the older male didn't work but only told the others what to do. Sometimes the older male barked, "Blahblahblah-blah," and sometimes he gave a speech, and when it was time for him to do that, everyone had to stop and listen.

Dog knew the speech very well by now. The bushkie had seen a pillar of light. The light had risen up from the ground. The light had called to him. The light had blessed him and named him the speech maker, the one who gave and the one who took away. The light had risen up from the ground, a pillar of light blazing and growing until it hallowed the earth and inseminated the sky, the sky a new father, the earth a new mother. The bushkie had seen the light, and once, when he commanded it to appear, the others had seen the light, too.

At this point, the others had to join in. Had the female seen the light? Yes, she had to say. She had seen the pillar of light. Had the boy seen the light? Yes, the boy had to say. He had seen the pillar of light rising from the ground. Dog knew they were telling the truth. Their voices often lied about other things but not about this. About this, they were confident.

Dog knew what made humans happy. Stories made them happy just as stories made Dog happy. Adenine, guanine, cytosine. The double molecule, ribbony, twisty. Playing with Luke, pretending to be mad, pretending to be sad. Genes, mutations, replications. Humans liked stories, and Dog liked stories, but humans turned their stories into the world. Humans needed, Lucia said, to make their mark on the world. They had the gene for mark, stamp, push, move, alter, rearrange, shift, gouge, transform. They needed to *assert* themselves. They needed to build circles of rock, and they needed a story to go with the circle. They needed to make little crosses of wood, and they needed to make big crosses of wood, and they needed a story to go with the cross.

No, the story came first, Dog reminded himself. They needed the cross to go with the story. They needed Luke to go with the story. The bushkie had seen a pillar of light. Now he needed Luke to be tied up. Sad, scared Luke. No pretending this time. No game of being angry. Luke was really sad.

Dog reminded himself that although he felt hungry he should watch, not hunt, not eat. He thought of a rabbit: adenine, adenine. He remembered being a pup. He remembered the den all over his body, his skin, his hair, the warmth of his mother and his siblings. Someone touching him constantly. His mother nuzzling or his sister licking (she thought she was licking herself) or his brother bumping, bump, shove, touch, caress. When someone entered the den from outside, when his father nosed carefully down into the tunnel, even the fresh air felt like a touch. Everything in the world wanted to touch him. The dark safe world wrapped around.

What a shock to leave that world into sunlight. Now his mother growled and nipped. Stay away. Don't do that. With his own sharp teeth, Dog bit at the bright new world. He bit his father's tail, and his father growled. Stay away. Don't do that. Now Dog was separate from his mother and siblings. He was separate from their skin and warmth, from these rocks, those plants, this sky.

Now the other direwolves saw how different he was. The fifth claw didn't make them angry. But the way he intruded into their thoughts. They had their own thoughts, which he could hear, and that was good. That was a good way to hunt and stay together. But his thoughts seemed bigger than theirs. His thoughts were too loud. His thoughts confused them. Now his mother growled more fiercely. Stay away. His siblings whined. Stay away, stay away, until he was big enough to scavenge on his own. Then they drove him into the mountains where the air was cold. No, don't follow us. They drew blood. He whined and crept forward on his belly. They drew blood. His mother grabbed his neck. Yes, she would kill him.

Epinephrine, cortisol. Dog remembered being lonely as Luke was lonely now. Heart pounding. Worse than hunger. He climbed higher into the mountains, higher into the cold, for this was in the north, where there was rain and snow melting on Dog's guard hairs. This was a long time ago although his memories of the den felt so new. He could almost smell his mother, his sister. Oxytocin. Dopamine. He smelled them sometimes on Luke/Lucia, direwolf mixed with human.

Luke! Lucia! Dog called.

Dog knew he was older than most direwolves, older because he lived with Luke, not alone and not in a pack. Because of Luke, his teeth hadn't snapped off in a fight. Because of Luke, his hindquarters were unscarred. Because of Luke, his stomach didn't ache with parasites. Once Lucia had made him eat a certain plant—guanine, cytosine—so that worms streamed out of his anus, twisty and ribbony, not a double helix. Once a snake bit his nose, and Luke had stayed with him for days and nights, bringing water, stroking his fur. Don't die, Luke said. I need you. Don't die.

Dog remembered hunting rabbits. The rush of hot blood filled his mouth. Nothing so right as blood in his mouth.

Dog remembered leaving the lab. He was Lucia then. He had been a woman all his life, dressing like a woman, using a woman's soft voice. He had breasts. He had a vagina. But he didn't feel like a woman. Inside, not a woman. He didn't believe really that he had a uterus, that he could have children. He didn't have sex with men. He was really a man. What could he do? People were born certain ways, without the right parts, with too many parts, with parts cross-wired, not quite sure if they were male or female or even human. Sometimes alone in the lab, Lucia became Luke. She was happy in the lab. Then why did she leave? Dog couldn't remember. These were not his memories. Perhaps she went on a quest. Perhaps she went north to see snow and there she became Luke as often as he wanted. There he could be Luke for years and years. There he could be Lucia, too, if he wanted, when he wanted. There he found Dog, almost dead from loneliness and snow.

Luke was lonely now. Scared. Sad. It was hard to stay and watch, hard to be still. Dog remembered eating a giant beaver. Even its tail was enormous. There was so much meat and so much of it fresh. That was such a happy day.

Dog remembered eating prickly pear fruit, how the tiny thorns bored into his lip. He remembered looking at numbers, scrolling down the computer screen, the rates of mutation in the northern tribes, the rates of mutation in the southern tribes. No one lived near the bad radiation, in California (what was California?) or the Northeast, the nuclear reactors overheating and melting down. Nuclear, nucleus. The way the double helix acted as a radio sending and receiving information, a super-functioning biocomputer, the organizing agent at the center of each cell, the DNA in each cell creating the biohologram.

Dog remembered the snake bite, how much that hurt! Cortisol. Adrenaline. He felt fear like the color red, a sharp pain in his hip, an insect boring into his ear. Heart pounding. *Bam, bam, bam.* He had the scavenger gene, the runaway gene. He was afraid of what he would not do.

Ashamed of himself, Dog looked over at the two humans also watching the bushkies, a male and female hidden on a rock ledge. Dog remembered he couldn't go hunt. He couldn't eat because he had to stay here.

CHAPTER SIX

BRAD

"Bushkies," Brad said sourly. Bushkies were loners, they didn't travel together, they didn't form groups. The bushkies chanting below were a brief isolate pack, formed by some rare pattern. They disgusted Brad, although he knew his feelings were irrational. Bushkies were chemically damaged. It wasn't their fault. They were no different from children born with failing organs or without a limb. These children compensated for their disability or they died. A few grew up to become bushkies. It wasn't their fault, but Brad blamed them anyway. No, he corrected himself, not blame exactly. A minor neurosis. Bushkies scared him. He was not one of them. He was different, but he was not one of them.

Clare touched his arm and jerked her head. She began to inch backward slowly, her rump raised.

Brad studied the four bushkies. The man kneeling in the circle of stone lifted his head, and Brad could see that parts of his beardless face looked misshapen, as though he had been beaten. Brad looked more closely at the younger man on the ground, who wasn't simply sitting but had curled around himself rocking back and forth. Only the bearded chanting man seemed vigorous—easily holding up the half-conscious woman, his voice booming, happily singing the chant of the dead.

Clare hissed. Brad gripped his spear and lowered his face to the slickrock, pebbles, and thorns. Raising his rump, he also began inching backward.

They moved far enough away to whisper and not be heard.

"We should go," Clare said. "Get our packs. Back to the river."

Brad was surprised. "Do nothing?"

"Bushkies. They have nothing to do with you—with us," Clare said. "I shouldn't have followed these people."

"The old man. We could help him," Brad argued out of habit.

"It's too dangerous. This isn't what we should be doing."

Brad could hear the frustration in her voice. She was his teacher and guide. She had to protect him. But what would she do if she were with someone else, someone she could trust with a spear? "It's my decision, isn't it?" Brad whispered.

Now Clare looked surprised. "Yes, but you should follow my advice."

Brad paused at that. She was right. He could be injured or killed. She could be injured or killed, and then he would be alone. The bushkies could be injured or killed, and how would she feel about that? In truth, one of the above was almost certain to happen if he and Clare interfered.

After all, they were only bushkies.

"Let's see what they are doing now," Brad said, more as a delay than a decision.

But then, by the time they had inched back to the hiding place, the bushkies had already started. The younger bushkie was on his feet and throwing stones with enthusiasm into the circle. The woman lay tumbled and still on the ground. The leader of the group chanted as he wound back his arm. One of his rocks, the size of a fist, hit the old man on the shoulder. Almost immediately another rock struck his forehead. Brad heard a high-pitched cry as the bushkie jerked back and bobbed forward, immobilized somehow by his kneeling position. It was just a matter of waiting. Another stone to the head. Another and another. It would all be over soon. Beside him, he could hear Clare take a breath.

In his mind's eye, Brad saw the grotto, that dizzying twist of perspective. The webbed feet twitched as though the animal were still suffering and not yet dead. Brad could see the yucca twine looped around its legs, tying them to the cross, thorns nailing flesh to wood. The limbs had been pulled apart, white belly lifted. Bits of quartz and mica winked in the dim light. Beautiful jewels. Glittering stars. Brad knew the reference, not just to the old Christian theology but to all of human history. The sacrifice of the innocent, the Aztec temples, the Holocaust, the African wars. There had to be pain. Torture and ritual. It was the bearded man's vision below in the stone circle, in the miniature grotto. There had to be blood. It was the way to power.

Brad hated that story. Also, if he did nothing now, Clare would never fall in love with him. Before he could think too much, Brad stood up, positioned himself, adjusted his eyeglasses, and threw his spear.

He missed the bearded man by a good distance, the spear sailing into the bushes beyond. But now in the space between the two rocks, Clare was standing, too, and her weapon went to target—the bearded man's right shoulder and chest. With hardly a pause, she darted backward and was gone, reappearing to Brad's left as she half ran, half slid down the gravelly slope. Brad literally gulped and followed her.

The bearded man roared, flailed, and moved forward, seemingly energized by his unexpected wound. The younger man also moved forward and suddenly had a knife. Brad slipped as he came down the rough incline and saw most of what was happening from his new seat on the ground. Clare started circling the bearded man, angling toward the teenager. From somewhere she also had a knife.

Then with a shower of rocks and pebbles, clattering and spattering from one of the cliff faces, a dark shape hurtled past both Clare and the boy and knocked the bearded man over, the spear sticking up and swaying almost comically. The shape, the animal, held the man down with the weight of its body while slobbering teeth and heart-stopping growls seemed to shock the victim into a faint. The bearded head lolled to one side. Brad shut his eyes and when he looked next, the younger man with the knife had vanished from the scene. The woman lay in her heap on the ground. The man in the stone circle found his voice and was croaking heartily, "Good boy! Good boy!"

As easy as that, the rescue was over. Brad got up and limped over to Clare. They watched in disbelief as the fully grown direwolf bounded away from the unconscious bushkie, leaped over the stone circle, and trotted toward the old man. The powerful animal slobbered over this human, too, licking and whining.

Brad exchanged a glance with Clare.

"Please, untie me!" the old man mumbled, ducking his head to fend off the glistening tongue.

Clare looked down at her knife and at the direwolf. She looked at Brad and then at the unconscious bushkie. "Watch him," she said as she climbed over the stone wall. As she approached the old man, the direwolf turned and snarled, hackles rising. Brad estimated that its teeth were at least ten centimeters long.

"Come on," the old man said to Clare. "He won't hurt you."

Clare actually laughed.

"Watch the bushkie!" she reminded Brad, and Brad nodded. He would. But he didn't. He was watching Clare instead.

Unfortunately, the woman was dead. No one could guess when she had died or why, although the three of them compared notes. Brad had last seen her conscious when the bearded man began his speech. Clare remembered how the bearded man had tossed the woman down at one point, her head hitting the ground. The old man, rubbing his arms, said the woman had always seemed sickly, breathing hard, her face blueish.

"I think she had a bad heart," Luke said.

The old man had introduced himself, not really a bushkie but more a hermit or bachelor bull. He had been on his own for many years, living off and on with the Colorado tribes, but mostly alone.

"A bad heart?" Brad stood over the body. The woman was so young.

"Born that way," Luke replied.

"Would one of you help?" Clare asked sharply. "I'm going to take out the spear now." She knelt by the unconscious bushkie and braced herself for pulling. If the bushkie was lucky, the tip of the spear would slip free and the wound could be cleaned and bandaged. Otherwise, they would have to dig into the flesh and cause more damage, with more loss of blood and chances for infection. In case the bushkie woke up, Clare had already tied his feet and hands, using the rope that had once tied up Luke.

"I'll do this," Luke told Brad. "Watch for the other one. I don't think he'll come back. But we should be careful."

As if on cue, leaning against Luke's leg, the direwolf growled. Brad couldn't help himself. The hairs on his neck stood up.

"Good boy," the old man cooed.

Brad tried again to catch Clare's eye, but she was busy with her patient, who shrieked as the spear came out whole, tip included. Luke moved swiftly to stop the bleeding with a fistful of grass, pressing down on the wound. Clare had already cut the edge of the woman's deerskin skirt into a strip she pushed under the bushkie's chest, lifting him up, wrapping the bandage around him twice. The man didn't struggle but only stared at her with bulging eyes. He didn't seem to know what was happening now or why, and he didn't react to Luke's hands or face, the man he had recently tried to stone to death.

Brad had to admire Luke's lack of emotion. The old man did his job without fuss.

Later, they made a stew of the javelina head and some herbs Luke found and tubers Clare dug up. As they ate around the fire, Luke talked about his capture and the days afterward when he was tied and helpless. Brad guessed the old man to be in his early seventies, wiry and strong, well muscled, without any facial hair—although he couldn't have been shaving, so that must be a mutation.

Brad was intrigued. Luke had a certain serenity. What was he doing living alone?

"The man is delusional," Luke was saying. "Before The Return, he would have been given drugs."

"You think we should be taking care of him," Brad asked, "people like him?"

Luke shrugged. "How can we? We don't live in that world any-more. And should we, in any case? How much should we muck-a-luck? We've been asking that since the supervirus."

Brad noted how easily Luke slipped into discussion, the age-old questions. "So we send the bushkies out to die. We don't interfere."

"We don't interfere," Luke said. "And we hope they die before they have children. We hope all the damaged people die before they have children."

Brad turned to Clare, unnaturally quiet as she added another stick of wood to the fire. "What will happen now," he asked her, "when we take him back? What will the elders do?"

"I don't know." His guide also shrugged. Of course, they had to return to her tribe now, taking the bound bushkie with them. Brad wondered if this had ruined his quest. Would this reflect badly on her?

Luke put his hand on the direwolf's neck, the ridiculous animal lying right next to him. "I can travel with you," the old man said. "I can tell them what happened. I owe you that. There will be a lot of talking and explaining to do."

"Yes," Clare said. "There will be a lot of explaining to do. Your Paleo, though . . ."

"Dog," Luke corrected. The direwolf raised his head.

"He won't get along with our dogs," Clare promised.

Luke agreed, "We'll have to make some arrangements."

As the fire died down, the Milky Way arched more clearly above their heads, a thousand stars like a river without water, pouring out light. Brad stretched and looked up, feeling reverent and humble and pleased by that. Clare also stretched in her skins by the fire and fell asleep.

"You're from the lab," Luke broke the silence, adding more branches. The flare lit his face. "You live there permanently?"

"That's right," Brad murmured, wondering if he had said he would take the first watch or if Luke was doing that. "Were you there before you went out on your own? Doing your service?"

"I told you I was from the north. But once I also lived in the lab." Luke paused, and Brad understood the old man had something important to say. "I think I knew your mother. I was a woman then."

The branches crackled, *pop, pop, pop*. Brad sat up, his heart beating in his ears. If he had known how exciting quests could be, he would have gone on one long before. The fact that Luke was a woman—had been a woman in the lab—was surprising but not shocking. These things happened. Hormones got confused. Wires crossed. It was something else making this hammering in his head. "You seemed familiar!"

"You were only a child when I left. You could hardly talk."

"It's not that I remember you," Brad said. "But you seem familiar. Did you know my father, too?"

"We all knew your father."

"You were there when he left."

"No, I didn't know about that. I was gone by then. But I was at his wedding feast. I ate his meat, of which there was always plenty. Your father could hunt a raven in a storm." Luke paused again. "I watched him carry your mother on his shoulder, over his heart, and break a clay pot under his foot. He said it was an old custom from his tribe."

Brad had heard that story before, from his mother and others. His mysterious father from a distant place. His beautiful mother born in the lab. He felt a light descent, a mantle on his shoulders, skein without weight, unaffected by time. Without moving, he drew the mantle close and warm in the night.

"You knew my mother better than my father? When you were a . . . woman?"

"We sometimes worked together. The Council agreed we could look at patterns of fertility in the tribes. So we talked a lot about the work, and other things."

Brad made himself more comfortable, bringing up the horsehide around his back and settling closer to the heat. "What other things? Were you born in the lab, too?"

"No, but I was a child there . . ." And Luke began his story.

River and roof, the Milky Way arched above their heads.

CHAPTER SEVEN

CLARE

Clare waited for Brad by the elder's tent. From this rise, she could see the rest of their summer and fall camp, some fifty tents contained within a meadow rimmed by foothills and pink cliffs. Although the clustering of tents looked random, Clare knew why some people chose to be near the communal kitchen and some far away. She knew why this elder was nearest the stream that ran the meadow's western edge, why that tent had been set off alone, why the drying racks were closest to a widow and her children. A few of the tents were larger than others. A few had smoke holes for a private fire. All were decorated with designs of orange ocher, mineral blue, and limestone white, lines of charcoal gray and devil's-claw black. All could be easily dismantled, the poles and skins stored in a nearby cave when the tribe made the move to their winter camp, a larger valley to the east.

That would be soon, Clare thought. She had to finish up her work with Brad soon. And where was Brad? She had agreed that the odd dark man could stay in the foothills with Luke and Dog only if he came into camp every day for the rest of his lessons, to consult with her and, more importantly, with the elders. What a mess this was. Brad's quest in doubt and the bushkie a prisoner—in restraints, guarded—something that no one in the tribe liked. No one wanted to take care of a bushkie. Especially no one wanted to deal with these problems when it was past time to pack up their solarcomps and everyday goods, store the rest, load up the travois, load up the kids, and start walking.

Pushing the closed tent flap from the inside, the elder emerged, a stocky eighty-year-old woman with two long silver braids. She carried a gathering basket. Only Brad was still missing.

"I'm sorry, Grandmother . . ." Clare used the honorific title. In this case, the woman was also her mother's mother.

Her grandmother waved the air. "Don't waste time apologizing. I've read all the files. Listen, sweetheart, it's not you. This guy has been missing his appointments with elders all his life."

"He promised he would be here . . ."

"This guy makes promises. But I'm not waiting for him. There are some things I want to get, a half hour from here. Upstream."

"Watercress?" Clare guessed.

"It's fresher in the morning. We'll be back by noon. We can talk on the way."

Clare thought they should take another hunter with them, but her grandmother was headstrong and already walking. Clare followed like a sullen child. This final assessment—what the student had learned, what he or she had done as part of that learning, what he or she would do differently now—was the least favorite part of any quest. Of course, usually the *guide* didn't have to do any of the talking. Usually this was the *student's* job, evaluating his or her actions and answering any questions from the elder.

Behind her grandmother, Clare tried to see inside the tents they passed. Maybe Brad was hiding in one of them. She scanned the kitchen area and trail to the latrines. She walked slowly, hoping still to see him in camp, perhaps with Luke, perhaps cadging some food.

How could she justify a successful quest? She had counted on Brad's arguing his case. He was charming when he wanted to be. He was clever. He was persistent. And she had already coached him on what to say.

"You're slow as a turtle," her grandmother stopped and waited, but kindly, in full elder mode.

Clare caught Jon's eye as he approached them carrying a skinned rabbit. His braid of brown hair had been wrapped into a bun, like a topknot, and his muscled chest glistened as though oiled. He looked happy to be alive on this beautiful morning, happy to see her, lifting the rabbit slightly in tribute. Clare shook her head. She felt chagrined, not happy to be alive on this beautiful morning. It was embarrassing. The quest had been cut short. Maybe the elders would count the week traveling back to the tribe, but that was complicated by the presence of the bushkie, bound and then gagged, not to mention Luke and Dog. They hadn't reached the mountains or worked on Brad's relationship with water. She hadn't had time to prepare the peyote and stop for a vision. After that one javelina, Brad hadn't done any serious hunting. Inevitably, her grandmother would declare the quest a failure, and the Council would ask Brad to repeat it. But not with her.

"Begin at the beginning. Tell me everything that happened," her grandmother said as she nodded at Jon. Everyone liked Jon.

They walked farther, to the privacy of the stream area, away from anyone who could overhear. Clare thought back. What had been her first mistake? Certainly that was when she had followed the human footprints. The lizards were unnerving, and she had sought the comfort of a tribe, not focusing on the present and what her student needed to learn. And then—her second mistake? Should they have not interfered at the stone circle? Let the bushkies kill Luke? Clare sighed loudly. This was unfair. Brad should be here, too, answering these questions, facing up to her grandmother.

Sheltered from the wind under a juniper, Clare sat by the peyote as it boiled, the round half-dried buttons turning the water dark brown. She would strain this water, save it, boil the buttons again, combine the two solutions, and reduce that to a cup of darker brown, a bitter liquid with enough mescaline to open the door.

A branch sagged in a whoosh of wings, sending down a scatter of hard purple berries. The raven barked a *ka-ka-ka* as it jumped from the tree to the ground near the small fire. Confidently, the bird waddled toward her, ruffling one black shoulder and opening its black bill. Clare knew that Jon would be close behind. People had started to complain about this newest pet, especially since pets were more or less against the rules. Dogs were the exception, but just a few, carefully bred and trained. Most wild animals were manageable only when young and became a nuisance as soon as they started growing up, never fully domesticated but never wild again either. This was not Jon's first offense. Clare could remember the raven before this one—a very loud bird—and the crow and scrub jay before that.

"May I join you?" Jon asked rhetorically, ducking under the tree and sitting cross-legged. Now the raven waddled toward him, opening and closing its beak. Predictably, Jon took out a handful of pine nuts and began tossing them to the bird, one by one. The hunter gave a *knocka-knocka-knocka*, a passable imitation, and the raven gave a *knocka-knocka-knocka* back. The bird got a pine nut. Jon gurgled. Clare had to widen her eyes. He was getting good. The raven cawed in response. Jon cawed, too, but this time he seemed to be saying the wrong thing, for suddenly the raven flapped its wings, croaked, and hopped until it could get enough lift away from the juniper and up into the sky. Jon was left with his handful of pine nuts.

Clare raised an eyebrow. Jon shrugged. He nodded at the clay pot, the peyote, the boiling water. Clare nodded in return and asked him to sing.

He had such a beautiful voice. She melted a little, as she always did when Jon performed alone before the fire or sat next to her when they sang as a group. His range was extraordinary, surprisingly high as he pretended to speak in the peyote button's voice, the spirit of the plant promising inspiration, welcoming the human into its world. In this song, the peyote spoke first and then the human, and now Jon dropped a register, deeper and stronger. Peyote, human, and next a sparrow. Then a saber-toothed cat. Then a tiger beetle. Jon knew the making-peyote-tea song better than Clare, and she was content to let him take the lead while she came in on the chorus or echoed his words in the parts that were a round.

The hunter swayed as he sang and Clare stirred the tea. How strange, really, that Jon was a mute, that he had never heard the Paleos whispering emotions in his head—I'm hungry, I'm thirsty, I'm eating you up. Somehow this hadn't made him less sensitive to the world around him. In fact, he was a true animist, believing in the unique consciousness of peyote in this song just as he believed in the unique consciousness of the human, consciousness everywhere and in everything, an essence in each pine nut and lice-infested bird. In each louse.

Clare, herself, believed in chemistry. For a short amount of time, the hallucinogenic properties of the peyote button shifted brain waves. Synapses sparked. Neurons fired. It was a new kind of reception. Clare stirred the tea and thought that Brad's animism was probably much like Jon's. Ironically, as different as they were in other ways, the physicist and the hunter had this in common.

She helped end the song, harmonizing with the final chorus, and felt Jon's stare on her lifted breasts. Actually the two men had another common interest. If she were younger and more susceptible, she would be blushing—the notes of sex so strong in the air.

"Can we meet tonight?" Jon exhaled, as if still singing.

Clare thought and nodded yes. But she wasn't excited about making love outside, in the cold, on the ground. "In my tent," she amended. She had been gone weeks, first to fetch Brad at the lab and then the aborted quest and back. Her tentmates owed her some private time.

Whoosh. The raven returned, flapping nearby. It knocked. It gurgled. Someone else was coming up the trail to the tree. Clare watched as Jon scrambled out from under the juniper branches and then straightened and stood, his compact body seeming to expand. The muscles of his arms flexed, and he lifted his head, his reaction just short of being silly.

As usual, Brad and Luke were talking as they walked. Dog wasn't with them, and Clare felt relieved. The direwolf made people nervous.

She was still annoyed at Brad, although naturally he had explained away his earlier absence. By not coming to see the elder with Clare, he had pointed to himself as the irresponsible party, the person at fault. He had turned Clare into another one of his victims. She couldn't be blamed for whatever had happened. She couldn't control such an aggravating man. This condescending strategy—getting the elder to pity Clare—was bad enough. Almost worse, it worked, and Clare's grandmother had decided that the quest didn't have to be repeated, for this would only shame her granddaughter. Only the peyote ceremony still had to be done. Also, Brad had to agree to another quest in three years. On this point, the elder was stern. No more tricks! No more trickster!

"Ah!" Brad looked a little startled at Jon's pose and the sight of Clare stirring tea. The tall loose-limbed man also ducked under the juniper branches to sit beside her, and Luke came, too, so that Jon looked foolish standing apart from them and by himself. It would have been natural for the hunter to take his leave now. But stubbornly Jon bent down and rejoined them around the clay pot of liquid.

The aroma of peyote mixed with burning wood mixed with the smell of the three men, especially Luke. The hermit was fastidious in many ways, brushing his teeth and keeping his hair braided, but he did not, surprisingly, bathe very often.

"Have you heard about the bushkie?" Brad asked. "The elders made their recommendation, and the Council agreed."

Something squeezed in Clare's chest. Killing the bushkie was a reasonable solution although it was something her tribe had never had to do before. Still, a Colorado tribe had executed such a man, and there had been many such executions in the Russian tribes. Naturally the Russians did things differently—gambling excessively, for example, but forbidding fermented drink. Naturally the three populations had their varying cultures. The Quakers, of course, had never "murdered" anyone and would vigorously protest. Emails would be sent around the world.

Luke seemed to guess what she was thinking, and not for the first time. The old man reminded Clare of her grandmother. "They are only going to banish him again," Luke assured her. "But this time they are taking him farther south, to the peyote fields. It's unlikely he'll meet up with other bushkies or live very long. But he will have that chance."

Brad said nothing.

"It's the right decision," Jon spoke.

"So he can kill someone else?" Brad asked.

Jon answered as if the lab rat had said this out of fear. "Don't worry," he soothed in the imitation of someone talking to a child. "He'll be very far south."

Brad didn't even bother to reply. There was an awkward pause—the raven *knock-a-knock*ing from a branch, the branches moving in a wind—and then Brad spoke to Clare. "I've asked Luke to be there when I take the peyote."

She felt another internal squeeze. Brad had turned to Luke as his mentor. They talked together often. The man was clearly the preferred teacher. She stirred the tea again. "If you want. It's not customary."

Luke coughed up a wad of phlegm, turned, and spit it at the base of the tree. This helped relieve some of the tension. Clare recognized it as an elder's trick, suddenly farting or blowing a nose. A good reminder. We are all just bodies, mucus and gas.

So she put her jealousy aside, explaining where they should meet the next day, a sweet sandy spot by the stream. They would be close to camp, safe from predators. The water would be musical, the afternoon warm under the yellow trees, the willow tips blushing pink. Later, Brad could walk to a nearby hill to watch the sun set and the rise of Venus. Clare wasn't hoping for any dramatic revelation. Since Brad had missed so many quests, this would be his first experience with peyote, and she preferred something mild and unexciting. She explained the process. The tea would taste awful, but he should try to not vomit.

Now Jon did get up, for this was quest business. He left with a meaningful look at Clare and a nod at the other men. The raven flapped and cawed and followed the hunter, who walked with triumph in his straight back and shoulders. The black bird soared into the blue sky, high and higher like a totem spirit, like the man's twinned half. Clare shook her head. The bird was a pest they would have to live with. No one could make Jon give him up.

The Mute Mammoth, submitted by Dimitri Wu

My subject in this paper is how The Return was influenced by the Paleos. Everyone knows the story of the first cloned teratorn and the first scientist who could hear him and how that scientist clapped his ears and said, "For God's sake, give that bird something to eat!"

After that, they cloned a lot of Paleos and established the Pleistocene Parks and did a lot of new scientific experiments. Paleos were a popular subject which some scholars have described as a cultural obsession. The idea that we could listen to what animals were thinking and feeling gripped the human imagination. Pleistocene scientists like my great-great-great-great-grandparents were revered and they were also very strong-minded. They insisted on cloning the giant shortfaced bear, for example, even though no one wanted them to do that. Then the supervirus happened and these same Pleistocene scientists emerged from their antique bunker outside St. Petersburg and were practically in charge. What would have happened if this had not been the case? If only the computer scientists in North America had survived? Or only the Costa Rican Quakers?

One interesting thing to remember about the conference in St. Petersburg is that the majority of the people who attended from around the world were receivers, not mutes. Most people think that receivers were especially drawn to Paleolithic research because it was so new and exciting to be able to communicate with a saber-toothed cat or a direwolf. In this way, the Paleos themselves influenced who was at this conference. Later this conference influenced everyone else and that is why we have The Return. The Paleos are why we are who we are today.

Here is one more thing to think about. Many thousands of years ago, as the Pleistocene came to an end, human beings hunted the Paleos to extinction—killing off the small groups struggling to survive the newest climate change. When the big game died, many of the predators and scavengers like the teratorns died with them. There are many questions around these extinctions. How did we kill these animals when they could hear us and we could hear them? Did we learn tricks of keeping silent? Did we have more mutes then, and did the mutes alone hunt these animals? Did some animals learn the trick of not being heard and are those the animals that survived? We will never know. My grandfather believes, however, that killing off the Paleos was the first big mistake humans made. Suddenly no one could hear each other anymore. Our lives changed after that. We turned to agriculture and civilizations rose and civilizations fell and civilization almost destroyed us. For this reason, out of regret, we do not hunt these animals now.

I will end this paper with a personal story about my relationship with mammoths. Last summer I was watching a herd as they ate grass in the big meadow near Blackhorn Mountain. The big females twirled their trunks around a clump of dry stems, kicked at the base, and pulled. Then they beat the clump against their knees to knock off the dust and chaff. As they chewed, they twirled their trunks around a new clump, kicked, and pulled. I could hear their dissatisfaction. This grass was dry. The younger females and the adolescent males also ate the grass and found it dry, while the very youngest mammoths just kept playing. They were still nursing and didn't care much about grass. They wanted only to bump against each other and see how far they could explore before their mothers called them back. Sometimes the mammoths rumbled out loud and sometimes they called out with their minds, and I could hear both. It was like being in a roomful of people, hearing all kinds of conversations. With Paleos, of course, I didn't hear words so much as feelings and ideas like come-back-immediately or here's-some-really-good-grass-at-the-base-of-this-little-hummock.

I also lay in some tall dry grass on a nearby hill and watched for a long time. Just when I was about to leave, a bachelor bull came trumpeting and flapping his ears through the spruce trees. Everyone got very excited, flapping their ears and trumpeting, too, even the younger females who could not breed yet. The male dribbled urine down his legs. His penis was swollen so that it looked like a fifth leg, and his face was also swollen from the glands in his cheeks. His smell was so sharp it almost made me cough in my hiding place. This bull began to chase some of the females who could breed and they kept outrunning him or, if he did catch them, they would turn and twist so that his long penis could not reach their vulva. I realized then that the bull was mute. That I couldn't hear him. I saw then that the females did not want to mate with him. They only wanted to mate with other receivers. The big bull roared and trumpeted and squirted urine. His penis whipped back and forth like a snake as he came closer to where I lay watching. Finally, he lowered his head, his penis drooping on the ground, and he seemed very unhappy. Truthfully, I felt sorry for him.

Bachelor bulls sometimes act crazy, destroying every-thing they can reach, trampling trees and living crea-tures. The mammoth herd suddenly seemed worried about this since the females began to move, even though they really wanted to keep eating. My friends laugh at me and say that mammoths do not like or care about humans, but I think the matriarch of the herd sent me a warning now to go away. She sent me this thought: go-away-stupid-boy. Go-away. The matriarch was sending out her hurry message, hurry-hurry, to all the herd, to the females and calves and adolescents, but she was also talking to me. Go-away-stupid-boy. She didn't want me to be trampled by the big mute mammoth.

CHAPTER EIGHT

DOG

Dog leaned against Luke's leg, wanting to be stroked down his back and sides. Instead Luke scratched between Dog's ears, which was nice but not completely satisfying. The touch was too light. Luke was not really paying attention to Dog. Instead he was watching and talking to his new friends, the male and female. The female, who was talking back, had just recently realized that Luke was also Lucia. The male lay on the ground holding his stomach. That male had known about Lucia for a long time although he did not want to mate with her—wanting only to mate with the other female. Dog growled to himself and also to anyone who happened to be listening. Luke behaved differently around these humans, less willing to play games, less interested in Dog.

The female was asking Luke about Dog, and Luke was explaining that Dog was like any other direwolf, only tame. That Dog didn't mind being with humans because he had imprinted on Luke when he was young. That direwolves were social animals and Luke had become Dog's pack leader. The female asked if there was something different or unusual about their communication, the receiving and sending, and Luke said no. He could sense what Dog thought and felt, not all the time, but some of the time, just like he could with any Paleo.

Dog pushed at Luke's hand. Scratch-harder. Luke did. Dog thought that Luke could be really stupid. Luke didn't seem to know how much Dog had entered into his thoughts, how much Dog understood about his work in the lab, how much Dog was now Luke/Lucia. Dog remembered being a pup in his mother's den, but he also remembered being a girl/boy and hiding away in a small room to examine herself. Himself. Not quite sure what to do. He remembered a wedding cake (what was a wedding cake?) and Brad's father—the male was called Brad—and the crunch of a clay pot under a man's foot. He remembered wheelboarding down a corridor in the lab (what was a corridor?) and feeling scared because this was so much against the rules. Maybe he didn't know all the words. Maybe he didn't remember everything or everything in the right order. But he still knew and remembered a lot.

He understood what the humans were saying now, for example. Brad lay curled on the ground, whispering, "Don't look at my TOES. Stop looking at my TOES."

"I think it's started," Luke said.

"Listen to the music," Clare told Brad. "Close your eyes. Listen to the water."

Dog smelled the peyote on Brad and in the clay pot on the ground. Guanine, guanine, cytosine, cytosine. The plant's DNA was new to Dog, and he crept closer to the man with the peyote curling like smoke in his veins. The peyote was a collapsed biohologram, no longer matter/energy/consciousness combined, zipping, unzipping, receiving, sending. Even so, the power of the molecules and the spirit of the plant began to re-form, absorbed now into living cells, receptors open, chemicals snuggling—an unexpected embrace. Fitting and locking.

"Where's the water?" Brad asked, his eyes shut.

"Put your hand into the stream," Clare coaxed. "Feel the coolness?"

"Don't look at my TOES."

"Let's take off his shoes," Luke suggested.

"Let's get him interested in the water," Clare said.

Brad opened his eyes, sat up, and looked at Dog.

Molecules traveled into Brad's brain, molecules crossing the brain barrier, quantum bilocality, sparking, connecting, opening, joining. Signals, messages. Synapses. Opening, closing, zipping, unzipping, opening, closing. Dendrites pruned. Dendrites blooming. Flowers blossoming. Dog smelled equations, the rich heat of blood, the sharpness of fox, tannin in oak. The numbers had smells, and Dog was dizzy because numbers were like stars: they had no DNA, they were real and not real, they were small and not small, they were still and not still. They made him feel like Dog and not Dog. The stars were water. He was spreading away from himself, dissolving in water.

Dog whined, but Luke couldn't hear him because this was not happening now, in present time.

Brad heard him. Brad whispered, "Don't be afraid." Brad held his hand like his mother had held his hand after his father had left to go hunting. His mother who died of cancer. Suddenly she was gone. Dog wept.

"If it's too much, shut your eyes," Clare said. "Lie down. Close your eyes."

Dog wanted to give Brad a gift. This was new.

Sometimes he brought sticks to Luke so that Luke could grab the other end and try to get the stick away from him. Sometimes he brought the carcasses of small animals and the bones of bigger animals just to show Luke he was a good hunter even if he was really only a scavenger. He brought Luke the bodies of animals and bones and sticks, but they were not gifts. He loved Luke. He loved Luke like he loved rolling in the dirt and shaking his fur and sleeping in the sun. He felt anxious when he was away from Luke for more than a day. He couldn't sleep that perfect extinction if Luke were not nearby. He would die for Luke if his genes would let him.

But he had never wanted to give Luke one specific thing like he wanted now to give Brad. What could that thing be?

Oh, Dog spoke to Brad. I know. And Dog thought about the peyote plant, and he saw the right frequency, the right amplitude, cosine and sine, and he gave Brad that image/sound/color, the whirling double helix, guanine, cytosine, adenine, thymine, how the helix opened and sent out waves and opened and received and how the biohologram of peyote unfolded in space, waxy skin, puckered indentions, plump roundness, respiration, transpiration. Dog had never seen it so clearly before. How the organization of matter/energy/consciousness was turned on by DNA.

Dog barked. Holograms were produced through interference, two or more waves passing through each other to create a pattern, the consciousness of the universe—waves and frequencies and interferences—projecting what was experienced as the physical world. The holographic principle. Einstein had disagreed. (Who was Einstein?) He had argued against it. But he was wrong. The great Einstein. The consciousness of the universe—waves and frequencies and interferences—projected as the unique consciousnesses of each plant and animal, turned on and organized by DNA. The universe holographically fractal. Dog barked again. Rocks and viruses! They didn't have DNA! How did they organize?

"Dog is the peyote god," Brad yelled.

"Listen to the water," Clare coaxed.

"He's in my head," Brad explained.

Luke reached out to grab Dog's ruff.

"Maybe you should take Dog away," Clare suggested.

"No!" Brad shrieked. "He stays with me!"

Dog had to laugh although no one heard him, and that's how it went for the rest of the afternoon and into the night. Brad played in the water. Brad smelled music. Brad took off his shoes. Clare and Luke took Brad to see the sunset. Brad was so happy. Brad lay down in his animal skins and stared up at the stars while Clare, Luke, and Dog sat around the campfire keeping watch. Brad looked at the three of them, each in turn, and felt such love—such compassion. The left and right sides of Brad's heart opened and closed, sending and receiving. The valves opened and closed, letting the world in, letting the world out.

At sunset, especially, Brad looked at Clare, her skin reflecting the last rays of light. The joy of love leaked from his eyes. Partly this was Dog's love for Luke, pure, unshakable, undying love, so that Brad made a noise of pleasure, a dog's noise, and Clare patted him on the shoulder. "Yes, it's very beautiful," she said. Brad put out his hands and cupped her face. "You are beautiful," he said, knowing for the first time what beauty was. Clare glowed in the raiment of her sweetness and goodness, her courage and humor, her smell of skin and sweat and menstrual blood. She glowed with her unique DNA, her unique consciousness, guanine, cytosine, and Brad wept for her and for his mother, weeping over their graves. The smell of dirt. Clare said nothing, letting him have this experience. "I love you so much," Brad said, and she nodded. She understood. The arc of the Milky Way, water and stars. George Fox. (Who was George Fox?)

And then earlier, before the sunset.

Brad looked across the stream and saw a glowing stick of light. The light floated above the sandy bank, horizontal, three meters long, topped by a composite of small flowers. The stick separated into three lines, one above the other. A Chinese ideogram. A symbol for something. Brad didn't know what. So many of the Pleistocene scholars had been Chinese, as well as Japanese, Korean, Mongolian, from all over the world. No one had heard from China for a hundred years. Two billion people gone. And now they were trying to speak to him.

"Do you see that, Dog?" Brad asked.

Dog laughed. Dog cupped his hands around Clare's face.

CHAPTER NINE

BRAD

Brad and Clare were having sex outside in a bed of grass away from the camp. Brad climaxed after Clare climaxed and then they dressed and lay together, holding each other until it became too cold and uncomfortable. The thorns of goathead pricked Brad's arm even through the leather shirt, and he felt a rock under his thigh. He didn't want to leave, yet he was the one who finally suggested it. Clare agreed a little too quickly.

They walked together to where Luke had built a shelter of willow saplings pulled together at the top and interwoven from top to bottom with other branches, strong enough to discourage any hyena who might come sniffing. At night, Brad, Luke, and Dog slept comfortably inside. Dog warned them of intruders, and Luke was good with his spear when he could jab close. Despite some scares, this had been better for Brad than crowding into one of the bachelor tents in the larger camp, sharing the other men's bad jokes and smells. Especially recently, Brad avoided any place where he might meet Jon, who was prone to glaring at him—a serious glare, the prelude to spontaneous action. Brad had dealt with this kind of jealousy before in the lab, but he had never felt so physically threatened. Even Clare was surprised and kept protesting that Jon was such a gentle man.

They passed the isolated tent where the bushkie had been kept a prisoner. He was gone now, and Brad thought of him alone in the peyote fields. Perhaps the spirit of the peyote plant would be of some comfort to him before he died of thirst or madness. Brad had to smile—remembering the peyote plant.

"Tomorrow the tribe moves to our winter camp," Clare was saying. "And I'll take you back to the lab."

She continued with the details of their five-day trip, what route they would travel, how fast they would go, what food and water they might find. Meanwhile, the tribe would begin the journey east and south to a larger valley near another stream. Herds of animals grazed these grasslands and browsed the forest edge—elk, camel, antelope, horse—with saber-toothed cats, lions, humans, and wolves competing for the meat. The glyptodont could be seen with its armor and poisonous spikes, which the tribes sometimes used for darts and arrows. Giant sloths and giant beavers were also common. The piñon pines were full of nuts. Some of the oak trees had edible acorns. Wild onion and garlic flavored their winter food. Clare boasted of bounty. Botany. Brad hardly listened.

"Just stay for the solstice," he insisted again. "If you don't like it, you can leave."

"I know I won't like it. And I've done my service in the lab."

Brad thought that he could talk to the Council and get them to request Clare's service again. Many adults came twice or even three times to the lab, helping with the work, building the solarcomps, monitoring the satellites. Clare had avoided that just as he had avoided the quest, but the right word to the right person—all done discreetly, of course. Clare would never know.

Brad grunted. Sex was making him stupid. How could she not know? The timing would be too suspicious. Clare took his hand, not understanding. Her fingers squeezed his.

Just before they reached the shelter, he said her name and touched her shoulder so that they stopped and turned toward each other. Brad pulled her close into an embrace. He kissed her standing up, yellow grass flowing around them, water flowing around a rock in the stream. "I want you to live with me," he whispered and kissed her again.

"It's . . ." Clare murmured. "I don't know how we can."

"Stay with me at the lab until solstice. Stay through the winter. Then we'll come back to the tribe and I'll stay with you."

"You," Clare pushed him away, looking toward the camp. Their relationship was not a secret. Still she didn't want anyone to see. "You hate living with the tribe. You can't wait to leave."

That was true, Brad thought. It was partly Jon. Who wanted to live with a great glowering stallion pawing at the ground? But more to the point, almost everything about tribal life annoyed him. It wasn't to his taste—all that physical labor and singing around the campfire. He didn't have the right skills. His hunting was marginal. He hurried too much when he skinned animals. He was awkward with children. Of course, he could carry things and cook simple food. But that didn't get him much praise. And those little lightweight solarcomps! They were dreadful! He missed his computer in the lab. He missed his work.

Besides, Luke and Dog were also leaving tomorrow, and then Brad would be friendless but for Clare. No, he couldn't imagine staying with the tribe much longer, traveling to their next camp, hauling all those supplies, setting the tents up again. He couldn't imagine coming back to live with them in the summer, either.

"Stay for the solstice," he repeated, drawing in Clare so her body fit against his. The tall yellow grass rustled and sighed. Clare smiled into his shoulder and rested her head. Habitually she touched the leather bag around her neck.

Brad knew he was losing her, the arc of their love already descending. In the distance, a condor flapped across the sun. Above the flank of a nearby hill, vultures circled, patiently waiting. Other scavengers hurried to join them as some animal lay dead or dying, and Brad thought of Dog, who might be hurrying to the site as well. He thought of Luke/Lucia, her hormones confused, all those years a woman in the lab wanting to be a man. People were born that way. Fertility was a concern for the tribes. And then—Brad marveled at the coincidence, the interlocking patterns—Lucia had become his mother's friend. She had watched over Brad when he was a baby and his mother was eager to be alone with her husband. Now, at Brad's urging, in their shelter at night, Luke became Lucia again, telling stories about the lab in a soft, high voice. She said Brad looked like his father. She said his father had been a great hunter.

Brad held Clare close. "Just stay for the winter."

"This isn't working," Clare said, referring to their sleeping arrangements. Brad had a bed in a small room in the lab, a very nice room with a window overlooking the enclosed inner courtyard. But Clare had been complaining that the room was stuffy at night because Brad insisted on closing the window. She said the bed was too small for the two of them. And the bed was too hard, not like the softer beds in camp made of grass and animal skins.

Clare wanted to make a tent for herself in the courtyard. Brad wanted her to sleep with him. Clare said he could sleep with her in the tent. Almost everything, Brad thought, was an argument. Even the winter solstice the next day had become a debate. Clare disapproved of the lab's preparations.

Now he pointed out the obvious. "You can't put out your tent until after tomorrow. We'll be playing games in the courtyard. There's the tree and the food."

Clare stared out the window. "It's like a sacrifice," she said. "You're cutting down and killing a living thing. For no reason."

Brad wanted to scream. "We've talked about this," he spoke carefully. "You cut willow branches for baskets. You cut saplings for spears. We all eat plants and animals. We consume the world, and the world consumes us."

"But we are careful about what we kill," Clare spoke with that insufferable righteousness of the tribes. "The solstice is a time of gratitude and thanksgiving. We eat our favorite winter foods and tell our favorite winter stories. We have races and spear throws. We try to have children who will be born in September."

"We do the same thing." Brad noticed he was grinding his teeth.

"And this tree?" Clare pointed out the window and looked grim.

"I've explained that," Brad began but it seemed hopeless. Every year, the lab chose and cut down a pine tree and placed it in their courtyard before the day of the solstice, decorating it with gewgaws, pieces of painted metal, curved nails—not just scavenged things but crafted ornaments made from scavenged material. The tree was like the lab, rooted in the past, but also reworked. Remade. The tree was silly and playful and that was the point. Not to be too serious on the shortest day of the year. Not to take themselves too seriously. Not to be like the tribes, Brad thought, but did not say out loud.

Clare looked at him—perhaps he had made a noise, perhaps he had groaned—before shrugging and putting up her hand, the signal to stop. The solstice tree was just one more bone of contention. They had a pile of bones between them.

She changed the subject. She was having trouble with her students, she said. Some of them had stopped emailing, and soon she would have to contact the elders in their tribe. She disliked doing that. In some subtle way, during the quest and with her move to the lab, she had lost control of the class.

Working hard, as hard as he ever had, Brad acted as if he cared. He asked some questions, and Clare seemed pleased with the effort, and they left the room together, the issue of sleeping unresolved. Outside in the courtyard, two children stood before the cut pine tree, admiring its ornaments. Clare looked at them but said nothing. Brad was relieved when she picked up her spear by the wall. A day of hunting would put her in a good mood.

They held hands for a moment before parting. Clare opened her mouth, and Brad was afraid of what might come out: *This isn't working.* So he covered her mouth with his, even though he knew people could be watching from the rooms three stories high that surrounded the courtyard, each room with its own small window. People could be watching from the corridor that led to the main lab to the east and from the doorways of the communal eating room to the west. People could be watching, and he was glad. He wanted everyone to see.

"Tonight," he said, touching her shoulder. Tonight he would take her to the radio tower, up the circular metal stairs that went to the very top, where they could look at the stars. "Tonight," he repeated and let her go, although his gaze followed her until she had passed the decorated tree—not giving it or the children another glance— until she was out the gate, her arms swinging.

A blonde woman crossing the courtyard saw Brad's expression and smiled with approval. Somehow Brad had redeemed himself at the lab. He had finally gone on a quest. He had hinted at a mystical experience, a peyote vision and Oneness with the universe. Above all, he had brought back Clare, competent and serious, heavy breasted and round hipped, still young enough to have a child. Although some tribal members sneered at the lab rats, Clare did not, and they appreciated that. She was quiet but well spoken when asked her opinion. She was a good hunter and got along with the lab's own hunters, something Brad had never been able to do. Even Brad's former lovers approved of her, as if their taste in him was now justified. Apparently he wasn't so bad if he could attract some- one as desirable as Clare.

Brad smiled back at the blonde woman—their affair was ancient—and remembered that he had promised to download Clare's student files from her old failing solarcomp into a new one. Like all new solarcomps, this would be made of recycled parts, mostly nano-plastic. Stopping before the solstice tree, Brad admired a perfectly shaped ball, a particularly clever ornament.

Plastic wasn't a concern. The plastic for solarcomps would never run out. The world before the supervirus had loved its plastic, which lasted forever, still piled up in buildings and storage sheds, still over-flowing the houses and hospitals and shopping malls, still filling the oceans and rivers and lakes with tiny disintegrating particles. And that was just the old plastic. The newer nanoplastic didn't even break down into smaller parts. For a very long time, they would have enough supplies to produce their solarcomps. The problem wasn't a lack of materials.

Brad thought about the Los Alamos Three. Thankfully, one of them had been a historian. Thankfully, the Pleistocene scholars and Costa Rican Quakers had also understood the importance of the worldwide web, the treasure of human knowledge. They had to know the past so as not to repeat it and, yes, they had to honor the past, too—like the lab honored this solstice tree. They couldn't throw out all human achievement. At the least, they had to know where they came from, the story of the supervirus, the existence of the Paleos, the origin of The Return. Moreover, they had to keep connected. They had to stay united, one large tribe, joining their resources of intellect and moral clarity. The satellites in space would last many hundreds of years. The web was in place, bathing them in waves of knowledge, history, information, instantly translating Russian into English, English into Russian, Russian into Spanish, Spanish into English. Maintaining the web was almost effortless. The web, the satellites—they were not the problem.

Suddenly irritated, Brad stalked toward his office at the far end of the east wing of the courtyard. The problem was education. The problem was labor. The tribes didn't appreciate the skills needed to repair a motherboard, much less build one. People like Clare and Jon and that tough-as-a-glyptodont grandmother elder still depended on computers for communication—for being human—but they didn't like to work on them. They spent a year or two at the lab and then avoided further service. The Costa Rican Quakers, of course, had a good balance. Their rotation system was exemplary. But the situation was desperate among the Russians, where the culture was so strongly nostalgic. Sometimes Brad wondered how many solar-comps the Russians even had left. When would they run out?

Alone in his office, alone with his own private and somewhat specialized computer, Brad felt himself relax. He twisted his back, loosening his shoulders and neck. He wanted to tweak some of his old work on the Theory of Everything. The quest had provided insights after all. In fact, he felt rejuvenated, something to do with talking to Luke under the stars. The old man had been so calm and wise. Perhaps it was the balance of male and female. And Clare, of course, this new energy had something to do with Clare. And the peyote vision. Something to do with Dog.

Brad opened to his favorite screen image, Albert Einstein, his childhood hero. His mother had set him the problem of Einstein's equation when he was twelve and asking too many questions about his father. Energy and mass were different forms of the same thing. Pure energy was electromagnetic radiation—waves of light, radio waves, X-rays—traveling at a constant speed of roughly 1,078,260,480 kilometers per hour. Energy at rest equals mass times the speed of light squared. But why square the speed of light? And what about energy in motion? Figure it out, his mother had said, and when Brad did—what about antimatter? she asked.

In those years, his early teens, his favorite book had been the twenty-first-century biography of Albert Einstein, which put the scientist at a turning point in history. Because of Einstein, people in the mid-twentieth century knew that matter and energy were the same thing. Everything was the same thing. Science as mysticism. Scientist as saint. Einstein represented a new way of seeing the world until finally in 2059 came the realization that thought could also travel in waves. The living proof was a hungry bird, a teratorn weighing 15 kilograms and standing 3.3 meters tall. Now the existence of a third property "apart" from matter and energy—unconscious consciousness immanent in the electromagnetic waves of the universe—threw the old string theories out the metaphoric window. New ideas and new equations started to make sense. That iconoclast Bohm, and others, started to make sense. Experiments with DNA and the holographic principle revealed some of the secrets of organized life and became the basis for a panpsychism, a TOE that went beyond anything Einstein had imagined.

Idly, Brad called the old biography to the screen. The author had emphasized Einstein's tragedy over his genius, highlighting the scientist's final years, when he had ignored mainstream developments in modern physics, suspicious of the new school of quantum mechanics, dismissing even the strong and weak nuclear forces. The book had won every prize of its chaotic time, making Einstein come to life as a mournful King Lear, Fool, and Prometheus, eternally foolish, eternally suffering. The pathos had appealed strongly to Brad.

He studied the famous photograph of wild hair and deep-set eyes. If only Einstein could have seen the work that continued after his death and built on his ideas. In Brad's adolescence (and, Brad admitted, for a long time after that as well) he had had daydreams in which he talked to Einstein, in which he sat with Einstein on a grassy hill or quiet spot in the lab and brought him up to date. At first, the great scientist had argued, as he had argued in his own lifetime—not ready to see the indivisible interconnectedness of the universe. Patiently, Brad had explained. Step by step. And Einstein listened with growing interest. His questions were probing, brilliant, as were Brad's answers. In the end, the great man was so grateful. So impressed. They began to collaborate. Almost they were like father and son.

And what did Einstein often say to Brad, speaking to him in particular? Brad spoke out loud, softly in his office. "The most beautiful thing we can experience is the mysterious. It is the source of all true art and science. He to whom this emotion is a stranger, who can no longer pause to wonder and stand rapt in awe, is as good as dead: his eyes are closed."

Brad closed his eyes. He remembered Dog's gift. The double helix. Amazing. Three golden lines. Mysterious. Unfortunately, almost everything else about that day was a blur. Brad opened his eyes and began opening his computer files, skimming through yesterday's advances, refreshing himself. Energized.

Later in the afternoon, a least favorite colleague bounced into the room—no one ever knocked at the lab. But Brad didn't feel the usual annoyance, not like before. And the colleague was not bouncing so much as hurrying. "There's someone here," she breathed, noticeably exhaling and inhaling.

A figure pushed at her from behind so that she half fell further into Brad's office.

"Luke!" Brad stood up. Luke looked terrible and smelled awful.

The least favorite colleague caught her balance and turned toward the wild-haired, wild-eyed old man. Brad noticed she had already steadied herself and was preparing a defense. Lab rats weren't as soft as the tribes imagined. They exercised. They trained for their quests. They hunted their own food.

"It's okay, Judith," Brad said to the woman. "I know him."

"I have to talk with you alone," Luke squeaked, clutching a leather sack to his chest.

"It's fine," Brad assured the woman again. "He's fine. He's from my quest. Thank you. Thank you."

"I'll be close by," Judith said. Brad nodded. That was nice of her.

As soon as they were alone, Luke closed the door and squinted at Brad craftily. "Only you can help," he whispered. "The only one. Dog said you would know what to do."

It shocked Brad to see Luke so disheveled. And where was Dog? But, of course, Luke couldn't bring the direwolf into the lab. The first thing to do was arrange a bath and food for the old man. Then, obviously, Luke needed to rest. Things had gone badly for him. The blonde woman could find a spare room.

Now Luke was emptying his leather sack on the floor, and Brad was stepping back as Dog's head tumbled out, lips pulled back from the gums. The yellow teeth still looked ferocious. The blue eyes were open and clouded. A fly escaped into the room.

Luke crouched and petted the direwolf's bloodied fur, above the edge of the neck where he had severed it from the body.

"He said you would know what to do," Luke repeated. "He told me what to tell you. It's all planned out. Just before he died. He told me what to do."

PART TWO

Because of Brad, Dog knew about the holographic principle, how everything in the world was a four-dimensional
image formed of waves that were themselves formed by
electromagnetic and quantum processes. He knew about
quantum non-locality, how the billions of cells in his body
were in constant non-physical communication, a complex
bio-holo-electromagnetic field organized by DNA into the
biohologram of Dog's body and Luke's body and Brad's
body. He knew about DNA from Lucia and from his own
research and study, and he knew about radio waves from
some deep mutation in his brain, from his birth to a direwolf in a northern cave.

CHAPTER TEN

CLARE

Clare was appalled. At first she couldn't speak. And Brad couldn't return her stare. Literally, he couldn't face her. Clare turned her attention to Luke, who was also appalling. Since she had last seen him, the old man had become a real bushkie, his gray hair matted, his eyes unfocused as he patted the head of a decapitated direwolf. The former Luke had been trim in loose-fitting leather. But now he seemed to fill up Brad's office, sitting on the floor like a big animal in a small trap. His smell and the smell of the dead Dog permeated the room, for he had been here all day, hiding, talking. What he proposed was crazy, crazier than any bushkie had ever dreamed, crazy and irresponsible and absolutely forbidden by the Council.

"We'll have to modify the transmitter in the tower," Brad said.

Then Clare realized that Brad was not avoiding eye contact because he felt ashamed. Brad was simply turned inward, obsessed with his new plan, this sacrilegious *experiment*. Brad was actually listening to Luke and encouraging him. Clare sat down in Brad's office chair, tired from walking all day with the other hunters, walking and finding little game, three javelinas and a single coati. It wasn't much, considering the number of people they had to feed. It wasn't unexpected, either, since the lab rats never moved to another camp but scoured the same hunting grounds over and over. All day, Clare had felt oddly dispirited, sorry about her quarrel with Brad that morning. At some point, she had made her decision. She had something important to tell Brad and she would not wait any longer. So she had come immediately to his office, not cleaning herself, not helping the other hunters skin the animals.

"Brad!" she spoke loudly to get his attention. "You know you can't do this."

They both looked at her, and suddenly Luke did not seem so unfocused.

"This is . . ." Brad hesitated. "An extraordinary opportunity."

"Then ask the Council first. That's why we elected them."

Of course, Brad didn't bother to answer that. They both knew what the Council would say. "Right," Clare agreed. "Because it is wrong. Because we don't do this kind of thing anymore."

Luke said, "You can't let Dog die."

Clare pointed to the object on the floor. "Dog has already died."

The old man flinched.

"Don't be cruel," Brad chided, and it was as if he truly could not help himself now, as if he truly had no choice: he began to lecture. "We know DNA uses radio waves to create the organism's natural bio-hologram. We know that after death the biohologram is no longer cohesive." Brad started to move about the room, but Luke was in the way, so the lab rat gestured instead, also pointing to Dog's head on the floor. "Obviously, in Dog's DNA, the switch for matter and energy no longer works. But the switch for something else might, for what we call the unique consciousness of the organism. Dog thinks it does."

Brad corrected himself. "Dog thought it did. Before he died. He believed that his own DNA, with the right radio wave, could be turned on again and that it could, ah, reanchor, reassemble the unique consciousness that had been formed up to the time of his death." Brad was speaking very fast now to prevent Clare from interrupting him. "Dog had an extraordinary gift. An insight into the structure of DNA and the genetic pattern. I saw it myself when we were joined by peyote. I saw it myself, Clare! Dog knows how to turn on his own DNA. He knows the right frequency, the right amplitude, sine, and cosine."

Clare wanted to yell back that she was not a buffalo. He had already explained all this, and she understood the basic concept. They wanted to send radio waves into a dead animal's head. They wanted to recreate Dog's connection to the panpsychism that unites all things. Consciousness that travels in waves. The unique consciousness that emerges and evolves with the biohologram of each DNA-based organism and that dissolves when the biohologram dissolves. They wanted to disobey one of the primary rules of The Return, the Council, the elders, and the last hundred fifty years—not to interfere with the natural order. Never to muck-a-luck again. And yes, she yelled, this was punishable. They could be severely punished for this. They wanted to do something humans had never done before, something no one knew anything about, something Brad was doing only because he thought he *could* do it, because this . . . mutation had whispered to a bushkie before he died.

"Luke isn't a bushkie." Brad pretended to be indignant for his friend.

Luke spoke from his place on the floor, "Dog told me what to do. I heard him. I know what to do. But we need Brad's help."

Brad explained again that Dog needed his insights into DNA to be translated into numbers and the numbers put through a computer that would moderate the radio signal. Radio waves varied from one millimeter to a hundred kilometers. They were as variable as DNA itself. Everything had to be finely tuned.

Clare couldn't believe this was happening. "No one cares about that!" she heard herself shrieking. "No one cares *how* you do this!"

She couldn't believe she was here in this stale stuffy room filled with scavenged materials, ugly plastic, ugly metal, ugly walls. She couldn't believe she was screaming at a poor crazy bushkie and the decaying flesh of a cowardly direwolf. This wasn't her. This wasn't her life. She should be with her tribe. She should be striding through the yellow grass, the winter sky a blue bowl over her head. The cool air. Rich smells. Mountains like humped animals in the distance. She should be walking through this precious world they had miraculously been given back, the only world they would ever have, spear in hand, alert in the moment.

"It's not the *how*," she said and actually stamped her foot.

The family of ground sloths murmured sweet nothings to each other. The big slow animals weighed at least two hundred kilograms and were the most pleasant-tempered of all the Paleos, perhaps of any animal on earth. Despite their claws, they would also be the most defenseless except that their meat tasted terrible, a nauseating flavor even teratorns scorned. Saber-toothed cats, lions, and bears taught their cubs, and wolves and hyenas taught their pups: don't bother. And so the giant sloths were left alone to spend their days eating leaves and roots, cooing back and forth all the while, a constant reassurance between parent and child, sibling and sibling, wife and husband. Here-I-am. Sweetling. Here-I-am. Don't-go-far. Don't-worry.

With her back against the rough trunk of a pine, Clare rested and listened to the murmuring sloths. Deliberately, slowly, she chewed a stick of elk jerky. Soon she would get up and hurry on again, across the land, almost running but not quite running, covering as many kilometers as she could, walking until nightfall, when she would sleep in another tree, not bothering to hunt or put out snares or make a fire. She wasn't comfortable traveling this distance alone, but she had no choice. Deliberately, calmly, she thought of Luke and Dog. Naturally Luke had come to depend on the direwolf for company. Naturally the bushkie had been distraught when his beloved companion died. The loss of such a friend had pushed the old man/woman over the edge. He was to be pitied. Poor Luke. Poor Dog.

Clare felt better now. She touched her stomach, her center. She knew who she was. So many things at the lab had been wrong—not big things, little things, but still so many of them, surprising her. The solstice tree with its round ornaments. The jokes the hunters made as they sat around a campfire. The way they cooked their meat in clay pots, with many of the herbs she knew, but still tasting wrong. The strange vegetables that came from their gardens, squash that was too big, and something called beets. Clare had been in service at the lab before, long ago, but she didn't remember feeling so alienated then. Of course, she thought now, she had been younger, less observant and more flexible. Also she had slept and eaten mostly with her own group, the other tribal members in service. She hadn't really been paying attention.

This time—paying attention—she was disturbed by the differences. Brad's status, for example. He was a man who avoided the quest and mocked the Council. Yet people at the lab tolerated him. They fed him although he did not hunt or gather food. They let him follow his interests, working for days alone on his computer with his equations and his Theory of Everything. They ignored his rudeness and bad behavior. In truth, they treated him like an elder although he was still in his thirties and brash and inexperienced and selfish and headstrong.

Alone now and calm, Clare admitted that elders were not always or even typically people whom other people liked and admired. And Brad *was* like an elder in some ways. His knowledge did not involve the skills of The Return. Instead, he had studied history and philosophy and literature. He understood quantum physics and panpsychism, the basis of their worldview. He commanded a breadth of information, and sometimes he used the past to think about their future—how they would keep scavenging, what they would run out of, what they would not. Clare suspected the Council consulted fairly often with Brad and listened to his ideas. They tolerated him because they needed him. One Council member had even made love to him.

Clare rose, put on her pack, and began moving through the landscape, effortless, smooth, running but not running. She sent energy into her legs. She pushed energy into her lungs and through her body. She kept alert watching for other animals who were also moving through the landscape stalking her or simply watching. She drank sparingly from her leather bottles and was happy when the springs she had been told about were actually there, when she could drink as much as she wanted and refill her bottles. She saw lion tracks and felt anxious. She saw an antelope herd but did not hunt them. That night, she climbed a large oak tree and built a nest, tying herself to the branches. Her legs twitched from exertion.

Before sleep, she thought of Brad's father, who had left the lab much as she was leaving. Perhaps he had gone back to the northern tribes or become a bushkie or died in an accident or been eaten with relish by a saber-toothed cat. No one knew. The hunter had stayed four years, a married man and then a father. When Brad was still a child learning to walk, the hunter announced he had to go and would not likely return, and Brad and his mother had never heard from him again. That was the end of the beautiful lab rat and the brave hunter. Clare could see how Brad had made this into a story, a polished tale, a touchstone. Now she was leaving him, the end of another story, the brave lab rat and the beautiful hunter.

In the morning, Clare was sick, vomiting up acid and taste of elk, and she thought about the baby growing inside her. She must have gotten pregnant in the weeks after the peyote ceremony. She was almost certain the child was Brad's, since she knew when she ovulated—when she desired sex more than usual—and she remembered that night, giving up her doubts and grudges, giving herself eagerly to Brad, that night and all the nights afterward, excited by his strangeness and declarations of love. Of course, the possibility remained that Jon was the father. They had lain together, too, a few days earlier.

Clare heaved one last time, wiped her mouth, and drank some water. She wouldn't be sick again until the next morning.

That's how it had been with her first child, Elise, sick every morning for three months, sick but happy, sick but laughing. She had made her husband laugh with her. They were not much older than teenagers. "I've never seen anyone throw up and smile," her husband said as Clare coughed, spit, her stomach knotted. She was sick but not tired, not worried, not like so many other women. It was her first baby, the whole tribe petting her and making a fuss, her mother and father and grandmother happy. The pregnancy had felt easy. Even the birth, always dangerous, had felt easy.

Then the midwives put the baby on Clare's chest. Elise had squirmed her face upward, found a nipple, and sucked hard. The little hands fisted, fists flailing. After a while, the sucking and gasping for air seemed connected. Suck, gasp. Suck, gasp. After a while, the midwives murmured and took the baby away, into the light, and Clare knew the meaning of bereft.

Her life had been full. Now it was empty. She called out for her baby. She told her husband, kneeling by the bed of skins, "Get the baby!" She could hear the midwives murmuring about skin, blue skin, and gasps for air. Heart damage, a hole in the heart. It was common enough.

Later some of the people—Clare's mother—had blamed Clare's husband. Children like this did not live long. Clare's husband should have suffocated the newborn, who would only suffer, not thrive. The midwives would have helped. Everyone in the tribe would have helped. The child would disappear. A quick sorrow.

But "Get the baby!" Clare had said and her husband had done what she asked although no one expected the little gasping girl to live past her first month or first year. No one expected her to live two, three, four more years. Weaker than other children, smarter than other children, brighter in spirit than other children, Elise had glowed like a candle in a tent, sheltered by parents who clung to the belief that she would grow up like any other child. She would flourish like any other child. With every day that passed, they worked to deceive themselves.

Some of the people blamed Clare's husband for not killing the baby that first day and then for not getting Clare pregnant again and then for dying himself so soon after Elise died. Apparently he had climbed the cliff to reach an eagle's nest. Many people liked such feathers for their pipe, and the fall could easily have been an accident. An accident, the tribe said, although they all saw the grief in his carelessness. They all suspected he had been blinded with tears.

For this, Clare had also blamed him—not for leaving her alone but for still having tears. She wondered if her husband had loved their daughter more than she did. For her part, she had felt empty the day Elise finally grew too big for an organ turned wrong and leaking blood. She didn't have any grief left when they put Elise in a tree to be eaten by birds. She had felt almost nothing, only going back later to sit under the ravens and crows cawing and swirling until the other women had to lift her up and force her away. Later, she didn't recognize Elise's bones. They didn't seem like her child's bones, so small and hard and white, and she watched her mother and grandmother wrap them in a skin and bury them in the ground, and she still felt nothing, comfortably detached. This little packet wasn't her daughter.

Clare did not want to think about Elise now. Elise wasn't a good daytime thought but something Clare saved for darkness, when she could bring up memories and relive them just as she fell asleep. She didn't want to think about the new baby either, not yet. She certainly did not want to think about Brad and what he planned to do with Dog's head, the physical proof of his latest equations.

"We'll finally know," Brad had said. "We'll know if it's true." Desperately, Clare had argued back that they already knew enough. They had enough truth. Desperately, she had begged him not to do this, even ordering Luke out of the room and having sex with Brad, using the most obvious and oldest trick: do this for me, please, for my love. The next day, she had threatened to leave. She had threatened to tell the Council. But nothing worked. Nothing budged Brad from his stubborn desire.

And he knew she wouldn't tell the Council. She wouldn't be the one to betray him. Didn't she understand obsession? For four years, she had kept alive a daughter who should have died at birth. Didn't she understand delusion?

Clare drank, wiped her mouth, and slung her pack over her shoulders. She wouldn't tell the Council, but she couldn't stay at the lab with Brad either. She believed in The Return, their charted course. After the supervirus—*a bed of bones, a sea of ash*—humans had to find another way. They had to go back to what had worked for tens of thousands of years, and they had to go forward with a new humility. Their old compact with the earth. Their new compact with the earth. They were part of something larger than themselves. They were part of everything, not separate, not gods, not above the world, not interfering with the world.

Clare began walking fast, effortlessly, wanting to reach winter camp the next day. So many people had suffered and died so that she could be here, right now, in this moment, this beauty. Brad would fail. His equations would be wrong. Someone would discover what he was trying to do. Hunters would be sent to destroy his equipment, his computer. They might imprison him, as her tribe had imprisoned the murderous bushkie. Dog's supposed insight would be revealed as the hallucination of a dying animal. There were so many ways this *experiment* could end badly. Clare had no doubt. Brad would not succeed. But that wasn't the point, not for her. Freedom was not unlimited. You didn't do something just because you could.

Clare imagined a game trail worn through yellow grass. Suddenly the trail forked. Perhaps one way led to a pond and another higher into the mountains. Two trails went in opposite directions. It was never meant to be. She and Brad had met so strangely. Crucified lizards. The way he cupped her face, the peyote god on his breath, the direwolf listening. A polished story, a fable.

She swam across the land, a swimmer in grass.

Social Problems: Assignment Five, submitted by María Escobar

I have decided to turn in another paper for extra credit. I feel that my last papers were not exactly the best I could do and as I have said before I really need a good evaluation from you so that I can go on my first long quest this summer. This quest is very important to me and if writing an extra paper will help you evaluate me better then I am very happy to do that.

Global warming is not really a social problem now but it was a social problem in the past, and so I think that counts. At the beginning of the twenty-second century, people were only using viral technology as well as wind and solar and hydrocell and they were not emitting much carbon dioxide into the air. But like the web says, "The damage was done." Most of the planetary ice was gone, the oceans were higher, many cities along the coast had flooded, there were new deserts, and there wasn't much land for gardens and growing food. People starved, drowned, and died of thirst or disease. Many species went extinct, even as the scientists were still busy cloning the Paleos. Cloning by then was so easy that they could have cloned all the species going extinct because of global warming but no one bothered because there wasn't enough room for them anymore.

Here in Costa Rica the weather got hotter and drier and we still have a lot of fires which destroy the jungle. We also have a lot of storms around the coast but since no one lives there it doesn't matter. We don't go thirsty and after the supervirus killed off almost all the humans, the plants and animals recovered fast so we have plenty to eat. The good news is that malaria and other diseases are hardly a problem at all now, although we don't know why.

Global warming was a huge and terrible mistake and everyone feels very bad about it. I think it was our worst mistake, even worse than the supervirus because the supervirus killed off only humans and global warming killed off so many other animals and plants. Once when I was a kid, I apologized to the planet for doing this and I had a ceremony where I cut my finger and let drops of blood soak into the earth. Actually I cut myself too much and it started bleeding a lot and my parents were mad at me. But that's just the kind of thing kids do. What's done is done. The important thing is that we learned our lesson.

CHAPTER ELEVEN

DOG

Dog remembered dying with a greater clarity than anything he remembered about being alive. In those last moments, his body was deliriously busy, bladder emptying, heart pumping, right and left atria filling with blood, priming the ventricles, ventricles contracting, propelling blood to lungs, aortic and pulmonary valves opening, atria filling—and then not filling. Where was the blood? The heart waited to contract. The non-beating of the heart. Where was the rich hot blood?

Time flowed differently in those moments of death, consciousness twisting gently apart from matter/energy, the double helix zipping and unzipping. Einstein had discovered that gravity could warp the curve of space and time, that time slowed near a large mass such as a sun or planet or black hole, that time was affected by matter. Now Dog understood that time was also affected by consciousness.

Dog knew about Einstein because of Brad. Because of Brad, Dog knew about the holographic principle, how everything in the world was a four-dimensional image formed of waves that were themselves formed by electromagnetic and quantum processes. He knew about quantum non-locality, how the billions of cells in his body were in constant non-physical communication, a complex bio-holo-electromagnetic field organized by DNA into the biohologram of Dog's body and Luke's body and Brad's body. He knew about DNA from Lucia and from his own research and study—and he knew about radio waves from some deep mutation in his brain, from his birth to a direwolf in a northern cave.

He knew about the five relatively unimportant dimensions of time, which might not be so unimportant. His brain waited impatiently. All the cells were impatient. Where was the oxygen? The cells cried out as one. Where was the oxygen? Excitement grew. Suddenly the optic nerve had no choice. Dog could no longer see. No more images formed of light waves refracted by air, cornea, and aqueous humor, inverted and then reinterpreted by the brain. He would never see like that again. Suddenly he could no longer hear. Or taste or smell. The cells growled, scavengers waiting for food. A teratorn hopped forward on the ground. A condor flapped to sit on a branch. A spiral of vultures twisted in the sky. But the birds in Dog's brain would get nothing from this meal of nothing being sent to them by nothing, a heart with no blood. Before their scavenger eyes, the tiniest scraps of oxygen disappeared. The bones of the beast were hollowed, the marrow crunched. No oxygen, no food, no prize. Dog gasped.

He couldn't see. He couldn't hear. He couldn't smell. It wasn't so bad. The very absence of these things had a new richness and meaning. He watched his DNA zipping, unzipping, the deflating hologram, signal waning. The last waves of consciousness released. Like bubbles in water.

Dog's mouth filled with bubbles. The giant shortfaced bear had bubbles in his saliva, too, Dog remembered. He had seen them just as he turned his head before the darkness closed in. The bear had surprised Luke and Dog, charging from a screen of quivering aspen while Dog was distracted by the scent of a deer carcass bloated with gas. It was clever of the bear to hide his thoughts and to hide in that scent, so close, waiting while the direwolf came closer, closer, closer, and sniffed the bait. Behind Dog, closely, Luke limped up the grassy hill and called him away. Luke's hips hurt. The deer was putrid. They would find something better to eat.

Close, closed, closely. Dog played word fetch. Dog loved a putrid smell and was thinking of rolling in it. He didn't care if that would annoy Luke. In fact, Dog was still angry at Luke, who had surrounded himself with humans, Brad and Clare, his real human pack. Now Dog would roll in the bubbling, falling-off, insect-filled ribs of the deer and that would make Luke curse and yell, and that was good. Luke had become too calm and wise. Dog missed the crabby old man. He missed their games.

But Dog didn't get this last bit of fun, this last roll in bubbling rotten flesh because just then the giant shortfaced bear broke through the screen of quivering aspen, pulling apart the white-barked trees as if they were grass. Dog turned his head to look. The huge animal towered over him, a living mountain of hair and muscle and catlike face yowling and spitting. Long heavy claws swiped the air and across Dog's back, flipping him over, swiping through his stomach and chest.

Very quickly, Dog began to die, his stomach and intestines quivering like aspen leaves, the blood rushing through his veins to fall on the ground, pulled by gravity away from the stunned madly beating heart, blood that would never return, never loop again. The perfect circle of his veins and heart had been cut. Dog felt the loss of perfection. The blood poured on the ground as the giant shortfaced bear grabbed Dog by the neck and stood up on her two flat back feet. She held Dog in her mouth as if he were a pup, shaking him back and forth with delight and fury. Dog himself had shaken things like that, sticks or small animals. Once he had tried to shake his father's tail.

Luke was close behind him on the grassy hill. Dog! Dog! Luke screamed even as he turned away from the bear and began pumping his legs, his pack bouncing against his back. Dog felt the waves of Luke's fear. The horror and grief.

The giant shortfaced bear also enjoyed those emotions. She almost dropped Dog in order to chase after Luke, but the human was running surprisingly fast. The joy of eating Luke was in the future, and the giant shortfaced bear was having such a good time eating Dog now.

In these last moments, just before dying, Dog didn't really want to hear the thoughts and feelings of the giant shortfaced bear. But they were so close, and she was so loud. She was so thrilled to be hurting him, slicing him, shaking him. All the tension in her body fell away, the release of that desire which had built up painfully in the last few weeks and the satisfaction settling in like the digestion of a big meal. Not all giant shortfaced bears loved to kill as much as this one did. But as a species, they were prone to pathology.

Brad began to lecture. Brad knew a lot about the animals and plants of The Return because he had read so much. His access to the computers in the lab was unparalleled, and his work schedule unusually light. He had considerable leisure time. Brad's voice explained to Dog that all too often giant shortfaced bears were psychopaths, the wiring of the carnivore slightly wrong, the pleasure in the kill misdirected. Oddly enough, these bears were predominantly scavengers like Dog, lacking a bone structure strong enough to bring down large animals, while lighter prey like horses and camels tended to out-maneuver them. The natural competition between scavengers could have been the reason the bear chose to trick and catch Dog. More likely, however, she was simply following her psychotic urges to kill something, anything, and Dog was available. Giant shortfaced bears, Brad concluded, should never have been cloned. They were genetically flawed.

Dog had to agree. The bear's DNA shimmered in the darkness. Thymine, thymine, thymine. And there, gossamer, the fragile chromosome—a too-thin wall, certain electro-positively charged molecules, certain proteins easy to break apart.

The bear let go of Dog's neck and Dog floated to the ground, the bear snapping up a bit of loose intestine. Grunting, the bear dropped to all fours and began to feed more seriously, a chunk from Dog's flank, a prod at the gaping stomach wound and then a daintier bite. She didn't want to hurry this.

Dog wasn't in pain. That first surge of adrenaline had been swamped by shock. Almost instantly, neurochemicals in the brain were produced and released. Dopamine. Serotonin. Systems shutting down, some of them quiet, some fussing a little. He couldn't move his legs. Or twitch an ear. He couldn't regulate his body temperature. Without a stomach, he certainly wasn't hungry. Only his lungs kept filling with air and letting out air, his breaths moving shallowly in and out. His heart had one last beat. One more contraction of the left ventricle. Dog felt relaxed. He watched and waited.

A burst of light in the brainpan. Dog was walking with Lucia in a place of red rock and rimrock, sweeps of grass and towering buttes, places where the Warrior Twins had once walked, where the Pueblo people and Navajo people had lived centuries ago. Now Lucia was climbing a steep road to the top of a mesa, and Dog didn't understand why. This was human business—the shape of twigs left in a game trail—and he was content with that. He only had to follow Lucia.

At the end of their climb, at the very top, they moved away from the adobe pueblo cracked with heat and dwindling with rain. Along the edge of the mesa where the ridge rose slightly, at another jumble of rock, Lucia climbed again in the dimming light to a wide flat perch where they watched the sunset, the plain extending in all directions, the horizon bounded by hills and buttes, the view stupendous. Lucia turned in a circle, her hair loose. Dog puzzled over the word *stupendous* and the idea that a view could be important. The horizon flared in splashes of pink, orange, red, the dust in the atmosphere accumulated from years of drought in the deserts of the American West, wind sweeping over eroded land and brushing up the earth like a broom. The red ball slipped below the curve of the planet, and Lucia said out loud, "He's not coming tonight."

Apparently they had been waiting for someone. Now they scrabbled down rock, and Dog curled against his human, sleeping without a fire or tent. No hyena or lion, no saber-toothed cat or shortfaced bear would be hunting on such a dry mesa with its thin covering of grass and shrubs. No one would climb so high for this.

In the morning they set snares for mice, Dog sniffing and Lucia putting out the traps. For water, they used the rain collectors made long ago by the humans who once lived here, depressions carved in stone by the most ancient people and then, later, the nanobarrels. After two more nights of waiting, on the third sunset, another hunter joined them, a tall long-limbed dark man younger than Lucia. He sat beside their fire as Lucia put her hand on Dog's neck, telling him not to growl. Like other humans they had met, the man was interested in Dog. He studied Dog but did not offer a hand to smell.

"I know where a black bear is denning," the man said. "You can have the skin."

"A black bear on the mesa?" Lucia asked.

"A few animals come this way. Perhaps they're like you and me. Curious. Perhaps they need a safe place."

Lucia nodded, pleased. "How are your wife and son?" she asked.

"I don't know." The hunter shrugged. "I left a long time ago."

"Ah," Lucia was sad.

"Ah," the hunter was sad. Then he shrugged again.

The two humans sat and watched the sky. As the red sun dropped below the horizon, the hunter stood and began to chant. Grateful for the sun. Asking its blessing. Grateful for the gift. Asking the sun to rise again. Dog recognized the feeling, like when he smelled certain kinds of rot, like when he discovered a new DNA he had never seen before. Lucia listened patiently but without real interest. Dog could smell elk jerky in the hunter's pack and wondered if they would eat that soon. Dog lifted his face and put his nose against Lucia's cheek, and she reached out and cupped her hands around his muzzle and shook him lightly back and forth.

The next day they speared the small female bear with her cubs and gorged on the greasy meat. Dog was allowed to eat from the choicest parts! The hunter stayed with them helping scrape and tan the skin until one morning his pack was on his back, and he said good-bye. "North," he said, rubbing Dog's ears and chest and scratching Dog's stomach until Dog flopped over, spread his legs, and whined with pleasure. The hunter showed his teeth. "Beyond the farthest tribe."

A smell in the brainpan. Brad breathed in his father's odor as he leaned against the man's leg, sharp bitter sweat and dried blood from a deer his father had killed and carried home. Speaking to someone else, the man reached down and petted Brad's head, gently stroking the wiry dark hair. The hunter let his hand settle on his son's shoulder, the fingers warm and firm. Brad buried his nose in his father's leather pants. His mother said something. She stood close, nearby, laughing. Suddenly his father picked Brad up and was swinging him in the air, pretending to toss him to his mother but never actually letting him go. "Who wants this little boy?" his father was chanting and laughing, too. Brad giggled and squirmed so that his father had to hold on tightly.

Where was Luke?

Luke held tight to the trunk of a pine tree. He had climbed as high as he could to escape the giant shortfaced bear, his pack a burden but also necessary, with enough food and water to last for days. Luke closed his eyes, seeing Dog disemboweled and suffering, bleeding, dying. Lucia wrapped her arms around the tree and sobbed. She was old and useless. She was alone.

A cloak of sorrow settled over Dog's shoulders. He brought it close against the chill of night. Flashes in the brainpan. Memories of smell. But mostly touch. Luke petting him hard. Dog leaning hard against Lucia's leg. Dog curled against Luke's animal skins, feeling the warmth through the night.

Dog couldn't bear to be separated like this. He couldn't live or die apart from Luke, and he reached out with yearning, with love—Brad quoted an old and revered Quaker—"or something like love that doesn't split, the way love does, into loving and being loved." Dog knew this had happened many times before. Dying ground sloths reached out to each other. Dying humans reached out to each other. They couldn't bear to be separated like this. They didn't know what to do.

But Dog knew what to do. In a nanosecond, he had lodged himself in Luke's cerebellum. This took some effort and hastened for a nanosecond the dissolution of the matter/energy/consciousness that had been Dog, who died painlessly in the sense that time stopped for him and he lived only as thought—knowledge—inside Luke's brain. Dog didn't mind. It was only temporary.

CHAPTER TWELVE

BRAD

Brad wanted to chase after Clare. If he could talk to her before she reached the winter camp, he could persuade her that what he was doing was right or, at least, inevitable. Moreover, she had been the catalyst. She had made the decision to follow the tracks from the riverbank that led to Luke and Dog and the bushkies. She had stirred the peyote tea, wakening the plant so that Dog and Brad could exchange neurosignals, receiving and transmitting.

In that exchange, Dog had learned about the Theory of Everything while Brad—he admitted wryly now—had learned about the scent of rabbit and the pleasure of licking his own balls. The mutant direwolf had taken more than he gave when they played with their TOEs by the stream that afternoon. But now the animal was about to reveal to Brad something extraordinary, something humanity had always dreamed about, always pursued—immortality.

Brad caught himself. That kind of hubris wouldn't convince Clare. And that really wasn't what he was doing. This really wasn't about ambition or arrogance or assuming godlike powers or perverting natural law. (Brad could hear Clare accusing him.) This was . . . an opportunity. A wind blowing through the window of a room. An open door! "Unscrew the locks from the doors," a nineteenth-century poet had said. "Unscrew the doors themselves!" This was a relationship with the world: I know you. I am part of you because I know you, and I must know more. I must know everything I can know. I must reach the limits of knowledge. This was a thirst, and this was the real quest. Brad felt his heart swell. Of course, Clare would agree. Of course, she would return with him.

But Luke said no. The morning after Luke's return, after a long tiring night of discussion (and lovemaking), Clare had packed up her supplies, picked up her spear, and walked away from the lab. And Luke said they couldn't go after her. They didn't have time. Dog's instructions did not make sense to Luke and, for that reason alone, tended to slip away. Luke was struggling to keep Dog's voice alive, an effort that gave him a headache and made him cranky. They had to do this now. They couldn't waste time running after Clare.

Brad was seeing new sides to Luke, first a grieving old man and then a stern taskmaster. Luke became Lucia became Luke became Lucia again, the higher voice alternating with the deeper one, mourning Dog, dictating to Brad the numbers in his head, and organizing their trip to the abandoned city of Los Alamos.

At first, Luke had questioned the need for that trip—until Brad took him up the radio tower, showed him the transmitter, and explained what was required to modify it to Dog's needs. A new childish Luke whined, "Don't you have those things in the lab?" A new insistent Luke decided, "We'll leave tomorrow. Make your excuses."

Brad had to decide what those excuses would be. No one—no one—could know where they were going or what they were thinking of doing. A chance meeting in the courtyard with Judith gave him the lie when she asked about Clare and remarked, pointedly, that

she had heard them arguing. Brad whispered back as if in pain—
because he actually was in pain, because he hated letting Clare go—
that his lover had gone back to her tribe. He was going after her. He
and Luke. He had to hurry. They would be gone a few days.

His least favorite colleague looked sorry for him. "Just the two of
you? Is that safe?"

"Maybe not," Brad said. He felt a little ashamed. He was always
lying to Judith, who, in her way, had always remained loyal to him.
"But it's something I have to do. Don't let anyone know until I'm
gone."

"I have a good feeling," his least favorite colleague reassured him.
"Quarrels like this can make a relationship stronger."

In the distance, they could see airplanes. For one hundred fifty years,
the machines had sat in the sun and wind, not rusting or falling
apart as much as they did farther north where it rained more often.
At least from here, some of the planes still looked flyable, although
Brad knew better. All the rubber would be gone, tires included, and
the wiring corroded or eaten by rodents. Brad speculated, as he had
before, about what it would take to restore a plane and fly to one of
the population centers in Costa Rica or Russia. Fixing the battery
would be easy since most solar cells were not viral technology. But
he would also need to repair and restart the nanoengines. Then he
would have to reprogram the computers for flight and navigation. In
the end, what would be the point? Every human who wanted to be
in communication was already on the solarcomps. Everything that
needed to be said could be said.

And, of course, rebuilding a pre-supervirus airplane was completely against Council rules. Brad had to admit those rules were not
arbitrary. The Los Alamos Three had decided against such flights
when they still feared contagion or a new strain of the supervirus.
Abandoning motor transportation and guns had also been part of

the Great Compromise between the Paleolithic scholars and New Mexican scientists, which, generations later, still seemed to be working. Despite low fertility rates and mutations from the overheated power plants, humans were still here and the population stable. Some would say the human race was thriving. Clare would say they lived in the best of times, the best of worlds.

Following Luke down a hill, scaring up a herd of white-tailed deer, Brad thought of Clare and how she had argued with him, begged him, made love to him. Don't do this. Please. Don't do this. His refusal was ironic since what he wanted most (well, maybe not most) was her approval. He admired her tremendously. He admired her work, how she carried on the principles of the Los Alamos Three in the constant emails and grading of papers. How she persevered with students who didn't appreciate her efforts but only wanted a life of hunting and gathering, mating, art, ritual, sleeping, family—everything The Return promised, everything The Return fulfilled. Clare was right about so many things, and by midday, hungry and thirsty, Brad was wondering if she were not right about this, too. If the rules were not arbitrary, then why was he breaking them?

Luke interrupted his thoughts. "The quickest way is to follow the road." The old man had stopped and was pointing down an incline. "If you can handle it."

Grass, yucca, and scrub brush grew through the cracks of the twenty-first-century highway so that it looked more defined than actually present, designated by lines of abandoned solar cars skewing to the left and right of its center. Brad knew the cars contained the remains of people who had died from the supervirus in the act of fleeing. He knew he would find other human artifacts as he and Luke walked toward the city, not bones—those had crumbled into the earth long ago or been carried off by animals—but pieces of glass and plastic, photo pods, the treasures that couldn't be left behind. Some receivers said that places like this, the desperation of people, still emitted waves of sorrow. A smoky depression.

"I'll be fine," Brad said confidently. "And you?"

Luke grunted. "It's just mixing up with everything else. Dog doesn't care and that helps."

At first Brad thought Luke was referring to Dog's head, which the old man had insisted on bringing with him, wrapped tightly in his pack. Then he remembered the Dog lodged in Luke's head, that singular echo spouting instructions.

"Paleos don't care," the old man repeated, "about how many people died."

They followed the curve of the road past a few adobe buildings and then many adobe buildings, roofs falling, doors hanging, and a large burned area hit by lightning, only its charred walls left, ashy metal, and unrecognizable debris. More solar cars littered the streets torn up by roots of hundred-year-old oaks and juniper trees. Brad knew the shop he wanted, a two-story Electro built toward the edge of town. Most of Los Alamos had used adobe construction, cool in summer and warm in winter. But in the year of the supervirus, 2113, the newest buildings had been made of a nanoglass designed to let in light even as it moderated the sun's heat. Fifteen decades later, the elegant structures of stores like Electro were still standing, still responding to the seasons, still filled with things people had once needed. In front of Luke now, Brad found himself walking faster. Dog was really beginning to smell.

Brad thought of Clare again, how he had walked behind her and the bouncing head of the javelina. The thick straight line of her braid.

"I was here with your mother once," Lucia called out, perhaps to get him to slow down. And Brad remembered calling out to Clare, "Where will we camp tonight?" Trying to get her to slow down.

"We came for your eyeglasses," Lucia limped beside him. The speed of Luke's transformations was becoming alarming, his personality swinging back and forth in the space of an hour. Sometimes the old man crossed the borders of time as well as gender, speaking with the voice of a younger Lucia, a woman from the lab still doing research on the rate of mutations among the tribes. That woman chattered about broken chromosomes and lab politics from over thirty years ago, unaware that the results of her work had long been censored by the Council and that the politics of her day were irrelevant. By now Brad understood that Lucia had been in love with his mother.

"We took back a round ball for the solstice tree." The old woman's knees seemed to be hurting, and she stopped to rub them. "Your mother loved stewed rabbit with rosemary. There was wild rosemary growing in big clumps here."

Brad worried that Luke was going crazy. He didn't know if bringing Dog's unique holo-consciousness back would help his friend or not. Probably not.

"What's wrong?" he asked, meaning the limp.

"Arthritis." Lucia shrugged. She chatted about herbal remedies as they walked through the falling-down buildings, avoiding crashed cars and concrete upheavals. Brad saw a few non-native flowering plants and trees imported from the Mediterranean or South America, still surviving in isolated pockets. Despite the growth of vegetation, the rusted litter would be a jangle on anyone's nerves, he thought. It was no wonder that human scavengers got spooked. Soon enough, the Electro store was in front of them—doors open, locks disabled long ago—and Brad moved toward it eagerly, not noticing the lions until Luke pulled him back.

The pride had staked out their resting area in a grove of cottonwoods growing up beside the glass-walled store, the trees watered by a spring that also watered a thick understory of grass and shrubs. The sudden appearance of two humans interested the male, who rose from his comfortable lounge on the ground and padded forward, less than twenty meters from Brad. Two lionesses camouflaged in tawny coats lifted their heads. Brad saw more movement behind them, two smaller lionesses who also got up out of curiosity or deference to the male.

Brad stumbled and then was still. As usual, he hadn't been watching for animals. That wasn't his job. Someone like Clare always did that. Besides, he didn't associate this weird decaying city with hunting or being hunted. Luke's hand slowly released his arm. The two-story, glass-walled store was another thirty meters away, directly in front of them. The male lion stood to their right, a healthy animal in his prime, as long as Brad was tall and three times his weight. The lion opened his mouth, half yawned, shook his mane, stretched the muscles of his back and haunches, and moved forward with a mincing step. Brad could smell urine and a faint rotting odor, perhaps the lion's breath as he exhaled, bits of flesh still in his teeth.

Luke did the talking. "We are going over there!" The old man raised his arm and pointed at the open doors. The hand that held his spear also lifted, not yet ready to throw, but getting ready. "We do not want to disturb you, and you must not disturb us."

Brad almost dropped his own spear because his palm was so sweaty. He recovered in time and also prepared to throw his weapon, trying to look calm, trying to feel calm, imitating Luke. He had heard of this often enough, how hunters spoke sternly to the lions whom they met unexpectedly or who came to steal their kill. The voice you used had to be firm, half scolding, but not threatening or shaming. One hunter told Brad that humor helped. It was important to be good-natured. Naturally, all that depended on the lion's mood, too.

Luke was firm enough, but he didn't sound good-natured. "We are going over there now, and if you try to stop us, we will be angry. You have your place, by the cottonwoods. That place over there is ours. That is where we are going."

Slowly, Luke did just that.

Brad followed, walking backward so that he still faced the lions. In response, the male lowered his head and began lashing his tail back and forth.

"You have your place, by the cottonwoods!" Luke repeated. "We are going to our place, over here."

They edged, side by side, through the open doors. At their seeming disappearance, the lion advanced a few more steps with the two small lionesses close behind. The larger two females on the ground, however, had not moved again beyond that first lifting of their heavy heads. Suddenly one of them sighed and slumped forward as if returning to sleep. Brad took that as a good sign.

Now he and Luke were trapped in an Electro store with a pride of lions blocking the only entrance. Brad imagined running through these aisles with the male running after him. It would be hard to turn and throw a spear. The lion's padded feet might skid on the nanomarble, as might his own leather shoes. Skidding, falling, an arm bringing down a display of some pre-supervirus appliance. Something smashing on the floor. Then a lioness at one end of the corridor, another lioness at the other end. More metal and nanoplastic crashing. Luke shouting from somewhere.

"Where are we going?" Luke whispered, watching through the glass wall, his spear still raised.

Earlier, as they had walked along the highway into town, Brad had been busy changing his plans. Modifying the transmitter was too complicated. He didn't know enough, and he risked damaging the lab's radio. In any case, he didn't really need that kind of power or that long a wave. He wanted something smaller, more subtle, more like a microwave, which is why he had remembered this particular Electro store.

"The edutoy section," he said now, but did not yet move in that direction.

"They won't come inside," Luke assured him.

"Why don't you keep watch?" Brad suggested. "Just to be sure."

Brad felt himself breathing normally again. After all his fears, leaving the store had been anticlimactic. The male lion and four lionesses were in their original position under the cottonwood trees, but this time they barely twitched when the two humans emerged through the doors. Only one of the large females opened her eyes. Her tail flicked. Flick. Flick. Flick. Brad felt hypnotized by that flash of creamy skin as he and Luke walked backward toward the street, their packs bulging with boxes that Brad had grabbed somewhat hurriedly, if not at random. *Huh-huh-huh-HUH*. The male snored. *Huh-huh-HUH-HUH*. The rest of the pride slept or pretended to.

With the lions behind them, Brad stopped at the nearest safe open space, wanting to open his pack and sort through his treasures, rethink, and discard. This was not his first scavenging trip, and as he removed the packaging, he was no longer amazed at the pristine condition of something made and wrapped in plastic one hundred fifty years ago. Protected from the elements, most items looked new, if also absurd and irrelevant. While Brad studied his selection, Luke kept guard, still disbelieving.

"These are for children," the old man repeated.

"Well, they loved their children then just as we do now," Brad murmured, reading the instructions. "They wanted the best for them, and before the supervirus that meant the best education in science."

Ironically, they were at a playground for children. Nanotechnology meant that some of the equipment remained sturdy enough to climb on, although Brad had no interest in testing that. From his historical research, he knew this shrubland had once been a green lawn. Children had skated, swung, roller-boarded, hover-dived, shouted, cried, and laughed—all around him, thousands and thousands of children. There was no shortage of children then. There had been, in truth, too many children.

Brad felt a chill, his sweat drying in the winter air. Perhaps it was a reaction to their encounter with the lions. He tried to focus on the How to Make Your Own Panpsychism Radio kit. This one was for advanced students and promised that the simple resulting receiver would be able to get signals from complex crystals. Another kit—Brad looked anxiously in his pack for that one—helped the mute child build a receiver/transmitter for frequencies from the Paleos. The signals were not words, of course, since only human receivers understood in word images what the Paleos were thinking. But the instructions promised that the frequencies could still be seen and charted and that this would demonstrate the newest principles of physics, the world as a constant interplay of waves sending and receiving. Brad threw away the box, which showed the face of an absorbed young woman, and kept the contents. He wanted this one certainly, and maybe this next one.

But he felt strange. He felt like crying. A sadness weighed him down, his arms and legs heavy. He could barely move his hands to repack the supplies. He could barely speak to Luke without his lips trembling.

"You feel it now?" Lucia asked.

"I never have before." Brad fought to control himself before bursting into tears.

What a waste. The dreams. The ghosts. The innocence. Children laughing and playing. The pain and fear as the adults suddenly died and the children were alone and dying, too. Children shouldn't be alone like that. The nanoplastic slide was still orange, the climbing gymnasium red and blue. The colors horrified him. The incongruous scrubland of snakeweed and rabbitbrush. The entire world, natural and human-made, seemed to be mourning. Gray smoke curled, drifting up from the earth. Brad wiped his eyes and nose and grabbed his pack. "Let's get out of here."

He couldn't shake the feeling until the city of Los Alamos was well behind them and hidden by intervening hills. Even then, Brad looked to the east and felt an echo. Even the next day, when they could see the lab ahead, he felt a weariness. The children crying. The weight of grief. People had tried to tell him. He had thought them superstitious.

Luke took him straight to the office, where they ate the rest of their jerky while Brad worked on the kits. Judith knocked and wanted in, and Brad gave her a muffled excuse. He was fine. He was busy. A few others came by. Brad ordered them away. The smell of Dog's head was getting so much worse.

But the kits were easy to assemble and modify. Lucia recited her numbers and kept adding refinements, as if the Dog in her head could respond to new questions and situations. Brad put these refinements into the computer, along with software to translate the numbers and turn them into frequencies, amplitude and oscillation, sine and cosine. He had never done anything like this before, and yet it all seemed to fit together, his former equations, what Lucia/Luke knew about radio and DNA, what Dog knew about dying. Flicking the switch. Not the biohologram. But the other switch. The holo-consciousness.

The biggest problem was the minutiae of connection—connecting the numbers to the software, the computer to the radios, the radios to each other. Of course, the kits were from the same era as the satellites in space, the worldwide web. That compatibility turned out to be key, although at one point Brad also had to sneak out and steal a solarcomp, which he disassembled for its nanowiring. Some connections had to be physical.

He was too excited to eat now, too excited to sleep, too excited to stop himself. He fiddled. He rearranged. He talked out loud. Luke/Lucia and Dog sat and watched.

Eighteen hours later, Brad stood up from his work and stretched his back. His shoulders ached, and he swung his arms in circles, forward, then backward. On the floor, three transmitters from three kits were linked with wires to the computer on the desk. Extra parts lay scattered on the chair and table. Brad surveyed the mess and knew this would work.

Clearing a space in the middle of the room, he set the transmitters at equidistance from each other and told Luke to put Dog's gummy maggot-oozing head in the center. The ritualistic circle wasn't necessary, but it looked right and seemed to make Luke happy. It seemed to evoke a certain optimism. A human aesthetic, Brad thought. A sense of order.

At the computer, Brad brought up the program and set it to run. Then he sat down on the floor with Luke, both of them cross-legged.

Brad had to remember to breathe. Dog's head stared up at the ceiling. Brad turned the radios on, one by one. The transmitters sent out their signals. The computer moderated. The switch in Dog's DNA turned on. Reanchor. Reassemble.

Luke whispered, "Dog, come home."

Above Dog's head, a golden cloud formed, two meters long by another meter tall and wide—about the size of a direwolf. Brad found himself whispering, too, "The most beautiful thing we can experience is the mysterious." He sat cross-legged on the floor, rapt in awe.

CHAPTER THIRTEEN

CLARE

Meadow came out of the tent with her face averted. Clare's grand-mother followed close behind, and Clare could hear the boy inside crying. Two children in camp were sick. What incredible bad luck.

"The ants run up his leg," Clare's grandmother said in a low voice as she watched Meadow walk toward the stream. The elder was refer-ring to Meadow's nine-year-old son. A cut on his thigh had become infected, and the bacteria were in his lymph channels now, streaking red like a line of harvester ants. Hard knots had formed under the armpit, which was tender and hot.

"Fever?" Clare asked. The elder pointed her thumb up.

Meadow was a woman who understood illness and injury. She would have yarrow and aspen bark to reduce the boy's fever, with chewed willow to ease the pain. She would have made poultices to draw out the pus, and she would be careful to keep her son rested, warm, and hydrated. But Clare knew, and Meadow knew, that the child really needed antibiotics, a medicine once refined to an art and then an arms race between disease and its cure. After the supervirus, the first Council had decided against the manufacture of these compounds, and that ruling had been upheld again and again. Hadn't the men and women who produced the supervirus worked at a similar task, synthesizing molecules, altering nature? The image still caused a collective revulsion.

Of course, plants with antibacterial properties were allowed—echinacea, goldenseal, garlic—although they were hardly as fast or as effective. If the infection spread to the lungs, a mullein tea was good for pneumonia. Also Apache plume, dandelion, and poppy thistle. If the boy developed a urinary infection, juniper berries were a diuretic. The tribe had a store of all these herbs, dried and fresh. Meadow would be thinking frantically now: which to use, what to do? Her husband would also be thinking and praying to one of his gods. The boy's father was a polyanimist, believing in many spirits, the totem of every animal and plant. But which one could help his son now?

"I have to go to the other boy," Clare's grandmother was saying. She put a hand on her stomach. "Very tender. Some spasms. Fever."

"You don't think?" Clare was horrified. Her grandmother shrugged. Without doubt, all the healers in the tribe had been searching on their solarcomps, looking up symptoms and reading the old accounts. For appendicitis, the best treatment was also unavailable—antibiotics and surgery.

Her grandmother looked old and tired. But Clare didn't offer to go with her to the next tent to see the next sick child. Perhaps that was wrong. Clare put a hand on her own stomach, which bulged like the lip of a buffalo gourd. She reminded herself: These sick children couldn't harm her child. Bad luck wasn't contagious.

"Go to the hot springs," her grandmother suggested. "The water is just right for you. Take Jon."

The kindness almost made Clare weep. She almost reached out and hugged the other woman, nostalgic for the refuge of those soft breasts. Not everyone in the tribe was so nice to her. Some people still commented that she had not helped with the move to the winter camp. Some people seemed angry that she had stayed at the lab through the solstice. Jon was one of those people, although he pretended otherwise. He pretended to have hardly noticed her absence. He insisted the child she carried was his, even though Clare explained carefully that this was not likely true. He insisted he would claim the baby at the central fire—for where was the lab rat to say differently? Who else would raise the umbilical cord and promise a father's muscle, heart, tutelage? Jon insisted now that Clare sleep with him in a separate tent he set up for the two of them near the communal kitchen. He insisted Clare stop hunting large game. He insisted she not travel away from the camp for more than a few hours, even with other people. He insisted he was pleased to have her back.

Clare had started to avoid Jon during the day. At night, things were easier, when they couldn't see each other.

The elders wove a basket for Meadow's son, a flat-bottomed platform of yucca leaves and willow sapling with raised sides so the boy couldn't fall out. The corners would be tied to branches at the top of a tree, with the basket wedged firmly in place. Everyone went with the mother and father as they carried the small corpse to a large oak close to camp so that the tribe could see the birds wheeling in the sky, black dots rising and falling. Everyone helped the parents be strong as they lifted the basket to the top of the oak.

Meadow's husband had prayed to the consciousness of the cat, a good hunter in every form, African lion and native mountain lion, jaguar, ocelot, bobcat, and house cat—feral and fierce in its pursuit of small mammals. The husband had even prayed to the saber-toothed cat, who had a particular love of human flesh. He had prayed for the strength of the cat to hunt and fight the infection in his son's body, the bacteria that finally traveled to the boy's brain so that his neck stiffened and he complained of claws behind his eyes. The father had called to the cat, but the birds answered instead, red-headed vulture, black crow and raven, white-necked condor, tera-torn. The birds wanted his son, and to the birds he and Meadow gave the body. The two of them would watch the scavengers every day as they cleaned the bones bleaching white through the dry summer. Later, in a year's time, the parents would return to the oak and bring down the remains to bury or burn.

On this night, after the tribe went to hoist the basket into the tree, they sang a death chant around the fire: the familiar words and rhythm, the same for a child as an adult, for female or male, everyone the same. Clare was dutiful, sitting next to Jon. "What is given is taken away. Our lives that were given are taken away. Our children who were given are taken away. Our good fortune that was given is taken away. All is flux and change. All is fire. For souls, it is death to become water. For water, it is death to become earth. Out of earth, water arises. Out of water, soul."

The chant came from the early Greek philosophers, the earliest age of Western culture. Death was nothing to fear, said men like Heraclitus and Epicurus. There was no death. There was only one law, one divinity. Clare knew the chant well but had only recently learned its history from Brad, who could get quite excited by this continuity of thought. It was not odd, he had explained, that the tribes repeated these ideas so many years later. The Quakers, especially, had believed in tradition, the human heritage. Even the Russians still used this chant, one of the bonds between the three populations. Around the campfire, the men and women would also quote the Eastern mystics and the original tribes from this land, the Navajo and Pueblo people. The Blessing Way. The Warrior Twins. This was the bridge, Brad said, language and history, as much a part of The Return as knapping arrowheads.

Across from Clare, the mother of the dead child held a young nephew on her lap. The other children of the tribe, solemn and well behaved, sat next to their parents. For some of them, this was new—this death, these chants, and the basket left in a tree. Their eyes were anxious. Would their playmate, their friend, never return?

Clare went around the large circle, some of the faces shadowed and some lit by the orange and yellow flames. She felt a presentiment, an ache, a pride. Their group was still healthy, almost a third of the population under twenty, newborns to teenagers. Their group was still strong. Clare lingered on the faces of her mother, her father, her grandmother, her two uncles. She nodded privately at her girl-friends. She nodded at Jon's former wife, nursing a baby by her new husband. Some people were also watching her, she saw, nodding at her, a valuable pregnant woman. Their group was still united.

Brad was naïve, she thought, to think these people chanted with a sense of history. Life was too hard now, too engaging, to think about the past. How long would it be, she wondered, before her students refused to care about events before the supervirus, about countries and cultures that no longer existed? Why should they spend their time studying a broken heritage instead of studying something more important? Like tracks in the white sand of a riverbank. Like the meaning of a darkening cloud. Why even learn to read and write?

The child's death had depressed her. And yet—Clare rallied—the ceremony was an important one. Community. She was sheltered in its arms.

The next afternoon she went for a bath in the hot springs, something she had begun to do almost every day, waiting for a time when most people in camp would be busy or napping. Craving solitude, she was relieved to see that the pools were empty. A movement fluttered in her stomach, butterfly wings. Clare struggled not to cry. Women became emotional when they were pregnant. That was natural. The poor boy dying in pain. Clare remembered how he had once run through the tents, chasing other children and being chased. She remembered how proud he had been when she had whittled him a toy spear. He must have been five. How he strutted and got into trouble poking one of his friends. He had lived a good life in his short life. Clare's face streamed with tears. But that was fine. She owed him water, a child from her people, the Rio Chama people, another child lost.

The pools descended in temperature, the hottest next to the cliff face and source of the spring, the coolest near the river, which bounded the winter camp. Low walls had been built years ago, enclosing each of the four bathing areas, the rocks covered with lichen, ferns, and small yellow flowers that thrived in the micro-climate of murmuring heat. Clare avoided the pond clouded with steam and settled into water that was only lukewarm but better for the baby and still scented with growing plants. As she lowered herself, mud and algae stirred from the sandy bottom and coated her skin, her arms, her breasts, submerged now and greenish. She rested the back of her head against spongy moss.

And let herself drift, deeper, plugging her ears and closing her eyes. She heard the beat of her heart, steady, slow, *beat, beat*. In her womb, another heart was also beating. Clare tried to imagine that piece of flesh, whole and perfect, pulsing rhythmically. Such a tiny organ, small as the nail of her finger, smaller than this yellow flower. Alone in the warm water, in the darkness of thought, Clare listened—*beat, beat*—and prepared for the worst.

The baby would be born blue and gasping. This time Jon would take the baby outside and not return. This time, no one would suffer for weeks and months and then years. Jon would do what he had to do. He had promised her that. Damaged children should not be allowed to live. He had said this firmly. He would take the baby away and that would be best for her and best for the child and best for the tribe. He would protect her.

Clare had nodded yes. Yes! Elise! The little girl singing. The waiting. The hoping. Clare could not go through that again.

But perhaps this time would be different? Perhaps the baby would be just fine, crying, loud, then suddenly asleep. Clare stretched and unrolled. The pools were so close to camp. She didn't fear predators. She listened for any Paleos, who might warn her of danger. She willed herself to relax in the warm water. She curled and uncurled her toes. She smelled something in the air, the tang of a crushed herb. She lived in the best of worlds, the best of times. She lived in abundance. She made herself breathe deeply. She let herself drift. The baby pulled hard at her nipple. She almost felt that satisfying pain. She cupped her breast. The baby suckled, rested, suckled, the milk leaking from pursed lips. At last the baby gave a sigh, its stomach full, its tiny face opening like a bud. Oh, what a big yawn. Oh, what a funny face. The baby rested quiet and warm on her stomach, his skin dark against her skin, dark hair moist with the mighty effort of nursing. They slept together. They breathed together and dreamed together.

Jon was carrying the baby outside. But Jon looked so sad, his eyes wet, his steps slow. The baby was damaged, after all. In her dream, Clare drifted outside the tent, outside the bed where she had birthed her son, as she followed Jon to the stream by the camp. No one else followed him, and the bundle in his arms didn't stir. In her dream, Clare felt numb. This was for the best. By the musical water, the splashing and gurgling, Jon turned to the north, a good direction, the place of rain and snow. Delicately, he lifted the rabbit skin away from the child's sleeping face. For a moment Jon paused, controlling his emotion. Then his hand rose to cover the small mouth and nose.

Clare tried to scream. But her voice had no sound. She was a spirit in a dream. He had the wrong baby. This was a healthy baby with abundant wiry hair and relaxed brow. This baby wasn't sick and blue. This baby had suckled and rested and yawned and slept. How could Jon have made such a mistake?

Clare woke with a jerk, half rising from the pool.

Jon squatted beside her. He looked concerned. "Clare?" he repeated. "Are you all right?"

Assignment Six: What I Would Like to Do This Summer, submitted by Alice Featherstone

At first this seemed like a pretty unexciting assignment. I thought of all the things I would like to do this summer and they are mostly things I have done every summer and can describe easily, but they didn't interest me in terms of writing about them. Mainly I would like to travel; I would enjoy leaving the mountains of Colorado for the first time and going south to see your tribe and then even farther south, as far as the peyote fields. I know that won't happen because this kind of long travel has to be approved by the elders and usually we are too busy in the summer and can't spare a large group of hunters. Then I emailed you, and you said that this assignment didn't have to be something that is possible or going to happen, that we could use our imagination. I have plenty of imagination and suddenly this paper didn't seem so dull.

What I would like to do this summer is go to Africa. Such a trip will involve a number of challenging steps. First I have to find a boat and get it seaworthy, ready to cross the "great desert of the ocean." The best place from which to start is New York Harbor Two, the one built after the last rising of the coastal waters. This means I will have to walk all the way to New York which will take me many months. That will be a tremendously interesting part of my journey as I pass through places few people have seen in the last one hundred fifty years. The high radiation will mean that wherever I go, I can't stay long. Even so, I will get to observe how the Paleos have adapted farther north, where the herds of mammoths and mastodons cover the plains and it snows in the winter all the time, not the occasional cold we get in Colorado. The colder weather is also something I will have to adapt to, and I will be responsible, of course, for all my food, water, and shelter.

In New York I will have a new set of problems. A big city like New York will be really sad. Scavengers who have gone to the big cities here like Albuquerque and Denver have said that even the mutes among them sometimes feel a sadness, and this is something I'd like to experience for myself since I am a mute. In truth, however, I don't think I will feel anything. I think I will be able to walk "among the great fallen skyscrapers" (as the poets say) without a qualm. From what I have read, my main problem will be navigating the large rivers that would now be running through parts of the decaying megapolis, flooding the streets and the "canyons created by concrete and ambition." This excites me even more since I have never seen a large river, just the little ones here that we still call rivers.

Once I am at the harbor, I will have to decide which boat to use. I am sure that many of them will have been destroyed in the storms of the last century and some will be too old for me to scavenge. Some will have computer programs I don't understand. Some will have engines I can't fix. In this part of the assignment I am really using my imagination since I don't know how to use any computer but this solarcomp and I wouldn't have any idea about how to fix an engine; it could be that what I need is a large sailboat but I have read that this kind of boat takes more than one person to operate unless you are very skillful which, obviously, I am not. In the end, I would select and repair just the right vehicle, and then I would stock it with enough food and water to last the many weeks of being on the salty waves.

Then on to Africa! By now I would have sent out emails over the worldwide web and radio announcements across the ocean to anyone listening. We haven't heard "a peep" from Africa for over one hundred years but does this mean that everyone is gone? I think not. By the time the supervirus appeared, Africa had already seen the worst of global warming and people were already in survival mode. The messages we did get for fifty years were from a few humans who had immunity like the Quakers in Costa Rica and those emails were strange from the very beginning, especially since our computers had trouble translating their dialect. I think those people just stopped communicating with us because they didn't want to communicate with us anymore. They were still angry about global warming. They didn't agree with the Great Compromise by the Los Alamos Three, although they never explained why, whether they wanted nothing to do with the old technology or whether they wanted to keep all the old technology they could. Since they stopped emailing us, I assume the first. Having abandoned their solarcomps and their radios, I believe that they went out into the grassy savanna, into the desert, into the jungle and began living like their ancestors, like us, with spears and poison darts. Only maybe they went deeper. Maybe they went further. Maybe they have achieved a new spirituality and culture that would amaze and astound us!

That's my dream—to find out. I want to know what is going on in Africa and in China and India, too, when

I think about it. That's what I would like to do this summer; I'd like to go on a really long trip over the ocean.

The Stuffed Teratorn, submitted by Carlos Salas

Someone stood up in silence today and told a story from the heart, and I wanted to answer that speaker because I felt my own heart quake in response. But I was too timid, which we are not supposed to be when our hearts quake, and now I have decided to write you instead. Apparently when the scientists cloned that first teratorn nearly two hundred years ago, they kept the live bird to study, of course, and when the animal died, they stuffed it full of chemicals and synthetic matter so that it still looked like a real teratorn. The biohologram had deflated, the unique consciousness was dissolved. But the scientists kept this facsimile in their lab, like some strange dead hologram. This story disturbed the speaker in my Meeting, the image of a teratorn alive and yet not alive, the feathers real but nothing remaining behind the eyes. So the speaker asked this of silence: what were those scientists thinking? And I thought about that and wondered if one of these scientists, or maybe more than one, had simply grown very fond of this teratorn. They loved the bird. They wanted to see their pet every day. That's what I didn't want to say out loud: they did this out of love.

CHAPTER FOURTEEN

DOG

Dog had a new trick to show Luke.

Luke! Dog called out vigorously. Luke? He coaxed.

The old man was close to their campsite, but if he heard he didn't reply. He only spoke out loud to Dog now, never mentally and never at a distance. He didn't want to receive Dog's thoughts. He didn't want to send his own. Dog understood. Luke had regrets about bringing Dog back from the dead.

Lucia showed up a few minutes later, her face and arms scratched from checking her traps and crawling through hackberry. There was hardly any game so close to the lab, Dog didn't help with hunting anymore, and Brad was almost as useless. Suddenly Lucia had to spend a fair amount of time catching her food, and this made her irritable. "Stop yelling," she said to Dog as she sat down and began to skin the squirrel. "I can hear you. I'm not deaf. You'd think . . . someone like you . . . would be more patient."

Lucia didn't know what to call Dog. Pure Consciousness? Radio Wave Dog? Dog Number Two?

Dog understood. That's why he had learned this new trick.

Come here, he said.

Lucia stripped the skin from the squirrel's body. It wasn't much of a meal, especially if Brad showed up around suppertime as he had promised, spending the night and going back to the lab in the early morning.

Touch me, Dog said. But Lucia ignored him, intent on her task.

Lucia/Luke had not reacted well to Dog's earlier shifting golden form. For weeks, Dog's outline had seemed about to escape into the rest of the world, a blurry motion that made Luke nauseous. Once Dog could maintain his shape, he continued to shimmer with a golden light not even Brad could explain—the puzzle sent the lab rat back to his equations and twenty-first-century books on physics. The glow was barely noticeable now, and Dog felt good about that, although he still had so much more to learn. The DNA turned on. The unique consciousness reassembled. The unique holo-bioform was gone. But a memory of that pattern remained, an electromagnetic memory taking the form of Dog's body, remembering what to do and—then, suddenly—not remembering. It was so hard to keep your body shape when the actual molecules were not there anymore. Holo-hair, holo-skin, holo-muscle, holo-bones. Dog had to focus all the time. Lucia didn't realize how difficult this was.

Touch me, Dog repeated and barked insistently. He had just learned to bark a few days ago, and he practiced it with another surge of pride. Look at me! Sending sound waves into the air when I have no lungs or vocal cords! Dog didn't know how he did this. He suspected he wasn't doing anything that affected the physical world so much as the perception of that world. This was something he needed to discuss with Brad. Dog theorized that when he thought about barking, he sent that thought into the minds of all the beings around him, and if those beings had a memory or understanding of this sound, then they would hear it. The theory was testable if he and Brad could find someone who didn't have any previous memory or understanding of barking—or any similar animal noise. Although that seemed unlikely.

Dog knew Brad would be impressed with his theory, with his bark, with his pant, with his whimper. Dog could hardly wait to demonstrate. But now Lucia almost dropped her skinless squirrel in the dirt because hearing noises come from Dog, after months of silence, still startled her. "Oh, be quiet," the old woman said.

Perhaps she wouldn't like Dog's newest trick, either. Dog couldn't really feel hurt or sad about that. He couldn't *really* feel pride either, because he didn't have those hormones running through the blood vessels in his brain anymore, connecting with receptors, starting chemical cascades. He didn't have receptors. He didn't have a brain. But he had the memory of these things, and he focused on that, and he stopped feeling almost-pride and started to feel almost-anxious. He was worried about Lucia. Why was she angry? Had he done something wrong? Was something wrong with Luke/Lucia? Dog felt a surge of almost-love and that was almost-good enough.

He whined. Please touch me.

Lucia grumbled, stood up, and moved forward, ready to put her hand right through Dog's carefully controlled, fully detailed, and slightly translucent body. Instead she felt soft fur grainy with dust and the hardness of skin, muscle, and bone. Instead her hand stopped at that line where she felt Dog's flesh, a pressure back against her own flesh. Automatically, she moved her hand in the beginning of a pet down Dog's flank.

Then she jerked her hand away. "What are you doing?"

Dog stepped forward, banging his muzzle against her leg. He thought about that push and sent that thought into the air and minds of all the beings around him and he knew that Lucia could feel it now, the weight of a direwolf's body against her body—causing her to stumble back. Dog kept pressing forward and jammed his cold nose into Lucia's hand, the one not holding the skinned squirrel. He knew she could feel that pressure, that coldness.

Dog himself could not even be sure his holo-paws were completely touching the ground. He thought he might be floating a little. He concentrated. He did not have the physical sensations Lucia was having now—the warmth of the woman's palm, the satisfying pet that smoothed down his guard hairs. But he had the memories. He had the habit. The feeling would come later. It had taken him time, after all, to be able to see colors and shapes again, the cliff face that sheltered them from the wind, the pink-and-yellow sky and sun rising in the east. It had taken time to hear voices and bird calls and fire crackling. It had taken time to understand time, how one moment followed another, how he should pretend to sleep and then wake. His own sense of touch would come next. Everything was coming faster and faster.

Lucia gave a sigh. "Dog." It was a lonely world without her friend and companion. The old woman squatted and began to pet him in earnest.

Dog had to focus. He had to remember. He had to keep his paws on the ground. Eventually all this would become second nature. Tomorrow, Dog thought—with a powerful almost-desire—tomorrow he would work on smell.

Brad ate more than his share of squirrel stew, but Luke was in a good mood and hardly noticed. Dog, of course, didn't eat anything. He slumped next to Luke, head down as though he were napping, still practicing his skills and sending out those thoughts of gravity and weight, texture and substance. Luke kept one hand on Dog's neck, occasionally scratching Dog between the ears, occasionally grabbing and pulling a handful of fur to which Dog reacted by jerking his paws and snuffling.

Being physically present for Luke took all of Dog's concentration. He couldn't really talk to Brad until the old man had fallen asleep by the fire, not retreating to his tree house tonight but curled in animal skins next to Dog.

Brad also waited for Luke to fall asleep. Then "It's fantastic," he said. "Your fur feels dirty, you can growl. You're as scary as the first day we met."

Brad didn't have to say any of this out loud, because Dog didn't only receive word images or word feelings from Brad now but distinct and separate words, something that resembled speech, with intonations, prepositions, punctuation. A sense of distance. Dog could see how being able to talk like this—to focus on a specific and controlled idea rather than on what else you were thinking, on what you were *really* thinking—helped humans discuss and plan. He could hunt in the words like a lioness in the grass. And he could hide in the words like a rabbit in the grass.

This new form of communication had happened between him and Brad in the first few days of Dog's return, even when he was still swirly in form, still adjusting. Luke had felt only despair then. The reanchored and reassembled consciousness of Dog was too alien, too much bright energy. Luke had retreated. But Brad had kept trying, hiding the swirly shape in his office and then sneaking it out to this camp until Brad had been able to "talk" to Dog, until eventually and in some way Brad had talked Dog into his present shape, the habit of Dog.

"This will make Luke happy, won't it?" Dog asked.

"Oh, yeah," Brad said. "But, you know, still . . . you have to be patient. Luke hasn't been the same since you were killed by the giant shortfaced bear."

"He didn't like me being in his head."

"That disturbed him."

"I'm still there in his head. That part of me."

"Oh," Brad hadn't known this. "I guess there's nothing you can do about that?"

"No," Dog said. Luke/Lucia had always been a fractured personality. Now they were more so.

"So . . ." Brad hesitated. He had something important to say.

Dog suspected he could know everything Brad was about to tell him. All he had to do was go wheelboarding through Brad's mind. But Dog waited instead. He remembered how his siblings had hated his intrusions into their thoughts. He remembered his mother's teeth in his neck. Waiting was better.

The lab rat smiled, enjoying the anticipation. He smelled like a river about to rush its banks. "We did it!" Brad said, looking over at Luke first, and unnecessarily keeping his mental voice a whisper. "It finally worked."

Dog would have felt his heart leap if his heart hadn't been eaten by the giant shortfaced bear. Losing his concentration, he floated a few inches off the ground.

Forgetting that Luke was sleeping, he whined with excitement. If he had been a body still, he would have dribbled urine. (Tomorrow, Dog promised himself. That sharp and wonderful odor: urea, creatine.)

"I really had my doubts," Brad confessed. "The last few weeks have been so frustrating."

Dog agreed. He had also been almost-frustrated! First they had tried to duplicate the experiment with Dog's head by using a dried sunflower stalk from outside the office window. Dog hadn't gone back to the lab but had consulted with Brad at the camp, describing the dead flower's DNA, guanine, cytosine, receiving, sending, explaining all the things Brad could put into numbers and then into his computer. They had done everything right, Dog was certain, and yet that first attempt failed, the sunflower stalk on the floor, the radios humming, and no golden cloud of unique consciousness.

Almost immediately, Dog knew. And Dog was embarrassed. Months ago (a lifetime ago) he had seen a glowing stick of light floating above the arroyo, a flower stem three meters long topped by a composite of smaller flowers. Sunflower: guanine, cytosine, adenine, thymine. But this flower didn't have DNA. Months ago, infused with the peyote spirit, Brad had seen sunflowers above the musical stream. A Chinese ideogram. Months ago, before that, the bushkies had worshiped their own version. A pillar of light. Dog should have predicted this. Plants were different. Time worked differently at the quantum level. They had got the equations both right and wrong. *They had sent the sunflower consciousness into the past.*

Now it was a dozen sunflowers later. All sent back into the past. Dog had wanted to use a different plant, something simpler, algae perhaps. But Brad had said no. Brad kept trying with the radios in his office, newly obsessed. Dog could only wait in camp and work on his tricks to please Luke.

"Just like before, with you," Brad was saying, "the holo-consciousness formed above the subject. Glowing. A cloud." But this time the glowing cloud had lengthened almost immediately to take its shape as a sunflower, so then there were two—the glowing three-meter-long sunflower and the dried stalk. "I had to smuggle them out, too, just like with you, hoping no one would see me."

"Where did you take them?" Dog felt a yearning.

"We got away that night and went north a few kilometers. At first, the new sunflower stayed by the old one." Brad paused.

Dog remembered his own desire to be near his gummy head, a strong allegiance to that DNA. He wouldn't have believed they could ever separate. After a while, though, the rotting head became less interesting. A pattern of molecules just like everything else. Dog was different now. Dog wasn't made of molecules anymore. Eventually Luke buried the head under a tree.

"Then the holo-consciousness floated away, up," Brad went on, seeing that scene in his mind's eye. "I couldn't follow."

And Dog felt that yearning again to see the holo-sunflower returned in full bloom, each composite flower part of the larger flower, each ovule filled with seed. Where had that glowing consciousness gone? What a pity Brad hadn't managed to bring it here. Dog whined. No matter. No matter. Dog made his first pun. Pleased by that, he spoke carelessly. "We need an animal next. A mouse would work."

The burning wood popped, a spray of sparks. Brad looked at Luke, still apparently asleep, and opened his mouth—and said nothing. Brad's unique consciousness began to retreat from Dog, something Dog could feel like a swat on the nose. For Brad, this was all happening too fast. Brad wasn't designed to accommodate a future rushing at him so quickly, carrying him, lifting him, the water flooding over and through the bank.

In the distance, Dog heard a lion's cough—*huh, huh, huh*—not particularly close and not threatening. Brad turned in that direction but also was not alarmed, sitting right next to a blazing fire. Dog perked an ear. He hadn't expected a lion's cough. He hadn't manufactured it out of habit and memory, which meant he was actually "hearing" it, aware of sensations even though he had no physical way to receive them. What part of him had already known the lion was out there—a weak male thrown out of his pride? What part of him knew about the ocean waves pounding on the beach sand far away, the moon's reflection on that sand, the light broken into patterns? The crab scuttling in moonlight? The solar flare in space? What part of him could know everything? Dog felt himself enlarge and stopped immediately. Shrank. Withdrew. To what he had always been. To what the former physical Dog could know. To what Dog could do.

A mouse would be easy to transport. "We need an animal next," Dog repeated, but Brad was silent, and Dog understood: This was happening too fast. Also, Luke disapproved now as Clare had disapproved. Luke had regrets, a part of Dog in his cerebellum and the new Dog not so fun-loving, not so much a companion as before. The new Dog had these ambitious ideas, conferring with Brad, urging him into the rushing future. Why? What did Dog want?

Brad was wondering that as well.

The moon shone here as it did on that sandy beach, gilding the pointed leaves of oak, casting shadows on the rocks above the fire. Waves rippled although they were not made of water, light, or sound. Wave upon wave, the infinite movement. Dog rocked. Dog rippled. Dog brought himself back. He didn't want to dissolve into everything.

Instead he reminded Brad, "Remember Clare. This is how you will get her back."

Brad was silent. He wasn't sure.

"I am sure," Dog said and found the lie surprisingly easy. The trick to lying was to sound like you weren't. "If we do this, we can give Clare what she wants."

Brad brought his arms close to his chest as though he were cold.

Dog repeated, "We can give Clare what she wants more than anything else in the world." Dog pressed. "We can give her Elise."

CHAPTER FIFTEEN

BRAD

The equipment had been a problem, too big, too heavy, and confined to the office. Brad needed something he could take outside the lab. The first breakthrough was a smaller but more powerful solarcomp capable of handling the new software that converted what Dog understood about DNA into numbers corresponding to radio signals. The radios themselves were still bulky, filling half his pack, and Brad had resigned himself to back strain until he found a twenty-first-century website on miniaturization. Two radios could be combined into one. One could fit into the palm of his hand. This didn't even involve a scavenging trip, only stealing some materials from the production center where they rebuilt the computers. Of course, everything took longer than he had hoped. There were always setbacks, the daily wrinkle, the thing that couldn't be solved until he miraculously found a solution.

For a fact, Brad had never been happier in his work. He had felt something like this before in his twenties, a sense of excitement getting up every morning. But the mathematics then had been so abstract. After his mother's death, he only had those equations—intangible, not of the physical world. This time, he had to use his hands manipulating wires and building little machines. This time, he was not alone but always thinking about Dog. Would Dog be impressed? What would Dog advise? Brad wondered if this was how the hunters felt getting up every morning to manipulate the world. There were always problems to solve, tracks to follow, decisions to make: which animal to kill, how to protect the meat. Unlike his father, most hunters were gregarious. They worked with partners and in teams. Brad had spent his life envying them without knowing why.

Now he understood. He understood Clare better and thought of her often, wondering what she was doing and if she missed him. This year, the spring came with a rush, small white flowers hugging the ground, sprays of orange poppies in the grass. The tips of cottonwood branches turned luminous, and the elm trees dressed in lime-green. Brad noticed the new life growing around him and knew that Clare was noticing that life, too. She was alive with the warmth and promise of spring. She was thinking of red willow, its limber growth good for baskets. She was thinking of fresh shoots and leaves, garlic and onion bulbs, certain flowering plants rich in vitamin C. She was thinking of him, or so Brad hoped. She was hoping he would come after her.

And he was almost ready to do that. He was preparing to leave soon—when the blonde-haired woman came to see him. The Council member called out first and knocked on the office door. Brad was thinking about the nature of time at the quantum level. He wasn't quite sure how he had solved the problem of the sunflowers. He had fiddled and adjusted and fiddled and adjusted and suddenly the glowing stalk was no longer disappearing back into the past. But why?

And this wasn't the only mystery. Why did consciousness seem to glow? Consciousness wasn't matter/energy, so what caused that physical effect? Was the glow real or perceptual? And why had the sunflower become a sunflower so quickly when Dog had remained a hazy cloud for days? And where was that sunflower now?

"Brad!" The Council member called out again.

Brad looked around. He checked his computer screen. He prepared his face and let her in, shouting at the same time, "*Buenos días! Dobry den!*" It was a bit of a fad to learn Spanish and Russian although the computer translators worked fine and there was really no need.

"We have to talk."

"*Konechno!*" Brad said boisterously.

The Council woman pushed into the room and also looked around, not bothering to hide her interest. "What have you been doing in here?"

"Making a breakthrough. Solving the secrets of the holographic universe."

"Yes, that's what Judith said, exactly what you told her."

"Working on the natural harmony of general relativity, quantum mechanics, and panpsychism. The Council approved this. *You* approved it." Brad smiled warmly, permitting himself the flirtation. The Council woman really was special, with that yellow hair and gray eyes, an interesting throwback or perhaps a mutation. Her critics complained she had been voted into the Council because of her looks—that famous picture emailed to every solar-comp in North America—but Brad knew she kept the position for other reasons. Because she was smart, because she was ruthless.

Now she was frowning. "I don't think your usual work involves spending nights away from the lab or sneaking around the production center."

Brad tried the offensive. "You're spying on me? That's not our way."

The Council woman changed the subject. "Whatever happened with Clare?"

Brad turned sorrowful. "You know me. Things don't turn out."

The Council woman looked at him too directly. "I do know you. And I know something is going on. I can't imagine what. But I'm afraid for you, Brad."

"Afraid?" That surprised him, and Brad couldn't help himself: he glanced at his computer again.

"Don't presume too much." The Council woman followed his gaze. "You can't just do whatever you want to do. We've been tolerant, but we have our limits."

"Ah, yes . . ." Brad found himself stammering.

"I can't protect you," she said and shut the door behind her.

Brad started packing. He had been meaning to leave in a few days anyway. This was almost his own plan, almost expected. He still had some hours of afternoon sun and could get a decent start before having to spend the night in a tree. The solarcomp and radios were already cached halfway to Luke's camp. He needed to take only some clothing, the dried food he had hoarded, and . . . his little collection of things.

Before putting them in the pack, Brad unwrapped the leather bundle just to check: a half-dozen dead mice, an assortment of teeth, some tufts of hair. He thought of Clare again, that habitual movement, touching her neck for the leather bag. He found himself grinning, his mouth stretched so that it almost hurt. The Council woman really couldn't imagine what he was doing. Not in her wildest dreams.

As he rewrapped the objects, Brad noted that his hands were shaking. Also, he couldn't seem to stop smiling. He was afraid he might actually start to laugh. But none of this was close to funny. Perhaps none of this was temporary. He was leaving the lab. He was leaving his home. He had the strongest desire to go to his bed in the west wing and crawl under the animal skins and pull them over his head.

Luke asked, fierce, "Did you kill those mice?"

Still tired from the walk, hungry, too, Brad had known the old man would object to the new experiments. But he hadn't expected this question. "We're not monsters!" he protested, his indignation fueled by the fact that he had been tempted. Trapping mice and killing them would have been so much easier than finding mice already dead. In this case, that meant keeping watch on the lab's small cats, intercepting the mothers feeding their young, and getting well scratched in the process. Yes, perhaps he had wanted to just poison or stab or smash the damn-muck-a-luck mice. But he hadn't. He wouldn't. Killing an animal for an experiment and not for food or defense? That went beyond loathsomeness.

Brad glared at Luke. The man grunted and returned to skinning the ubiquitous squirrel. Luke seemed better, Brad thought, a little more centered, a little more like himself. Dog turned to nip a flea in his tail, and Brad felt the tension in the air lessen. Obviously, Dog didn't have fleas. But he had perfected this performance for his old friend. It seemed to be working.

"Let's get started," Dog said to Brad privately.

Brad looked down at the six mice, six in a row on a flat stone. He arranged the radios, got out the solarcomp, and fiddled with the software. Then he picked up the best-preserved mouse and carelessly, casually, put it on the ground next to the transmitters. The tiny bundle of flesh looked pathetic. Tiny lips pulled back from tiny yellow teeth, tiny eyes closed, tiny paws curled convulsively. Apparently, the death hadn't been painless.

"Give me the numbers," Brad said, also not out loud. Luke didn't want to be part of this. Luke went on making their dinner as Brad typed on the keyboard and fiddled some more and finally, without fanfare, turned the radios on.

He didn't expect the first one to work. It had taken thirteen sunflowers before he had gotten the consciousness of a plant to come back at the right time, the quantum level of time matching Newtonian time, the equation fine-tuned to the plant's DNA, the signals fine-tuned to the equation. A mouse should be harder, not easier. Now Brad was puzzled, but he couldn't stop and think about the puzzle, not with the shimmering and recognizable animal hovering in the air above its dead body and Dog growling with excitement and Luke suddenly coming over to stare.

The mouse in the air opened its eyes, feet twitching. Much like Dog in the first weeks, the animal was having trouble holding its shape, with bits of—what? mouse consciousness?—drifting off and drifting back, coalescing and not coalescing. Dog moved in closer as if to sniff, and Brad was afraid the direwolf would suddenly extend his jaws and snap up the swirly animal as a tasty meal. It was an odd image, consciousness eating consciousness. Dog seemed to be vibrating. The golden mouse became perceptibly more solid.

Brad looked up to catch Luke's eye. Luke turned away.

Dog said, "Do another one."

Brad tried to focus on the moment. He forced himself to remember that he had a plan, a testable theory. "I want to use the same mouse," he told Dog. "To see if its DNA will produce multiple consciousnesses."

Dog seemed surprised but agreed.

Brad didn't feel disappointed when he turned the radios on again and nothing happened. The shimmering mouse floated in the air. The corpse of the mouse lay in the dirt. The DNA had turned on. But it would only turn on once, producing for the last time the animal's unique consciousness shaped by matter/energy/time. The biohologram loop was already broken. The consciousness loop was now broken, too.

"Do another mouse," Dog insisted, and they did. Out of six mice, five retained their shape and the last expanded into a cloud, radio waves seemingly visible and then fading away in a golden shower of light. Brad squinted. The cloud was there. The cloud was gone. Where did it go?

"Where does the stream go when it enters the ocean?" Dog answered.

"No," Brad said. "You are not supposed to read my mind."

Dog let his tail droop. "Sorry."

"You're excited." Brad struggled to speak normally. "This is incredible. Amazing. But we are all tired. We should stop now."

Of course, Brad didn't feel tired. The adrenaline surge was too strong. But they had already accomplished so much, and he needed time to sort out his thoughts. Luke had started a fire, stubbornly cooking food, and the smell of meat and onions was noticeable. They should eat dinner, Brad thought. Five glowing mice floated ten centimeters above the ground, close to his feet, staying near their dead bodies and DNA. They didn't make a sound, and Brad knew he could put his hand right through them. The mice didn't look particularly confused or upset. But it was hard to tell for sure.

They should eat dinner. After that, the next step would be to study the floating mice to see in what ways they resembled Dog and in what ways they did not. They should slow down and eat dinner and study the floating mice.

This time, Dog didn't agree. "Do another animal," he said, insistent as a dog playing a game, bringing a stick, bringing it back again.

"We don't even know why the last one disappeared."

"The last one was me," Dog admitted. "I didn't help. I let it go. I wanted to see what would happen."

"You're influencing them?" Brad should have known. Similarly, he had influenced Dog. But why did that work? What was that influence? This was happening so fast.

"Please," Dog said. "Please, please."

Brad chose a bundle of camel hair. He didn't think they were ready for this. He muttered to himself, "We're not ready for this." Even so, he let Dog give him the numbers for the animal's DNA, and he plugged those numbers into the equations he knew by heart now, not bothering to fine-tune or modify, just letting the computer stream the data into numbers that modulated the radio signals and then turning the radios on, just letting the software do its work.

"What the muck?" Luke asked, jumping back into the fire and burning himself—they would realize later—as the shape of a glowing camel appeared in the middle of their campsite. This happened to be hair from a large male, as tall as Brad at the shoulder, taller at the hump, and much taller when the animal lifted his long neck and pulled back rubbery lips in a gesture of reaching out for food. Dog rushed to put his nose next to the camel's feet, up to the bumpy knee and skinny flank. Almost immediately, the golden blurry outline became more clear. There was less arcing and sparking, less radiance. Brad peered through the fingers he had put up to protect his eyes.

How could they stop then? They were producing these animals from the DNA in hair! Brad was stunned. He hadn't thought it possible, although Luke had warned him that it was very likely possible. Luke knew about DNA.

The horse hair came from a colt, long legged, ears up, the animal wanting to run and then stopping, curious, innocent and coltish and endearing even as pure consciousness.

The deer crowded against the colt, and Brad worried they would merge into each other, half horse, half deer. But both colt and deer seemed to know their boundaries, close but not touching.

In other ways, the golden animals hardly seemed aware of each other. Nor did they seem to notice Brad or Luke or Dog. They seemed to be—Brad searched for the right word—preoccupied. Busy adjusting.

The black bear was next, from a worn skin. By now Luke had stopped protesting. Briefly, he and the direwolf reminisced. They had killed a similar female a long time ago. The bear had been hibernating. They had been helped by another hunter.

Brad moved on to the teeth—another horse, a calico cat from the lab, a second bear. By now even Luke seemed caught up in the glory and the wonder. Creation. Genesis. The time for stopping was long past. Brad felt feverish. It was so easy. Dog fed him the numbers. The radios turned on. Another glowing animal. Perhaps it was the software, designed to be intelligent and getting better with every use. Perhaps it was Dog's influence. Perhaps it was something else. It was so easy. So quick.

Night had fallen, but that didn't matter. They didn't need daylight, surrounded as they were by the light of the camel, the horses, the deer, the bears, the mice beginning to move away from their dead bodies. The deer kept together in a herd. The bears kept close to Dog. The calico cat sat by herself and didn't watch the mice, absorbed in her own experience.

Later, and throughout his life, Brad would have vivid dreams that recreated this scene. The dreams were set amusingly in different cultural contexts.

The Christian God brought forth the beasts of the earth, the winged fowl and every creeping thing, and looked upon His work with pleasure, this great bearded God in the sky who said, "Lo, it is good," and "Be fruitful and multiply."

The Hindu god Brahma used thought to create water into which he let loose his semen, which became a golden egg, which split into two, male and female, splitting into two again and again and again and again until every plant and animal had come into existence.

P'an Ku was a Chinese being whose body turned into the world: the head the mountains, the blood the rivers, the left eye the sun, the right eye the moon, the fur the forests, the fleas on the fur the creatures of the forest.

Most often Brad saw himself and Luke shaping figurines from clay, shapes only a few centimeters high, which Brad threw behind his shoulder to land on a pile of other clay figurines all jumbled together. Very serious, very fast, the two men worked, making squirrels, bears, horses, mammoths, mice, deer, camels, direwolves, glyptodonts, on and on. Finally Luke grew big in size, taller than a pine tree, and sprinkled this pile with water from his penis, and the clay figures began to grow.

Sometimes Brad used nanometal to build a giant short-faced bear that reared on her hind legs, dropping and shuffling forward, leaving no tracks in the dust, without sound or smell. Ahead of the bear, a golden nanosnake twined through the grass—although the grass didn't part, the snake flowed up Brad's body into his mouth, his stomach, his colon, flowing out his anus. Then the bear was in him, too, moving through him without sound or smell.

Brad always woke from these dreams with a feeling of joy.

That night, he saved the saber-toothed cat for last, carefully placing the half-broken fang on the ground near the radios. Sending and receiving. The DNA turning on. The unique consciousness reanchored, reassembled. Luke stepped back as the huge animal swung her shining head back and forth, from Luke to Brad, as if trying to understand. No one knew why saber-toothed cats were so strongly attracted to human flesh. Maybe, Brad wondered for the first time, it was an actual form of love, more beneficent than anyone had supposed.

He brushed the idea aside. He was in danger of losing all sense of science and proportion. Reality was becoming too unreal. Finally, they had to stop. Finally, they were out of body parts and bits of hair.

Dog nudged the saber-toothed cat, who did not respond as quickly as the other animals, who kept wanting to disperse and fade into a cloud. Dog and the giant cat seemed to be conversing. Brad couldn't hear, although the other glowing animals came forward slightly, as if they could. After a moment, the saber-toothed cat stretched on the ground, her blocky head with the long curved teeth resting on her paws, her shoulders and front legs bunched with muscle, her paws cupped around her physical broken tooth, everything but the tooth softly translucent.

Now, at last, Brad was exhausted. He couldn't imagine sleeping, but he also couldn't imagine staying awake. He had to rest. He had to rest now.

Keeping watch for the night didn't matter. Not even the glowing animals mattered. Who would be here in the morning? Who would drift away? It didn't matter. No matter. Dog's pun.

Brad and Luke looked at each other. Neither was sure which one of them spoke. Too many waves in the air. Too many thoughts mixed up. Brad took his pack and put it next to the dying fire, the uneaten stew, and Luke joined him on the hard ground, their legs and arms mingling as they closed their eyes, their bodies touching— not something men like them would normally do, but something they did instinctively now.

CHAPTER SIXTEEN

CLARE

From the red willow near the stream, Clare could hear the noises of camp, the play of children or shout of a parent. For the sake of solitude, she was making the basket here and not in front of her tent, where too many people would stop and comment and chat. First she had cut the limber branches, dug a pond close to the stream, and put in the branches to soften. During this time, she rested and drowsed. Then, with an obsidian flake, she cut the end of each branch, took one side of the butt between her teeth, and pulled down the other side. The willow spilt in two, showing its white interior, smelling cleanly of sap. Holding the butt, she tore off the bark in another quick motion. These branches were young and easy to prepare and—biting and pulling, biting and pulling—she soon had a pile of long white strips beautiful to a woman about to make a basket.

Humming a campfire song, Clare tied three branches together and curled them into a circle for the base. With a bone awl and yucca thread, she sewed the branches to each other and slipped in strips of willow along the rim. To build up the walls of the basket, she began weaving in more willow strips horizontally. The morning was warm and the flies and mosquitoes scarce. In some ways, this was her favorite time of year. The clean white willow looked like snow, which Clare had never seen except in dirty patches high on a mountain peak in Colorado. The clean white willow looked like milk puddling in a baby's mouth after nursing. The clean white willow looked like the flowers of spring that covered the flanks of hills near the camp. The sharpness of willow tingled Clare's nose. In and out, she wove.

Apparently she had misjudged how many branches to collect. Sooner than anticipated, she needed more. That was also good since it gave her reason to stand and move, stretch her back, and circulate the blood in her legs and feet. At six months, she was much bigger than she had been with Elise. Already her stomach was a great melon, a camel's hump, a full moon, a certain mountain to the east, all the names the tribe used to tease and joke. Partly her size was natural in a second pregnancy, her muscles more elastic and easily stretched. She was also less active this time, or so it seemed to her. She had less energy, and the weight of this baby seemed heavier. She had trouble urinating. Her hair was thinning. Of course, she was also older now, thirty-two this September. And maybe this was simply a larger baby filling her camel's hump, a fat and healthy boy.

These days, her thoughts tended to follow old paths, the same worn game trails. She counted up the months and days. The baby, conceived in November, would be born at the end of fire season: a good season if the monsoons came and fires were few and small, a bad season if a dry spring and the lightning storms of summer combined with little rain. Clare had lived through bad summers, the fear of a grass fire sweeping through camp or catching a hunter unaware on the plain. She had lived with the smoke and winds of ash and soot, and she didn't like the idea of giving birth at this time. She would have preferred a September baby.

Like a bad-tempered glyptodont, she lumbered into the chest-high shoots of red willow, creating space with the force of her belly, stumbling and splashing into the stream. But glyptodonts were more graceful, Clare thought, as she put the knife between her teeth so she could bend back the shoots.

"Clare!" someone hissed from farther upstream.

Startled, she turned. The knife was in her hand now. A tall dark man came partially out from the stand of cottonwood trees. "Clare!" he sang.

"Brad," she said.

"Clare!" he urged.

"Brad," she repeated.

She started to move through the willow brush but stopped before she reached the very edge. Brad also did not rush into the space between them but withdrew back into the trees, gesturing for her to follow. He wanted to stay hidden. Briefly, Clare wanted to stay hidden as well.

Brad. At last. Now she realized how much she had been expecting him. How disappointed she had been when he had not come earlier. As far as she knew, no one had emailed the elders about problems at the lab—unnatural, unapproved experiments. She had heard no rumors concerning Dog or Luke or Brad. Whatever they had done was already done, in the past and seemingly unnoticed. So where had he been for the last four months? While the child grew bigger. While Jon claimed the child.

And what would he say now? What would he think?

Clare came out of the willow brush, aware of her dirty hair, the shapeless leather shirt that showed her stomach. She put a hand on that shelf and walked forward over the uneven ground, still holding the knife and wishing she had put it down.

Brad retreated farther into the shadows.

"No one is here," Clare said when she was only three meters away and didn't have to yell. "Where have you been?"

Silence from the cottonwoods. She couldn't see his face. Silence. And then, "You're pregnant."

Clare wanted to say something clever. "That's right," she replied.

"You knew when you left." It was not a question.

"Yes."

"You're having my baby." The dark man in the shadows reached out his arms, and Clare moved into them. "Well, maybe," she murmured. "Probably."

Brad didn't know what to do with her stomach and the way it interfered with his kissing her. Clare turned so she didn't face him directly because they needed to talk, not kiss. Almost against her will, she rested her head on his chest. "The baby could be Jon's," she said, to get this out of the way, "although I don't think so. Where have you been? What happened with . . ." She didn't finish.

"Dog." Brad stroked her hair. He seemed very pleased. Clare could feel him smiling. She breathed in his scent. Only Brad smelled like this. "That worked out fine. Everything is fine. Dog told me where to look for you, where I might find you alone. We've been watching the camp."

Dog told me where to look for you. Clare registered the words but asked only, "Why are you hiding if you've done nothing wrong?"

"I have something—"

He caught his breath and stopped, and now Clare could hear two other voices coming closer, two women chatting as they approached the stream, perhaps to find her, perhaps for water or some other reason. Camp was so close. People came to the stream all the time.

"Where can we meet tomorrow?" Brad asked, his arm squeezing her uncomfortably.

"Oh," Clare felt pressed. Where? But it was as if she had already thought of this. In the same way she had been waiting for him, she had also been planning, unknown to herself. How strange and how completely natural—she had been living a second life under the surface of this one.

"Downstream from here," she whispered, "three kilometers. Go past the hot springs to an old beaver dam. Up from the dam, in the rocks, you'll find a cave."

"Clare!" one of the voices called. "Clare!"

"Don't tell anyone," Brad said, and then he was gone, not very quietly, breaking branches and twigs.

"Clare! Where are you?" The women came into the clearing between the willow and the cottonwood trees. They called out, turning their heads this way and that.

"I'm defecating," Clare said and squatted.

They sang half the night, celebrating the full moon, the green plants in their full stomachs. Throughout the year, the Rio Chama people were careful to consume enough vitamins and minerals even if it meant chewing dry berries and herbs, eating scurvy grass and brewing pine-needle tea. But nothing was as good as the actual leaves and stems of mustards and sorrels, chickweed and beebalm, lambsquarter, vetch, and waterleaf, the lovely mess boiled until tender. Sometimes the greens were bitter, and they enjoyed that, too, the peppery flavor, the taste of anise, a sharp bite on the tongue.

The full moon rose higher in the sky as they passed around a bottle of fermented yucca drink, most of the adults getting a little tipsy. Clare sat by the fire with Jon's arm over her shoulder as he sang, his voice joining with the women on the higher parts, the voice of the dandelion or the moon, yet he could also take the harmony with the men, deep and masculine, the voice of the lion and the sun. He smiled down at her as she came in on the women's chorus. He squeezed her shoulder to tell her he loved her. Above them, the eye of the moon grew as wide as it could, eager to look down on the tribe and listen to their songs. The moon was a piece of fruit hanging ripe in the sky. The moon was the belly of a woman about to give birth. The moon was a gourd full of seeds.

"You are as beautiful as the moon," Jon whispered to her, something men had been saying for thousands of years.

Clare felt bad about lying to him. She felt guilty for snuggling up to him, smiling back and even squeezing his arm. But clearly Brad didn't want Jon or anyone else to know he and Luke were near the camp. That Dog was near the camp. *Dog told me where to look for you.* Clare didn't want to think too much about that.

The next morning she explained to Jon how she would be with her girlfriends the entire day as they walked to the west gathering baskets of green leaves. She hinted that this was a woman thing, a being-pregnant thing, something that might involve a few rituals. Maybe they would sing some special women songs, tell special women stories. Jon looked thoughtful and wise—still sleepy from the yucca drink. He was happier now, the larger she got and the longer Brad stayed away and did not email. Jon's friends and Clare's friends also pitched in to help Jon save face. They teased him about becoming a father, the fathers among them giving advice, and the men taking him on hunts where, Clare supposed, they did special men things, sang special men songs, told special men stories. Almost everyone in the tribe seemed to have forgiven her for leaving them to go to the lab. Now she was here. The present was what mattered.

Clare felt a sense of hurry. Even so, the sun shone well above the horizon before she finally set off with the other women, five of them walking and talking. One of the women told a story about her mother's cousin. Another had politics on her mind, an upcoming election to replace a Council member who had recently died. They all talked about the move back to the summer camp. That would be soon. Clare listened and nodded, and when they were far enough away but still within sight of the colored tents, she begged off from the trip, saying she was unwell.

The group fell silent. Two of her friends offered to stay with her.

Then Clare admitted she wasn't being completely truthful. She didn't feel unwell so much as she wanted to be private, to think about her baby's name, to idle alone in the hot springs. Now the other women looked relieved. They could understand that. Besides, they would go faster and gather more plants without her.

They all agreed that Jon was too protective. "He's like a mother ground sloth," Clare's best friend joked. "A heavy blanket," another said. "You want the warmth but then, suddenly, you're hot." "He's always been stubborn," an older woman spoke. "Remember all those damn-muck-a-luck birds? Besides, he's still angry . . ." She stopped, not liking where this would lead. "He loves you so much. He's so happy about the baby," she finished, and Clare nodded.

They watched her backtrack and slip over to the woods by the stream. They waved good-bye. Clare waved good-bye. Good-bye! Good-bye! Good-bye!

She stood for an extra minute, waving. Then she turned and walked downstream, fast but careful not to stumble over cobble or tree roots. She didn't want to think too much about what she was doing. Instead she focused on birdsong, recognizing the call of black-headed phoebe and yellow-breasted chat. There was the flash of a hummingbird, which always meant good luck. There were coyote tracks, and fox, a black bear and a badger, a mountain lion and direwolf. Clare stopped at the print, but this direwolf was normal-toed and unaccompanied by human footprints, probably a male running without a pack. She smelled something rotting in a hackberry—the odor enough to make her gag. She mentally marked a patch of sweet-root to gather later. She tried to be alert and present in the moment, despite what she was doing and whom she was meeting.

Scrambling up the rocks to the cave, Clare scraped her palm and sent small showers of pebbles below. A noise above told her he was there, and then a dark hand and arm were pulling her to the top, his glasses askew, the smile shy. She could only imagine what she looked like to Brad: misshapen and unbalanced. A stranger with a stranger in her womb. Suddenly Clare felt angry. She carried his son or daughter, something that belonged to him more profoundly than anything else in the world, and yet something that didn't belong to him at all—the child already claimed by another man. What did Brad know of this new heart beating, the umbilical cord pulsing with blood, new thoughts forming—the brain developed enough to think! The baby already responded to music! What did he know of vomiting and back pain and a clutching in her chest?

"Where have you been?" she asked, shaking off the lab rat's help once they were on flatter ground. The cave entrance was as she remembered, a clutter of boulders hiding a black hole that led into a deep low-ceilinged rock shelter. She looked around for Luke.

"She's here," Brad called at the same time.

And Clare had to stop herself from crying out as the old man and the direwolf emerged from the cave. Luke squinted as if just up from a nap. The sun was already hot and high, but Clare understood: You slept when you could, especially if you had been traveling through the night. Dog yawned ostentatiously, his pink tongue lolling.

Clare fought down her panic. Yes, this was Dog, the same brown and yellow coloring, the same extra toe. She remembered the stench of the rotting head. Had she imagined that scene in Brad's office? Out of habit, she put a hand on her stomach and spoke to the baby: It's all right. Don't worry. We're okay.

"You can touch him," Brad said.

Carefully, the direwolf came forward, and she put down her other hand and touched the top of his head. The fur felt gritty from the dust in the cave. She smelled that Dog smell, wet fur and meaty breath. Dog whined, as if wanting a real pet. Brad watched her. Luke grunted and went back into the cave to retrieve a pack, which he put on the ground against the trunk of a pine. Then he sat down himself.

Clare stepped back and looked at Dog more closely. She turned her head to see him from another angle, from the corner of her eye, to catch him by surprise. "Just tell me the truth," she said wearily to Brad. "Start at the beginning and tell me what you've done."

Before Brad would begin, he insisted she eat some jerky from Luke's pack and gave her water from a leather bottle. Then he explained methodically, step by step, everything Clare had missed. He didn't seem to hold anything back. He and Luke had scavenged for edutoys in Los Alamos. He had experimented on the head of a direwolf. And a sunflower. On twelve sunflowers. The Council had become suspicious. He had to flee in the night with his radios and solarcomp. He had experimented on a mouse. The next thing he knew he was surrounded by golden animals, surrounded by light.

The details were so shocking they had to be true. And then Brad was saying that he could bring back Elise. He could bring back Clare's daughter just as he had brought back Dog, just as he had brought back a camel, a saber-toothed cat, two horses, two deer, two black bears, a small cat, and five mice. Elise could be sitting here, bright and funny, four-year-old Elise chattering about her pretend-games and pretend-dramas, her little families of sticks and pebbles, laughing at her mother's jokes, asking to be tickled, asking for something good to eat. All Brad needed was a bit of Elise's hair.

Clare stared at Brad. She stared at Luke, who nodded. She touched the leather bag at her neck. That's how he had brought back the others. A bit of hair or bone. Dog would help. Dog knew what to do. Elise would be here again—her unique consciousness, a glowing Elise just like Dog. Brad would do this for her. Because he loved her. Because he wanted her to be happy and because he knew—he had always known—about the longing and the hunger. The hole in her life. Clare put her hands on her stomach. It's okay, she told the new baby. It's okay. We're okay.

She waited for the outrage to rise up and fill her chest and open her throat. She waited for the self she knew to say no. This was impossible. This was wrong. This was against The Return and the Council and the elders.

She remembered the moment Elise died. She remembered rocking back and forth in front of her dying daughter. Because Elise couldn't die. Because *that* was impossible. Your child couldn't die, couldn't leave you like this. Because you loved her so much. Because your love was so powerful. Your love protected her, would always protect her. Your love made everything possible. And then Elise gasped. Then Elise was still. They put her in a tree for the black birds to eat and buried her bones in a leather pouch near a white-barked sycamore. Elise was gone forever.

Had Clare ever believed that?

The new baby kicked. Don't worry, Clare said to her stomach. I'll protect you.

But she hadn't. She couldn't. She didn't. Had any of that really happened? Had her daughter really died? Would the new baby die? Would Jon kill the new baby? Of course, yes, Jon would kill the baby if the baby were damaged like Elise had been damaged. But that wouldn't happen. Clare wouldn't let that happen. Her love made everything possible.

And Clare felt a wind rush through her body, a wind so strong that all certainties swayed before it and blew away. Flux and change. Only one thing remained, one thing at the center. The baby in her womb, the baby she had lost. She wouldn't let them die. She wouldn't let them go. Brad had returned, and Dog had returned, and they were offering her something she couldn't refuse. She only needed to hold out her hand. Nothing else mattered. She only needed to take this gift.

Brad was explaining that Elise would not be like Dog right away. Elise would have to adjust to her new form, and so Clare had to expect some confusion and dissonance. Dog should be the first to go to Elise. Clare would have to be patient.

Clare felt the new baby turn over in her stomach. The baby was saying: I'm alive. The pine trees were saying: We're alive. The rocks, the buzzing insects: alive, alive. The world was so present, so real. Elise could be here, too. Elise was saying: I'm alive. I'm alive!

"Clare?" Brad asked. "Do you want me to bring Elise back?"

Luke broke in as if irritated. "What do you expect her to say to that?"

Clare remembered thinking: Freedom has limits. But this wasn't about that. She had never felt less free.

"Clare," Brad asked, "do you understand?" His voice was deep, serious.

And Clare thought of how smart her daughter was, how Elise would adjust much more quickly than Dog. Brad didn't know. Elise was a fast learner. Clare thought that they should have something ready for the little girl to eat, and then she remembered that Elise wouldn't need food. She wouldn't need water. She wouldn't need to breathe.

"I understand," Clare said. There was nothing to understand, nothing to think about. She watched as Brad went to the pack and got out his solarcomp and two radios. Luke closed his eyes. Dog panted like a dog on a hot day.

Brad looked nervous when he asked for the leather bag, when Clare took it off for the first time in six years and he took out the curl of Elise's dark hair. Gently, he put the hair on the ground near the radios. Clare watched and at the last moment thought quite clearly: This is probably a dream. This probably isn't happening.

"Okay?" Brad asked again.

Yes, she agreed. She agreed. She understood.

It's okay, she told the new baby.

Dog came up closer, near the hair. He and Brad fell silent. Brad typed on his computer. Luke kept his eyes closed.

Oh, Clare laughed, a barking noise. Elise shimmered in the air. That was Elise's face screwed up in protest and distaste, newly awake. That was Elise's hair messy and uncombed. That was Elise's naked body, the slightly distended stomach, the thin arms and legs.

The body, however, seemed uncertain, drifting off into space, partly dissolving. There was some sparking, some radiance. An electromagnetic shiver. Clare was standing now, walking toward her daughter. Brad stood, too, and blocked her way. Dog hovered near the child.

"Mommy!" Elise screamed. "Mommy!"

Clare didn't know if this were a real sound or a sound inside her head, but Elise was talking to her. Elise wanted her. Brad seemed surprised when Clare pushed him aside and kept moving forward. Elise flickered. More sparking, more radiance. Clare couldn't touch her yet. She couldn't embrace her.

"Wait," Dog cautioned. "Give her a little time."

Clare almost jumped to hear the direwolf in her thoughts, speaking clearly in a complete sentence. Brad had said that Dog would know what to do. Dog would help.

"Yes, I can help," Dog answered. "And this is wonderful. She can already talk to us! She knows you already. She wants you."

Of course, she wants me, Clare thought. Of course, she wants her mother.

A few hours later, as the shadows lengthened and the afternoon air began to cool, they all realized that this was a problem. Elise wouldn't leave Clare's side and that meant Clare couldn't return to the winter camp.

Clare said out loud what she had known as soon as Brad took the leather bag. Perhaps she had known earlier, the moment she saw Dog. She wondered how her body could contain these contradictions, this joy and this grief. She wondered why she wasn't herself sparking and dissolving. "I can never go back to camp," she told Brad. No one in the tribe would understand what had just happened. No one would approve. What would they do to Elise when they saw her? What would they do to Clare and Brad?

Now Clare had to go with Brad and Luke and Dog. Now she and the new baby and Elise had to flee, for they no longer had a place with the Rio Chama people. How lucky that Jon thought she was with her girlfriends and her girlfriends thought she was at the hot springs. It was important to go back to the stream now and erase the sign of her footprints. Luke could do that while she soothed Elise and got her ready for the journey. Dog could help with Elise while Brad packed and cleaned the area around the cave. Jon mustn't guess they had ever been here. They must make it hard for Jon to track them.

But they had to hurry. Clare gave her orders. It was late afternoon, and they should be on their way. How lucky that her people (her mother, her father, her grandmother) would be leaving soon for the summer camp. This would also make it hard for them to find her. How lucky that she would have a full moon tonight, the moon that looked after pregnant women, the moon like a gourd full of seeds.

Assignment Six: What I Would Like to Do This Summer, submitted by María Escobar

What I would like to do this summer is go on my long quest. All the smaller quests I have been on have just made me more ready for this one. I'll be fifteen years old, turning sixteen, and in my tribe we think of this long quest as my quinceañera, a celebration of who I am as a woman and tribal member. I want to be gone with my guide for at least a month. My friend Carlos had his long quest three years ago and he said it was wonderful. I know I will learn a lot on this quest and it will become a defining moment in my life! I am so excited to do this! My elders are waiting now for your final evaluation of my work during these last few years.

As soon as you send them that evaluation they can choose a guide and start the preparations. I hope you think that I have done well. I have really tried and I have also learned a lot from you! I hope you send them my evaluation soon.

PART THREE

Clare gave her death-shriek. Rabbits shrieked like this when they were being torn apart by hyenas. Clare remembered that sound. For a moment, she looked down from a branch in the juniper tree and saw herself, her mouth hanging open, her sweaty naked belly, and the top of Lucia's gray head. Lucia's shoulders twisted as she put her hand into Clare and tore her apart. It was such a shame. Clare had wanted to say good-bye to Elise. To Brad. To the new baby. She was so sorry to leave them.

CHAPTER SEVENTEEN

DOG

Dog was watching the humans dream. He had promised Brad to stay out of people's minds, but he felt this did not include the periods when they were sleeping, their thoughts so chaotic and relatively unconscious. Dog suspected his own reasoning on this subject could be called specious. He was rationalizing his behavior, a kind of lying to himself. That was interesting.

He just really liked watching humans dream. He liked to think, too, that he was helping Luke/Lucia by manipulating his/her dreams so that they were calmer and more knitted together. In his present form, Dog himself could not affect the physical world. But that part of him still in Luke's brain had become an actual part of Luke's brain wired into neurons, and Dog could use the Dog-in-Luke to nudge along a thought or connection. Yes, Dog-in-Luke could give Luke a little push. A little encouragement.

Dog only did this to make Luke feel better. Luke was a chameleon. Luke was a kaleidoscope. Luke was fractured. Luke was

Lucia was the lover of Brad's mother was the father to Dog was the wise man to Brad was the lonely old woman was the lost soul was the childless womb was the hunter was the midwife was the voice of humanity was regret was guilt was love for Dog. In his lifetime, Dog had known Luke as the person Lucia usually wanted to be. But Lucia had been dominant before and might be again in response to Clare's pregnancy. It didn't matter. Lucia was Luke was the lover of Brad's mother was the lonely little girl was the protector of mice was the researcher of mutations was the scavenger was the elder was regret was guilt was love for Dog. They all came together in dreams, and sometimes they fought like two children wrestling each other, like mighty Titans, and then Dog gave a little push—urging peace.

Dog understood that all humans were made up of such multiple parts, many things united under one thing they called "myself," fractured bits of consciousness assembling and disassembling. Luke was only more so. He contained more parts than usual, more hormones than usual, and that seemed to throw off the balance. Dog understood that he himself had once been made of many parts, his mutated heritage, the leakage from Luke and Brad and the giant shortfaced bear. All the stories he had heard, all the games he had played.

Dog saw an opportunity and gave a little nudge, retrieving an old memory: Luke throwing a stick and Dog bringing it back. Back and forth. A pleasing motion. Back and forth. Nothing at stake. Nothing that would change the world. This was a healing dream. Dog saw how it made Luke relax. The muscles in the man's neck loosened. The easy movement. Back and forth. Dog was still half-grown, almost a puppy. Luke was younger, and Dog made him laugh. The clumsy eager puppy. Back and forth.

Dog left Luke and moved over to Brad sleeping nearby, the humans in an arranged pile. Dog was always on night watch now, and no one else needed to take a turn. Dog would alert them to the first sign of danger.

Most of the time, Brad's dreams were practical. He worked on equations or some other problem he had encountered during the day. Tonight he was reliving the last few days, going over their actions, looking for mistakes. They had started off strong. Leaving the stream, Clare felt certain that any signs of her and the others had been erased, making it difficult for Jon to follow them. Elise was adjusting well to her new condition, already talking after only a few minutes, already able to float beside them in a coherent shape. Luke said he knew of a place to hide, a canyon not near any human trail. There would be water and game and a large cave for protection from the summer storms. The old man led the way, and they walked all that moonlit night.

Then Luke grew doubtful. He didn't recognize these mountains. It had been years ago, before Dog. The old man muttered to himself and began to move his hands secretly. Brad was not completely surprised. Luke still refused to look at Elise. Perhaps he was nearing a kind of breakdown. Things were happening too fast. The future rushing toward them.

On another level, Brad worried they were going too fast for Clare. She was huge! Surely this kind of speed was bad for her and the baby? In Brad's dream now, Elise began to scream, "Mommy! Mommy!" although she hadn't done this in real life except for that once when her unique consciousness was newly reassembled. Even so, throughout the day and night, she had demanded attention, trying to catch butterflies (her hands passed right through them) or asking about her father (not really understanding that he was gone, now and forever) or wandering away from her mother—so that Clare called frantically and Dog went to herd the girl back. Clare had looked increasingly dazed. They were traveling with a four-year-old who could float and keep an adult pace, who didn't eat or drink or need rest, but who in other ways was nearly uncontrollable.

With Luke becoming more vague and distraught, Brad had started making the decisions. He sat down beside the old man to draw a map in the sand. They agreed on a direction. First they would stop for part of the morning and rest. Brad gave the remaining jerky to Clare. He checked the water supply and set up snares before allowing everyone to nap under the shade of a scrub bush. He had never been in charge of a trip like this before, never had to worry about someone else before. He knew he was forgetting something, and as the sun moved across the sky, Brad discovered what that was: They hadn't provided themselves enough shelter from the heat. They should have gone deeper into the brush. They should have built a ramada of sticks and grass. Their punishment was waking to hot skin and dehydration. Now Brad decided they should drink the remaining water and push on to find more. Everyone felt awful but Dog and Elise and the golden animals following discreetly behind.

This was what happened in real life, a mistake followed by a decision, and their efforts rewarded by the green flags of a cottonwood tree. Gratefully, they camped by the spring, and Brad snared a rabbit for their breakfast.

In Brad's dream, however, things were not going so well. The spring was dry, and even the baby in Clare's womb cried out with thirst. Lucia sobbed and would not stop sobbing. Her old woman's neck bobbled like a turkey's wattle. *Wattle, wattle, wattle. Gobble, gobble, gobble.* Clare fell down a rocky slope and hit her head. The blood was old blood, not fresh, so that Brad thought distinctly, "This isn't right."

Brad looked down at his father and thought, "This isn't right." His father didn't look like the crazy bushkie Clare had struck with her spear. The blood around the bushkie's wound had dried dark. The bushkie groaned and when he opened his eyes, Brad was surprised to see that, in fact, the man *was* his father. Those were his father's eyes, sane and agreeable, the cunning eyes of a hunter. A man who could track a raven in a storm.

"I saw a pillar of light," his father told him. That was his father's voice, too, deep, serious. "I saw it rise from the ground, a stick of glowing light."

Brad recognized the paradox. He had sent the consciousness of the sunflower stalk back in time. The bushkie had seen that glowing stick of light and was inspired to form his religious band who kidnapped Luke whom Brad helped rescue—meeting Dog and leading to the events that caused Brad to send the sunflower consciousness back in time. Which came first, the light, the bushkie, or Brad?

In his dream, Brad began to think about time and paradoxes. What happened at the quantum level? How had he solved the problem of the sunflowers?

Dog felt bored since he knew the answer, and he moved again— over to Clare, sleeping next to Brad. Clare was dreaming about Jon. In Clare's dream, Jon lay sleepless in his summer tent, staring up at the night sky, the round hole where the poles came together. The round hole let in wind and moonlight but not enough, so that the air in the tent was stuffy and dark. Some people had already dismantled their skins, not needing them in this warm weather and preparing for the move the next day to the summer camp. Others wanted privacy for some reason, for sex or to be alone with their family or alone with themselves. Jon wanted to be alone with his anger. He stared up at the round hole of night sky and felt the tension in his body. His parents were dead. His first wife had left him. Clare had left him and then left him again and taken his child. He had seen the sign of her erased prints. She didn't want him to know where she was going or whom she was with. But Jon knew. The lab rat had come back.

Dog wondered if Clare's dream were true, if she could really see Jon as he stared up into the summer tent or if she were only imagining the scene because she knew Jon so well. Dog could check but he didn't. He was afraid of expanding and disappearing. He preferred to stay Dog. To do only what Dog could do.

Clare was worried about the future. The elders would send emails. The tribes would be looking for them. Jon would not forget her. He would not forgive her. He would keep searching. And where would she give birth? That was less than three months away. Who would help if not her mother and grandmother? And what if they met another group of hunters? How would they hide Elise?

Dog felt bored again. He couldn't nudge Clare to dream about something more pleasant. He couldn't influence Clare. Still, he didn't leave her for Luke or Brad. Because Dog knew that eventually Elise would join him. Elise also liked watching Clare dream.

Dog felt a thrill, an almost-thrill. He had kept track of the little girl all night. That was part of his job, too, listening for predators and babysitting Elise. For now she played with the golden animals following discreetly behind them—the camel, horse and colt, two deer, two black bears, small cat, saber-toothed cat, and five mice. Brad had told these animals to go away and hoped they would. Because they were evidence against Brad. Because they might lead a human hunter to him and Clare and Luke. Because they would certainly upset Clare if she knew they were still here, part of their new group. Brad hoped the golden animals would float away out of his life, like the golden sunflower, but Dog knew this was not going to happen. Dog understood the animals' compulsion to stay together and to stay near him.

"Don't let the woman see you," he had commanded them. "Don't let any other human see you." He was stern. "Stay behind us. Blend into the sunlight."

Almost immediately, the golden animals had also been attracted to Elise, and on this second night, Dog had introduced her to them. With everyone else sleeping, the child had started a game of freeze tag. The golden animals learned the rules quickly and seemed happy to be jumping and leaping and holding still, "frozen" by Elise's "touch" on the yellow plain. Dog was pleased to see Elise following at least one of his instructions, not running too much faster than a little girl could run, not doing too much more than a little girl could do (except for the floating part, except for the disappearing in and out of things part). He had warned both her and the golden animals over and over: Stay within your shape.

They agreed wordlessly. For the most part, they *were* wordless, mute like any non-Paleo. Only the saber-toothed cat occasionally spoke to Dog or sent word images, feeling images that seemed almost-angry, as though the big cat still resented dying and being eaten by direwolves, resented, perhaps, being brought back.

"Dog?" Elise asked, suddenly beside him and watching Clare dream. "Who is Jon?"

Dog wagged his tail. "A friend of your mother's."

"Why are we scared of him?"

"He wants to find us. We don't want him to find us."

"Where are we going?"

"It doesn't matter," Dog explained. "No matter. I go where Luke goes, and you go where your mother goes."

Elise seemed satisfied with this, and for a while they eavesdropped while Clare whispered urgently to her grandmother as they gathered watercress. The watercress looked crisp and tasty, and Clare yearned for a dish of watercress lightly salted.

"Dog?" Elise asked. "You weren't here . . . before, were you?"

"No, I'm new."

"I'm new, too, aren't I?"

"Yes," Dog said. "You and I. We are new."

CHAPTER EIGHTEEN

BRAD

Brad was getting good at rabbits. In the last few months, he had made a study of why rabbits went where they did and at what time of day, what snare worked best, how to kill the animals if the snare didn't, how to skin them, and what herbs brought out their flavor. He was becoming a rabbit expert, perhaps not as exciting as being an expert in deer or horse or black bear, but still satisfying—to bring Clare a bowl of rabbit stew and get a smile in return.

Clare was astonishingly large. With the birth only weeks away, she seemed as big as a ground sloth. Different parts of her were in discomfort, and those parts were sometimes out of her control or even her reach. In the evening, Brad had started massaging her ankles, the top and bottom of each foot, and each toe. He combed her hair with a comb she had made from bone, and he rubbed her stretched-out stomach with a paste of plants Lucia ground fresh every day. If Elise was behaving, Clare could relax, and he and she talked about the day's events—not about the future or anything else.

Clare would repeat that this was a nice spot, this hidden canyon that Luke had remembered, with its small spring and green bower of cottonwood and red willow. At the top of the canyon, a scatter of caves provided shelter from the heat and thunderstorms. This is so nice, Clare would say. How lucky we are.

By mid-July, the rains so far had been scarce, however, the summer dry. That was not lucky. Also, Elise did not always behave. This morning, as Brad sat on the ground and tried to check his emails, she kept walking through the solarcomp he had taken from the lab, walking back and forth as she whispered and scolded an imaginary being in her private game. When Elise walked through something, her form disappeared—in this case, her feet. When she wanted to disappear herself, she simply stood very still as though standing behind molecules of air. She was not interested in becoming more solid or, rather, in appearing to be more solid—like Dog—although Clare would have liked that, would have loved, in fact, to hold her daughter's hand and use the comb on that wild hair. But Elise only laughed and chattered, "Look, Mommy, what I can do!" And she disappeared. "Look, Mommy!" And she floated through a tree.

Clare had started making rules that Brad couldn't enforce. Now, for example, he was supposed to tell Elise to stop walking through his solarcomp. He tried. "Honey, Elise, stop walking through my solarcomp."

"I'm a giant antelope," the little girl said, "with giant white teeth."

"Mommy doesn't want you walking through things. It looks funny to the rest of us. It's very distracting now."

"Now Spider Woman comes down from the sky to look at the giant antelope with giant white teeth, and she and the antelope get into a fight."

"Someday we might meet other people who will get upset if you walk through things."

"The giant antelope pulls Spider Woman's hair, and Spider Woman's hair breaks into a hundred baby spiders! Not even the Warrior Twins can save Spider Woman!"

Brad recognized the Navajo story and admired the little girl's adaptation. He gave up on the scold. Clare wasn't here, after all, but busy in the cave preparing her birthing room. In truth, Clare was the only person who could get Elise to do what she wanted her to do, and then only some of the time. Brad had never realized how strong willed a four-year-old could be. He had often thought of himself as strong willed. But compared to Elise, he was a rabbit. The thought made him smile.

Elise smiled, too. She had been watching him. She loved to entertain people. "A hundred baby spiders," she sang, "going everywhere, in every direction . . ." Parts of her curly and slightly glowing hair began to break off, twisting in an imitation of baby spiders—luminous tendrils escaping into the air. She looked like Medusa, one of the old Greek myths, and Brad stopped working. When Elise started deforming like this, no one knew what would happen. She might dissolve entirely. She might not form back into the daughter Clare recognized. Brad had a sickening image of hands pointed the wrong way or eyes out of place.

"No, Elise!" he said sternly.

And somehow she knew he meant it this time. Her hair reconstructed, and she stopped pacing, her feet in the solarcomp, her naked legs blocking the screen. Brad guessed she was about to cry.

"Hey, look at this email!" he said. "This is really unexpected!"

"Whaaat?" Elise hesitated.

"Come around here, here behind me," Brad went on, changing the focus and font of the email text, adding some graphics, throwing in music. "We'll read it together."

Elise liked to pretend to read.

"Oh, it's from that wicked Council woman. What does she say?"

Brad knew exactly what the Council woman said because she said the same thing in every email. "Where are you? Contact me immediately." She sent these emails almost daily. Judith also wrote on occasion, asking the same question. A few of his other least favorite colleagues wondered instead about some of the things he had left behind. Could they borrow the chair from his office? Could they use his computer while he was gone? Brad worried quite a bit about that. He wasn't sure if he had wiped his computer 100 percent clean. He had left the lab so quickly. If someone like Judith were to look hard enough, she might find traces of the experiment, the work with Dog's head and thirteen sunflowers. Brad put that thought away. Of course, he never answered the emails. He didn't want to be traced.

"Come on," he coaxed Elise. "I can't read this alone."

"Elise!" Clare was calling, rolling like some slow-motion boulder down the path from the caves. Elise hopped right out of the solarcomp.

Late in the afternoon, Brad and Lucia went hunting. Small game was plentiful, but bigger animals now avoided the spring, and Lucia wanted something big, a horse or deer. She wanted to prepare jerky for the day they could not hunt, the emergency they could not yet predict.

"You're tired of my rabbit stew?" Brad joked.

"Really tired," Lucia said.

They walked through the tall grass that spread like water from the sheltered canyon, mountains in the distance, black birds circling in a blue sky. Brad suspected Lucia welcomed this escape as much as he did, away from the domesticity of camp, the burden of chores and children. The old woman led them to a small rise. From here, they could see the herds move across the plain.

Lucia seemed content enough, her white hair braided down her back and plaited with flowers like women liked to do in the summer.

Her lined face looked softer and fuller now that she had stabilized and was Lucia the midwife all the time. Deliberately, she belted her leather tunic to reveal and not hide her meager breasts.

Brad didn't want to bother with camels unless they saw a straggler. An antelope would be tasty. A young horse would be best. Brad brushed at the flies around his face and coveted, particularly, the tail of a horse. He'd certainly be a hero, bringing back a horse's tail. They could use it in the evenings for mosquitoes, too.

"We should clear more area around the cave," Lucia was saying, "in case of fire."

"Take out the brush," Brad agreed. With little rain, the grasslands were dry and thunderstorms building every afternoon. A fire would sweep across them, fast and hot, the small spring no protection. With a good enough firebreak, they would be safe in the birthing cave.

"We should work on that tomorrow."

Brad nodded and wondered if those were elk to the east. Or horses? He watched a sloping hill that reminded him briefly of a woman's thigh. Was that a shape against the hill, an older animal falling behind? It would be a long walk to see and longer coming back with meat in their packs.

"Have you noticed anything unusual . . ." Lucia paused, for once not the first to spot game, "between Dog and Elise?"

Brad glanced her way. So Lucia wanted to talk. Perhaps that's why she had suggested this hunt. He answered cautiously, "Only that sometimes she does what Dog asks. He's a good influence."

"A good influence," the old woman repeated. Her silence was now pointed. Then "What were you thinking?" Lucia said gently, not really asking.

Brad studied the sloping hill. What *had* he been thinking, bringing back Elise, knowing her presence would be impossible to hide among the tribes or in the lab? What had he hoped for? Another unique consciousness like Dog, someone who could help him unlock the secrets to the universe? Or maybe it had simply been all about Clare, her gratitude and admiration, her thigh against his in the middle of the night. Brad couldn't decipher his own motives anymore. He suspected he hadn't been thinking at all.

"Elise will get better," he said authoritatively.

"Grow up, you mean?" Lucia scoffed. "You think she can do that now?"

"No. Yes. Yes, she can learn." Brad hoped that was true. Certainly Dog's consciousness, no longer paired with his bioholo-gram, was still learning and evolving. A bit too much for comfort, Brad thought. But Elise had been a child when her bioholo-gram died, her unique consciousness shaped by the experiences and lack of experiences of a child. Certain hormones had never coursed through her system. Certain physical changes had never taken place. How much could she learn or change as a perpetual four-year-old?

Lucia shrugged. "Maybe." And started a new subject. "Do you remember the younger bushkie, the one that ran away?"

Brad kept his eyes to the east. Definitely those were horses. "Why?"

"He had to go somewhere. We have to go somewhere. After the baby is born."

Brad wondered why they couldn't stay in the small canyon by the spring, but Lucia was already explaining that. "Where we are is too good. Water and shelter. Likely other hunters use it, too, or will find it eventually. We can't go very far east or west, not closer to the radiation zones. We could head north to Colorado. But there are lots of people there. Too many, I think. That leaves . . . the peyote fields."

Brad jerked his eyes from the herd. They had sent the crazy bush-kie to the peyote fields. Exiled him. Probably killed him by doing so.

Lucia shrugged again as if to say—we are exiles now, too. We are bushkies now, too. "If we don't want to be found," she spelled it out for him, "we have to live on the margin. We have to hide."

No, Brad thought and turned his attention back to the grassland. No, he rejected that for himself and for Clare, for the child in Clare's womb. In the past few months, he had grown to understand Clare's defense of the bushkies, the ways they were different, the ways being different was not bad. He understood his own fears better, although he no longer felt afraid. He knew he was nothing like a bushkie. He had Clare. He was a husband. He was a father. When Brad thought about the baby, his baby, he didn't imagine an actual body, hands or feet or face. The baby itself was a blur—the category of baby. Still he felt something else that was specific, sharp as a spear. He felt the clarity of the future. He saw days and weeks and months and years, decades stretching ahead. His son, his daughter, walked confidently into that light. She moved with grace. She walked and held her own child's hand. She walked beside other men and women, her tribe, her family. She was not alone. She was not marginal. Brad felt fierce although his voice stayed even, without emotion. "Do you see the horses?"

Lucia had not, but when she looked, she agreed. There seemed to be a straggler in the herd. Brad could almost taste the sizzling fat.

Which was their undoing, the sizzling fat in the campfire and thin wisps of smoke from cooking that night and the next night, curing jerky. Afterward, Lucia berated herself, but really what could they have done—lived like animals without cooked meat?

Brad found the round circle of grass to the west, not far from the campsite. He was hunting alone this time and hoping for something small like a javelina when he saw the wreath hanging from the branch of an old oak, a solitary giant on the yellow plain.

Three bundles of long-stemmed grama had been braided and tied together, an easy enough message: the Round River people had stopped here.

Looking for footprints, Brad found those, too, four adults. They seemed fresh, although he was not an expert in tracking, not able like some to guess the weight of a person from the indentation of the heel. He could, of course, follow the tracks through the grass and along the game trail. When the prints turned and headed toward the canyon where Clare, Lucia, Dog, and Elise waited for him, he began to run, bursting through the screen of cottonwoods to their cleared site with its ramada and campfire, rack of jerky, and scatter of debris.

Clare had been sewing, and her bone awl and pieces of leather lay dropped on the ground beside Brad's solarcomp and a willow basket half-done. Clare was standing, a hand on her stomach. She looked miserable. Lucia sat beside a pile of greens, picking the leaves from the tougher stems, trying not to seem worried. Elise and Dog were nowhere in sight.

Four hunters from the Round River people were also standing, forming a half circle facing Clare. They still had on their packs as if they had just arrived. Or as if no one had yet asked them to sit. They seemed to be talking all at once but stopped when Brad rushed into the clearing.

"Brad!" Clare said. "We have visitors."

The two women and two men gave friendly smiles, nodding heads and keeping their spear hands lowered. They were tall, sturdy, and brown-haired. Brad also lowered his hands, his spear pointed down as he went over to stand by Clare.

"We saw your smoke last night," one of the men said. "We've just come to say hello."

"They know my cousins." Clare also tried to smile. The effect was awful.

"Is the birth near?" one of the women asked. "We can help."

Still no one asked the hunters to sit.

Where was Elise? Brad looked around, trying to be discreet. Where was Dog?

Clare shook her head slightly. What did that mean?

"We have all the help we need," Lucia spoke up. Her voice sounded musical, quite like an elder. "We're grateful for the offer, but the truth is, we'd prefer to be alone now. We're sorry to be inhospitable. We can't even offer you food."

"What?" one of the men said, confused.

"This is just the way it is," Lucia replied reassuringly. "This is a personal matter. You need to leave. We need to be alone."

"Your cousins . . ." the woman began.

"Tell them hello for me," Clare interrupted. "I'll email them soon."

"Mommy, can I come out now?" Elise's voice sounded from near the drying rack, and Brad understood. She was there in plain sight. The frame of saplings with its string of horse meat would not normally hide a child, only someone like Elise who could turn invisible behind a column of molecules. Elise was listening eagerly to the conversation. Elise could barely keep still, no matter what her mother had told her.

"No," Clare said sharply.

The Round River people glanced at each other.

"No, Elise!" Brad heard himself say.

"Mommy!" Elise whined and materialized.

Now there were gasps, high pitched from one woman, lower from the men. The second woman was silent but actually raised her spear. As Elise floated forward, the four hunters jostled back. The little girl glowed slightly. Her feet didn't touch the ground. Her dark curly hair twisted and twined in the air like snakes. Brad moved closer to Clare, who had turned visibly pale and who might even fall. He dropped his spear and prepared to catch her.

"I want to meet them," Elise said plaintively.

Lucia was standing, picking up Brad's spear, and speaking to the hunters, "You have to go now."

The hunters were talking all together, a swell of chatter like frightened birds.

"What should I do?" Dog spoke to Brad.

"We have to drive them away," Brad said. "Lucia and I will help. Get the animals."

CHAPTER NINETEEN

CLARE

Before the visitors came, Clare had been making a sling for the baby, using some leather from a deer's hide for the back and front and rabbit fur for the inside, where the baby would sleep against her breasts. She was making the kind of sling in which the child could face in, legs tucked against the mother's ribs, or face out, legs kicking in the air as passing adults smiled and cooed, and the baby smiled and cooed, interacting with the world.

For the front panel on the sling, Clare wanted the design of a swallow. Swallows were friendly birds not afraid of humans but swooping close as if to see—what are these humans doing? Sometimes swallows built their nests in human structures like ramadas or the adobe corridors of the lab. Moreover, swallows were easy to draw and recognize with their long forked tails. Clare had been using the bone awl to prick dots forming a line, the pattern of this bird in leather. Later she would fill in these holes with the black dye of devil's claw. She would use another dye, yellow from rabbitbrush, for the rump. She didn't have purple for the head and wings. Maybe she would use brown from walnut or a bit of cochineal if she wanted an accent of red.

It was important to keep doing her usual activities, to make art and decorate clothes and sing at night. Almost every day, Brad combed her hair so it was smooth and untangled, and she saw that Lucia did the same for herself, keeping neat and clean, brushing her teeth, plaiting her braid with flowers. In some ways, they were all simply part of a smaller tribe now, counting Elise and Dog—five fingers like the strength of a hand. Should she count Dog? Yes, yes, of course, if she wanted to count Elise.

Nearby, close enough to reach out and touch—if Clare could reach out and touch anything over her stomach!—Lucia sat on the ground, picking through mustard and beebalm, discarding the tougher portions and putting aside the rest for dinner. Clare felt grateful again that Lucia had some experience with birthing. The old woman had even helped at Brad's birth. That was a nice coincidence and perhaps meaningful. A good sign. Clare let herself think so. (Jon would see it as a sign, but she didn't want to think about Jon.)

"Lucia?" she asked, just to talk. "Can you see Elise?"

The woman shifted, leaned forward, and settled back, nodding. "She's outside the cave, with Dog."

"What are they doing?"

"I wish I knew," Lucia spoke darkly but then smiled. "Nothing, I'm sure. Playing one of their games."

"Do you think Elise . . ." Clare didn't know how to say this. Would Elise ever stop playing games? She couldn't grow physically. Clare understood that now. She understood what she had agreed to—what she had gotten back. Her daughter alive. But not quite the same daughter. Not quite human. Not a child who would ever physically grow into a teenager or a young woman. But mentally? Could Elise mature in some way as she acquired new experiences?

Clare let herself hope. Elise was smart. Dog was smart. Dog would teach her to be more like Dog, to keep her shape and feel solid under human touch, warm and breathing like any little girl. Maybe they could join with a northern tribe, people who didn't know them, who thought they were bushkies living alone. Maybe that was unrealistic. Maybe one day they could go back to the Council and explain. Brad was persuasive. He could be so charming. The Council would see that nothing really bad had happened. Yes, Brad had brought back the unique consciousness of Dog and Elise. That was wrong. But that was the end of it. He would promise never to do anything like that again. They would both promise. They would live at the lab. Maybe that was unrealistic. But they couldn't live with her tribe. Clare knew that. Not with Elise. Not with Jon. Maybe they would be allowed to live at peace on their own. That would be their punishment, to be their own small tribe, not harming anyone and not being harmed. She would be allowed to visit her family and friends. To see her mother and father and grandmother. As time passed, as this new child grew up to be a man, he would be allowed to return to her people. After all, none of this was his fault. He was innocent.

Clare could see Lucia watching her. Clare had never finished her question about Elise, but Lucia didn't seem to expect that. Lucia seemed to know how Clare's thoughts got sidetracked now (how she thought more than usual in parentheses, like some of her students, María, Alice, Dimitri . . . what were they doing now, what were they thinking?), how she couldn't finish one idea before starting another, how she lived round and round between worry and hope.

Annoyed, Clare struggled out of that circle. She was a writing teacher, after all. She could reason and analyze. Putting down the sling, she asked, "Where do you think Elise was before Brad brought her back?"

"Ah," Lucia was interested. "I've wondered about that. What happens to our unique consciousness when we die? We have always thought that it dissolves naturally, consciousness into consciousness, part of everything. Apparently it also exists in some dormant state as long as there is DNA." Lucia paused. "Maybe exist is too strong a word. It remains as potential."

"The elders say humans are the consciousness of the universe reflecting on itself."

Lucia pointed over to Dog. "Now we're not the only ones," she said dryly. The midwife was in one of her moods.

Soon after, they heard voices. It happened so fast, men and women calling out the traditional loud greetings before entering a strange camp. Clare recognized the dialect almost immediately. The Round River people. Elise floated down from the cave, and Clare told her to hide behind the drying rack. "Don't move or speak until I say you can!" Dog had already disappeared. The Round River voices came closer. Clare answered back, tremulously, standing up, holding her stomach. It's okay, she told the new baby. It's okay.

Suddenly Brad was there. Lucia took charge. Clare remembered one of the women. (They had met long ago, that summer with her cousins and uncle, the wildflowers so spectacular—she had wanted to weep with joy—and now apparently she, Clare, was no longer someone the other woman recognized.) Clare was about to speak. Remember when? Then Brad said, "No, Elise!" And Clare despaired. Couldn't Elise behave this one time? Clare felt a stab in her side, a painful ripple. Brad was right there. He wouldn't let her fall. Not now, she told the new baby.

The Round River people were shouting. But perhaps the woman would understand. They had traveled together. They had been friends. Clare decided to speak to her directly. She knew what to say: There is no reason to be afraid. Remember the summer we walked the game trails together? Remember how we laughed and made fun of my tall camel-cousin? You liked him then. Remember the camel's dance? This is my child Elise. My little girl. Let us offer you food. Let us sit down together. There is no reason to be afraid.

But before she could open her mouth, a direwolf rushed into the scene. That had happened once before, Clare thought irrelevantly.

But this time Dog could do nothing since he wasn't physically here. This time Lucia suddenly held a spear. This time Brad was shouting at her, "Sit down. Get down!" He practically pushed Clare into the dirt and then he was waving his arms as a herd of golden animals streamed through the campsite.

Elise shrieked with excitement. Clare saw a deer and a bear and a camel. She saw a small cat. She saw a saber-toothed cat huge and menacing and golden! She understood they were all like Elise. They were the animals Brad had brought back earlier, what he had described when he first told his story. She had thought them long gone, scattered across the plain. She had decided to forget about them. She had decided her world was too small for them (her world not much bigger than her belly).

Where had they been hiding? What were they doing?

The Round River people screamed and fled, their packs bouncing. We can't stay here, Clare thought from the ground like some helpless beetle set on its back. As soon as they could, the Round River people would email the rest of the tribes, let everyone know what they had seen, what had chased them away, and where they were. Not everyone would believe the entire story. But they would believe the part about Clare and Brad. Her mother would believe, and her grandmother would believe. Her tribe would send someone after her. Jon would volunteer. Jon was coming.

She had to leave the birthing cave. All that nice moss and bed of leaves.

Clare trudged under the hot sun. Thunderstorms built in the western sky, dark clouds billowing into white pillars. Perhaps later there would be rain. One step, two step. Lucia and Brad had all their supplies. She didn't even carry her own water. All she had to do was walk, trudge, move forward. That wasn't so hard even though it felt like she were moving through air as heavy as regret, knee-deep in a river, her feet being pulled from behind. One, two. One, two. The feet in her womb kicked. Brad whispered, "You should rest, you should drink." Nag, nag, nag.

Clare wasn't interested in arguing. Her stomach had not yet settled, rippling still, a small knife poking her from inside. But she was fine. She was fine, still two weeks away from giving birth. Water was easier to find in the rainy season. There was always some hole, some spring. Better to travel now, while she could. Better to get away as far as they could. Lucia was in charge of erasing their tracks, and perhaps that wasn't truly possible. Perhaps any good tracker could find them if he wanted. Or maybe a good summer rain would help them out. Maybe no one would come for days or weeks. Maybe Jon didn't care anymore. Maybe that was unrealistic. Still, there were so many possibilities.

Clare wasn't going to stay and wait. If she had to, she would have the baby on the plain of yellow grass. Lucia could build a shelter. Clare would have the baby and rest and then they would keep moving, Elise by her side, the new baby in the sling across her chest. The sling with the swallow, the pattern unfinished.

And it would be over. That would be done. Clare couldn't think past that moment. Lucia thought they should head south. That was fine. Clare didn't care where they went. She couldn't think of everything or make all the decisions. Not now—she felt a jab, the knife. Not now, she told the new baby.

Where Are You? submitted by María Escobar

Dear teacher, I am just wondering where you are? You will be glad to know that the elders in my tribe have decided I can take my long quest even though we have not heard from you in a very long time. The elders themselves looked at my work and said it was okay. I think they talked to the elders in your tribe. Everyone is concerned about you. I go next week and I will be gone almost two months! That is a long time for a first long quest. I think it shows a lot of confidence in me. My best friend Carlos is coming too and I couldn't be happier. I hope you are also happy and well.

One Last Question, submitted by Dimitri Wu

I understand that you are not my teacher anymore and that our class has been disbanded, at least for a while. I am saddened by this because I think I was learning a lot. My writing skills were improving and I felt that some of your assignments had really made me think about things I hadn't thought about before. Not all the assignments, of course, but some of them.

My last question to you concerns something very upsetting that is happening in my tribe. Someone (who I will not name here) wants us to start using guns to protect ourselves from the tigers in this area which have grown more numerous. This person's son died from the attack of a tiger and was eaten and so this person has very strong feelings. The rest of us have strong feelings, too. This is against The Return, against our pact with the earth! This person says we should use guns in self-defense to kill the tigers who have grown to depend on and demand human flesh. He says we should not use the viral-powered or even the nanoguns but only the old ones, from the twenty-first century, with their bullets and simple mechanical parts. We don't have any of these guns now, of course, but he says he can scavenge them. He knows where they are and he could learn to repair them easily. He says we would only need a few, for protection, to save our children.

But I say no to him and his allies. Because where will that end? This is a matter being discussed among the elders, and I know about this because my grandfather is an elder. He does not think we will ever take this to the Council because it is so clearly a bad idea. He says that people have had these ideas before and they are always dismissed because they are bad ideas. Still I worry. I worry in my soul. What do you think? I feel sure you will agree with me.

Some Strange News and a Confession, submitted by Carlos Salas

I heard about something very strange recently and immediately wanted to write you a paper on this topic. Apparently you have left your tribe, and no one knows why or when you will return. In the meantime you are not accepting any more papers from us. I will tell you the truth: At first, this made me angry. It seemed that you should say good-bye to your students and not leave us so concerned about your well-being. Then I realized that maybe you had no choice or that even if you did have a choice—and you chose not to contact us—there was nothing I could do about it either way. I could only choose to be angry or not. I decided as a Quaker not to be upset and simply to do what I really wanted to do— which is to keep writing to you whenever I feel like it even if you can't or don't or won't answer back.

So this is the strange story I heard. Two hunters in one of our tribes recently returned from the eastern coast where they went walking along the beach. They claim they saw a mammoth there walking across the wet sand. As you know, the southern edge of the mammoth range is just south from where you live and does not extend all the way to Costa Rica because it is so hot and humid here. Of course, we have our Paleos like glyptodonts and giant sloths and teratorns and even some of the earlier species like the dawn horse and small hippo, which aren't true Paleos since they came from the Eocene. Also they aren't very interesting because they aren't telepathic. But we don't have mammoths or mastodons or some of the bigger mammals like giant beavers and giant sloths. But these hunters said they saw a mammoth, and they are both reliable men. I think the story would end here except the hunters went to look more closely at the mammoth and they noticed it wasn't leaving footprints in the sand.

The elders in my tribe are not sure what to do now. They don't want to call these men liars, but they don't believe them either. The men are upset that people do not trust them now. They say that the mammoth didn't pay any attention to them and the thoughts and feelings they heard from the mammoth were quite calm and ordinary. Finally they say that the animal turned and walked into the ocean. They never saw it come back out.

This story has caused quite a lot of tension in my tribe. My thought is similar to the one I had when I was angry at you. We cannot change what has happened. Either these hunters saw this mammoth or they did not. But we can choose to believe them or not believe them. If we don't believe them, then they are unhappy and we are unhappy. If we choose to believe them then they are content, and we are left with a feeling of trust and wonder. I am wondering then why so many people don't believe them. Why don't we just choose to be happy that a mammoth has come to our land at last even if it did walk into the ocean?

This is the kind of philosophical question I have sometimes written to you about before. Sometimes I have written papers that I didn't send because I didn't want to burden you with too much work and because I didn't think they were good enough. I am going to be honest again: I have actually written a lot of papers I didn't send. I guess I felt shy sometimes. But now I have decided to keep believing in you as my teacher. Now there is no reason for me not to show you all my work and no reason not to send you all my thoughts. I send them out into the wide web bathing us at all times, "washed in the web," as we say, and I can only believe that you will someday see them. This is my choice.

I'm Confused, submitted by Alice Featherstone

If you are not our teacher anymore, I am wondering if we will be getting someone new. Who will that be? When will you let us know? I feel like we've been abandoned like baby coots.

CHAPTER TWENTY

DOG

Dog wanted to be alone and that was unusual. Most of the time, he wanted to be with Elise and Lucia and Brad and Clare. When he was younger, he had wanted to be with his brothers and sisters and parents. He was a sociable direwolf, touching and being touched, his neurons happiest in a crowd. Now, however, he wanted to be alone so he could think about what he really wanted, who he really was, and the answer was clear. He was Dog, the same Dog as before he lost his physical body. The same personality. The same habits.

He wanted to think about that. He was the habit of Dog. Just as his switched-on DNA had been able to resurrect the holo-form of paws and muzzle and teeth and flank, so the same DNA had resurrected a holo-personality, the Dog he knew and others knew. Brad and Luke had helped remember him into being Dog, as he and Clare had remembered Elise into being Elise, as he had remembered the golden animals into being horses and black bears and mice—although not all the mice, Dog remembered, not the one he had deliberately let go.

Dog knew that he could also let go. He could let the edges of himself slip away and dissolve. Briefly, if he wished, he would know everything that had ever happened or ever would happen. The African tribes. The moons of Jupiter. He could know the future. Would the Council punish Brad? Would Jon find them? Would Clare survive the day?

Maybe Clare would not survive the day. Mothers died giving birth. This birthing had started in the early morning, a few hours into their third day of walking. First Clare made a noise as liquid spotted her leather skirt and dripped onto her legs and feet. Then she lay down in the tall yellow grass and wouldn't get up but only held her stomach. The group was close to a series of pools in an ephemeral stream. They knew this from the maps on Brad's solar-comp, and also some of the golden animals could almost-smell the fresh water. But Clare didn't want to walk even that short distance. In any case, birthing too near a source of water wasn't always a good idea. So Brad had begun to build a shelter under a juniper, rearranging branches and using yucca stalk and grass against the wind. Lucia began to organize her supplies. Elise began to fret at her mother's odd behavior. Everyone was busy. No one was paying any attention to Dog. No one watched him wander off in his holo-form from the juniper that had become a birthing bed.

Dog didn't mind. He could wait to find out what happened to Clare. He wanted to think about being Dog. He didn't want to dissolve or know the future. He remembered his mother's teeth in the back of his neck. It was better to be like everyone else.

Where-are-we-going? The saber-toothed cat suddenly paced beside him. In his past life, Dog would have been terrified with such an animal at his side, a predator four times heavier than a direwolf, stronger and meaner. Now he felt comforted if also a little sorry that the other golden animals had found him so quickly, the black bears shambling close together, the camel mingling with the horse and deer. Still this was to be expected. They were a herd now, a pack. And he was their leader.

Where-are-we-going? the saber-toothed cat repeated and shook her blocky head with almost-irritation. Days ago, Dog had stopped her from chasing the Round River people too far past the campsite. Let them go now, he had said. We don't want to frighten them more than necessary. Dog wondered now if the saber-toothed cat was still sulking about that. She had also kept her personality, like Dog, like the other animals—although it was hard to tell with mice. The habit of being themselves.

Nowhere, Dog said. We're waiting.

The saber-tooth had a short stumpy tail, which she bobbled now. Feel-that? the saber-tooth asked.

Dog sent out a tendril of consciousness, not too much. He didn't want to spread himself out too much. Yes, he felt another one, another golden animal coming into existence, and he yearned toward it even though the giant sloth was far away in the radioactive west. The sloth had died and then returned because she couldn't bear to leave her babies behind, because her love was so great. The babies would still die, suckling fruitlessly at her decaying breasts. The sloth had known that. She had just wanted to be with them.

Yes, Dog thought. Yes, yes. This was not the first golden animal he had sensed dying of disease or violence or accident, speared or clawed, head crushed, heart stopped, an animal who at the moment of death, all alone, without Dog's numbers or Brad's radios, had turned on its own DNA. Its unique consciousness reanchored! Reassembled! Re-formed.

Dog had a theory about why this was happening. A hole had opened in the universe. The thirteen sunflowers, Dog, the golden animals, Elise—especially Elise, the universe reflecting on itself—had opened a hole. What Dog knew, what Brad could do with his transmitters and solarcomp, unconscious consciousness now also knew. Water poured through the hole. Dog liked this metaphor. Water enlarged the hole and flowed into the den. Claws did the same thing, scrabbling out the entrance to a gopher's burrow or a badger's home. The world breached, boundaries broken.

Dog didn't know why only some animals could turn on their own DNA or why some of those animals then chose to dissolve and some to keep the habit of themselves. As he sent out a tendril, sensing the ground sloth, he felt the presence of a human being—across the ocean, on another continent—who had also died and returned, turning on that switch, the water rushing in. He yearned to be with the sloth. He yearned to be with the human.

The hours passed. The golden animals were careful to stay in their shapes, walking the plain and following game trails as though they were ordinary physical animals. But no longer looking for other predators or prey, no longer worrying about any of that.

At some point, the saber-toothed cat spoke again, I-miss-the-girl.

The others agreed, the small cat, the grumpy camel. They missed Elise.

Dog heard the swoosh of wings overhead. A raven flew low and fast, black feathered in the blue sky, dark and light. It seemed to Dog that every day he felt more keenly the beauty of the world. He recognized beauty wherever he went. Beauty behind him. Beauty before him. Beauty all around him. Perhaps that was Brad's influence. The raven cawed, and Dog remembered Jon. Dog had seen Jon, too, when he had uncurled a tendril and seen the ground sloth. Dog quickened their pace back to the juniper tree that was also Clare's birthing bed. Jon would probably be there by now.

Clare was still alive, and Dog was happy about that. The golden animals stayed behind while Dog went into the shelter of branches and yucca stalk under the tree, almost-smelling the blood and sweat. Clare had birthed one twin but the second seemed to be causing a problem. Lucia looked at Dog, her face hollowed and strained, a baby in her arms. Dog noticed that this infant girl was a receiver, while the boy still in the womb was a mute. For the second time that day, Dog sent out a tendril of consciousness, peeking into the boy's mind and then quickly withdrawing, momentarily blinded by the neural blooms.

A good distance from the tree, in the direction of water, Brad was on the ground and Jon stood above him holding a spear. The men had fought. Dog could see signs of broken grass and scuffed dirt, a bit of blood on rock. The spear pressed into Brad's chest, and the muscles in Jon's arms tensed. Elise floated nearby, sparking and spinning in a full-scale tantrum. It was too much, her mother in pain, this strange man. Elise cried without tears, hysterical and unable to stop. Jon looked up at Dog's approach but didn't move the spear. Still, he recognized Dog and came as close to snarling as a human face could.

The hunter looked exhausted. Dog guessed that he had been running hard, pressing himself, forcing himself faster and faster to find Clare and Brad. If he had started as soon as the Round River people sent out their emails, then he had taken only days to travel what Dog and the others had done in weeks. Had the tribe approved his pursuit? Dog wondered—because Clare would wonder that, too. Or was Jon acting alone without the elders' guidance?

"Dog, help me!" Brad said but not out loud. As well as a spear pressed to Brad's heart, Jon also had a foot on the lab rat's throat.

"What can I do?"

"Scare him? Rush him? No, wait. Don't do that."

Dog didn't think so either.

"Take away Elise."

Dog understood. Jon had begun to scream at Brad, berating him for ignoring the Council, for insulting the elders, for interfering in the world. Yes, Jon screamed, they had found his computer. They knew everything. Brad was a monster! Like the monsters who had created the supervirus! Brad was just like those people! Brad was responsible for everything! The guilt pressing down on them! The grief everywhere!

"Blahblahblahblahblah," the hunter screamed and pressed his spear into Brad's chest—all the while, looking secretly at Elise, horrified by the ghost of the little girl he had known six years ago when she was a child of the Rio Chama people. Perhaps Jon had once played with Elise. Carried her when she was tired. Felt sorry for her as the sick baby of deluded parents. "Blahblahblahblah," Jon screamed, terrified, while Elise's hair twisted into snakes and she floated a meter off the ground, a golden glimmer crying without tears.

Dog couldn't do anything to stop Jon from pressing on the spear or stepping on Brad's throat. But if he took Elise away, maybe the hunter would calm down.

Naturally, Elise didn't want to go. A gust of dry wind swirled through the yellow grass, rattling seed heads, and Jon's foot slipped down harder, perhaps harder than he realized. Brad, at any rate, was losing consciousness.

So Dog tried something he had been playing with, a new trick not yet perfected. He created a bubble outside time. This had to do with time at the quantum level and the way it shifted at certain wavelengths. Concentrating, Dog could manage about five minutes.

Before Jon killed Brad, Dog had five minutes to convince Elise.

"Elise," he coaxed, "let me show you something. Come with me."

Dog had offered to show Elise things before, about how to be like him, for example, solid to touch. He had tried to teach Elise how she could have her hair combed, how she could make footprints in the sand, how she could sit nicely on a rock. But the little girl had never been interested. She would rather float and be invisible and startle people and make them jump. She didn't want to return to what she had been before, when she had gasped for breath, when she was sick and weak.

Dog had an inspiration. "Elise," he asked, "remember food?" He took a second to steal some memories from Brad. What did humans like about eating? Fat, of course. And sweetness. Ascorbic acid. Ripe berries. Prickly-pear fruit. That brightness in the mouth, the quick energy. "Remember honey?" he asked.

And Elise did. She stopped crying.

"Come with me," Dog said, "and I'll show you how to taste honey."

She floated closer to him. They seemed briefly to tangle together, and in her eager response Dog's own memories came rushing back, the live rabbit under his paws, that first bite and salty wetness, hot blood . . . he took the memory and made it almost-real. He felt the gulp down his throat. He shared that first giddy gulp with Elise, and they came together again, closer than before, and surprisingly Elise also began to nose the corpse and wolf down the hot living blood, much too rich for a human. In her enthusiasm, she entered into Dog's life, pushed right in. She was stronger than Dog in many ways. She pushed right in, and Dog said yes. She could have all his meals, every one. Marrow. Antelope flank. Rotted muscle. Intestines. Elise wanted more. Dog remembered Luke and Lucia and the meals he had shared with them. Rabbit stew, javelina, tubers, onions, sizzling horse meat on the fire. He called up memories that were not his. Sun-ripened grapes juicy and tart. And honey! Honey! Pure glucose, addictive, delicious, dripping from the comb. All she could eat. All Dog could eat.

Now the golden animals surrounded them, flowing, shimmering, wanting to eat, too, wanting to join the game. Dog knew this would upset Jon even more. The golden animals brought their own memories. Cellulose. Grama grass. Hackberry. A woman's flesh. They delighted in the irony, cat and mouse, saber-toothed cat and human child, direwolf and deer and horse. At one time, they had eaten each other. They were eating each other again.

The five minutes were nearly up. "We can keep playing," Dog said to Elise, "but we have to leave."

Elise didn't hesitate, and Dog led them away from Clare's birthing bed, from the drama unfolding under a juniper tree, from the hunter pressing his foot on Brad's throat. Dog hoped Jon would not kill Brad. He hoped the second twin would live. He hoped Clare would live, too.

CHAPTER TWENTY-ONE

BRAD

At night, hiding under his bed of animal skins, Brad read that Albert Einstein's brain was kept in a jar in the basement of the Smithsonian, a major storage unit in what had once been the United States of America. Einstein's famous biographer said this wasn't true but then hinted that it was. The storage unit denied the story. So Brad went on a quest to find Einstein's brain. First he had to walk across Texas, a country pulsing with radiation—the unmanned nuclear plants overheating and exploding. He traveled a hilly landscape of breasts and then started fording rivers: building a raft, fording a river, building another raft, fording a river. The water teemed with carp and alligators. Later there were manatees and flamingos. Finally he came to the major storage unit in what had once been an important city. Calling out for his mentor, he wandered through corridors that resembled the west wing of the lab but were much more grand. There, as it turned out, Einstein's brain was not hidden in a basement but prominently displayed in a large room on a marble table next to a vase of flowers.

Nearby stood a statue of Marcus Aurelius.

Marcus Aurelius, as I live and breathe, Brad thought to himself. In the second century AD the Roman emperor had written, "Everything is interwoven, and the web is holy: none of its parts are unconnected." He had written, "I am made up of substance and what animates it, and neither one can ever stop existing. . . . Every portion of me will be reassigned as another portion of the world, and that in turn transformed into another." He had written, "Nothing can happen to me that isn't natural."

How had the emperor known? How had he known, fighting the barbarians on the northern edge of his empire, coming into his tent filthy with the gore of battle—not literal gore, but spiritual karma from the prisoners he had condemned to death, from the soldiers he had sent to die horribly, from the barbarian men, women, and children he had sent his soldiers to kill horribly? Old Marcus Aurelius: "One world made up of one thing. One divinity, present in them all." He was not even a great philosopher, just one more king scribbling down his meditations, someone who really had no time to be a philosopher what with constantly going to war to protect and expand his borders, what with ruling over one-sixth of the world's population, a few free men, their less free families, and many, many, many slaves.

The Roman emperor had repeated what others had said before him, Heraclitus and Epictetus, the Stoics and pre-Socratics, and how had they known? How did so many tribal people know, ancient peoples like the hunters and gatherers around the world that The Return tried so hard to emulate, like the Pueblo people of the American Southwest who breathed into stones and said hello? Old Marcus Aurelius: "Everything is interwoven, and the web is holy: none of its parts are unconnected."

His statue standing next to the jar with Einstein's brain.

Brad got out his solarcomp and transmitters, and in a few minutes, the radios were humming. Thunderstorms sparked through the night sky. Lightning flashed again and again. The DNA switched on, and Einstein's consciousness shimmered in the air. Wild waving white hair and round spectacles formed immediately. The professor was dressed in a twentieth-century dinner suit with pressed trousers and shirt and jacket with golden pocket watch and fob. Brad was so relieved. He had so many important questions to ask. He knelt before the great scientist and begged, "Can you untie me?"

Brad tugged at the yucca ropes and felt the painful scrape. His arms were bound behind him, and his shoulders ached horribly. His ankles were also tied together, and he couldn't stretch out his legs unless he lay on his back and lifted his feet into the air, crushing his hands. Most of the time he curled with his knees to his chest, in a hole under a mesquite bush, perhaps a collapsed badger den that Jon had found and furiously enlarged. Brad groaned and tried not to wake up. He had already spent some of yesterday in the sun without water, and he dreaded the next long day, when the flies would come and torture him with their prickles, their bites, their lazy walking on his burning skin. The flies would not kill him. The sun would kill him. Even so, he dreamed of a horse tail.

Einstein's consciousness shimmered and looked inward. What did it care about lazy flies? Einstein had a big decision to make: Should he dissolve into all of consciousness or resume the habit of himself? Albert Einstein thought deeply about this.

But the statue of Marcus Aurelius came to life and embraced Brad. "My poor boy. I think of you so often. You and I are so much alike."

Lucia was shaking Brad's arm.

"Where is he?" Brad opened his eyes but couldn't see much without his glasses and with his head cracking open, *krack, krack, krack.* Was he in the middle of a thunderstorm? In fact, he seemed to have his face pressed into earth. Grass and dirt fell from his eyes and nose as he strained upward.

Lucia's voice was close, next to the shallow pit. "He went to get water."

Water!

"How is Clare? The baby?"

"Sshhh!"

"What is he going to do with her? With me?"

"Quiet now."

"I'm thirsty."

Later Brad woke for a brief lucid moment and realized that this conversation had never happened. He would not have been able to speak to Lucia, to ask her the questions that swarmed him like flies, because his throat was too parched, his mouth sewed shut with a dry paste. But something else *had* happened, obviously. Now there was an uncomfortable weight against his back and some new unwelcome warmth against his skin. He pushed against the weight and felt an answering push. Perhaps the badger had come back.

CHAPTER TWENTY-TWO

CLARE

Clare's waters broke, drenching her thighs and feet, splattering on the dirt and yellow grass. Her uterus contracted strongly, and she lay down on the ground and felt a rush of gladness. Okay, she said to the new baby, if you insist. If you must. If you really want this now. At last, it had begun. At last, it was nearly over. She was tired to death of lumbering about like a giant beaver on land, awkward and grotesque, her weight in front of her. Her uterus contracted, and she made a noise, happy. Now she could focus on something other than worrying if this child would be healthy. She could stop thinking about blue faces and gasps for air. She could stop thinking about Jon and Elise and the Round River people and her mother and grandmother. She could focus on the pain. There it was. A jab, a stab. What a relief. She had something to do now.

Clare stumbled to the nearest juniper tree and let Brad build a nest around her, yucca stalks and yellow grass and bent branches. Walls against the dry wind. Lucia swept the ground under the tree free of needles and leaf litter and put down fresh grass as a new floor. The smell was lovely. So familiar.

At first the contractions came hard and fast, and that was good. But then they stopped, and that made Clare nervous. She lay under the shade of the tree, sweating in the summer heat, feeling nervous. What if the baby was like Elise, with a damaged heart? What if damaged hearts were the only thing she could make as a mother? Who would gently smother the child? Not Brad, Clare knew. Lucia? Luke? And then—would Brad and Dog try to bring back a golden baby shimmering consciousness? Absolutely not, Clare thought, sitting up in agitation and half falling over. They couldn't! They shouldn't. They wouldn't. Where would it all end? What had she done, bringing back Elise?

Her uterus contracted. She gasped.

She lay back down, gasping. This was good. This was better than thinking.

She lay on her side. She didn't want to get up, as Lucia suggested. She didn't want to walk around.

She didn't want to crouch on all fours.

She wanted to stay where she was, with the pain.

She began pushing, but it wasn't going to be that easy. Sometimes she whimpered, not because she was asking for help but because it felt good to whimper, to complain, to let herself loosen, a little out of control. It was better not to be in too much control. Let the muscles loosen. Let the body take over. Cry out! Complain! Be a little different from the usual Clare, who hadn't complained even as a child when she broke her arm or as an adult when a stallion dislocated her shoulder and bruised her purple and black from chest to thigh. She had been too self-conscious to cry, too proud, too strong. But now those qualities were not what she needed. Now she needed to focus on something other than herself. Now she needed to be a little weak, letting herself relax and weaken, letting the baby do what it wanted to do.

Lucia left the shelter to talk to Elise and Brad. Clare complained about that and felt resentful. She wanted Lucia for herself. There wasn't enough room for the others.

Then Clare decided that she did want to be on all fours.

But that seemed to change the gravity of the earth.

Then she decided that she wanted to squat and press her back against the rough bark of the juniper tree. A branch almost poked her eye, and Lucia cut away more of the branches, giving her and Clare more space, filling the air with the smell of sap, the sharpness of juniper. It was almost over!

But now Brad was gone. Where had Brad gone? Water? He was getting water? Was that really necessary? But she couldn't wait for Brad. She didn't want this other person inside her anymore. She wanted to be separate. She wanted it to be over.

"Where's Brad?" Clare asked again, between harsh pants that came from everywhere in her body, all her body a breath.

"Let me do this first," Lucia said and guided the baby out. "It's a girl," Lucia whispered. "Oh, she's so mad." Clare opened her eyes when she heard the furious wail *wah, wah, wah, wah*. "What a temper," Lucia rejoiced and smiled hugely at Clare, who smiled hugely back and slid down the tree bark, very slowly, while Lucia cut the cord and cleaned the baby of Clare's blood and the baby's waxy coating. The little girl sighed with the loss of the womb, her anger turned to resignation.

Lucia gave the baby to Clare to nurse, and Clare pinched a nipple, smearing drops of watery blue colostrum over the tiny lips, the thin liquid rich with nutrients, better now than the milk that would come later. Lucia waited for the afterbirth. Clare stared at the baby. Until, in a burst of energy, the newborn grabbed hold of Clare and sucked hard, and Clare startled, and the two women laughed. This was such a strong little girl! She was small—Clare had already noted that, surprisingly small—and raw-skinned and ugly for having been born a bit early. Her hair hadn't grown in yet, and her eyes were gray. Her tiny face scrunched with the effort of sucking. But she didn't let go, and she didn't gasp for air.

The two women were blissful just watching her. Clare felt more contractions, and Lucia said, "That's fine now. Almost done." And Clare had another desire to push and another, and Lucia was ready with fresh grass, and then Lucia was staring up at Clare, over Clare's still mounded stomach.

"That's not the placenta. I think there's another baby."

Clare shook her head. Not true.

"No, I see a buttock. It's coming the wrong way."

No one in Clare's tribe had ever birthed twins. Clare had never met a twin, although she knew of twin teenagers in Colorado who had been caught and killed with their family in a stampede of buffalo. A few times, occasionally, a midwife suspected that a second fetus had died and been absorbed in the womb, but that was always early in the pregnancy. Twins were so rare. No one had mentioned the possibility to Clare, and she felt surprisingly indignant. Why hadn't anyone told her this could happen?

Another pain, a new wave, and Lucia took the baby from her breast.

"Am I going to die?" Clare wondered.

"It's a breech birth," Lucia snapped, "not a snakebite."

She began to massage Clare's stomach, trying to push the child's buttocks up and to the side, turning the baby around, pushing sharp shoulders and a head against Clare's intestines and diaphragm. Clare was being wrung from the inside, the way her mother and grandmother squeezed yucca leaves and beat them, wringing the rough loops of fiber, squeezing and twisting.

"This isn't working," Lucia said. "I'm going to put my hand in now."

Clare gave her death-shriek. Rabbits shrieked like this when they were being torn apart by hyenas. Clare remembered that sound. For a moment, she looked down from a branch in the juniper tree and saw herself, her mouth hanging open, her sweaty naked belly, and the top of Lucia's gray head. Lucia's shoulders twisted as she put her hand into Clare and tore her apart. It was such a shame. Clare had wanted to say good-bye to Elise. To Brad. To the new baby. She was so sorry to leave them.

At some point in the next two hours, Clare didn't die. She knew that vaguely but wasn't always grateful. Then she *was* grateful, holding the baby boy as he also nursed at her breast, more gently than the girl, for he seemed as exhausted as Clare was. Still he sucked and slept and woke to suck again, healthy like his sister, who snored contentedly at the other breast. Clare and Lucia were too tired to laugh, although Clare felt as though her body had been undone and then stitched back together with something like joy. Bright threads of joy held her painfully in place.

Lucia left the juniper tree shelter and Clare slept, too, curled on her side, her arm lightly covering the babies next to her.

And then Jon was there, taking one of them away.

Clare struggled awake when she felt the boy's absence. The girl yawned and stretched at Clare's breast, getting ready for the next adventure of the day—to nurse again. But her brother was gone. He was moving through the air, and then he was being held against Jon's chest, although Jon was not looking down at him and marveling and adoring. Instead, Jon kept his eyes on Clare's face.

"Wake up," Jon said.

"Give him to me," Clare croaked, her mouth so dry. She struggled to sit and see Jon better. Here she was, still under the juniper tree, the smell of birth stronger than before, the smell of her own skin stronger than before. The little room of green had been just the right size for her and Lucia, but now Jon made the space seem unbearably cramped, his face too close as he knelt beside her and held her son.

"Where's Brad?" Clare asked. "Where's Lucia?"

Where is Elise? she thought.

The baby boy began to squirm. Perhaps the pressure of Jon's hands wasn't quite right. Perhaps the heart in Jon's chest, which the boy could hear and feel, was beating too fast. Soon, Clare knew, the little face would pucker. He would wail, *wah wah wah wah wah wah wah*, surprisingly loud for such a tiny body.

"Give him to me," she urged.

"Your . . . Brad's gone," the hunter hesitated before saying his name. His voice went up slightly in pitch. "We fought and he ran away. He ran to save himself. He knows the Council and the elders are angry. He knows he has to answer for what he's done."

Clare tried to understand even as she watched the boy and brought the girl into her breast more tightly. Quickly, thankfully, her daughter latched onto the nipple. Already, so soon, she was skilled at eating. Meanwhile her brother was moving his head and mouth urgently to the side, searching for a nipple of his own, trying to suckle Jon. The hunter didn't seem to notice.

Clare knew, of course, that Jon had found them yesterday. After the second baby was turned—after she didn't die when Lucia put her hand inside her—the midwife had begun acting strangely, going outside, talking to someone. "It's just Brad," Lucia had said then because, after all, there was still another baby to be born and Clare didn't need any sudden bad news. But once the boy was cleaned up and the placenta out and put aside, once the children were safe, small but strong with all their fingers and toes and with clearly healthy lungs—Lucia confessed. She didn't know where Brad had gone, or Elise, but Jon was here. Jon had been sent by the Council and the elders to bring them back to the lab.

"I need Lucia," Clare said to Jon, trying to think, watching her son, willing the boy not to cry, willing Jon to give him back. Had Brad really run away? It didn't seem likely. Probably he was close by, also watching and waiting. Brad would have some plan. He would keep Elise safe.

The hunter stared at the girl on Clare's breast as if she were a piece of fat sizzling on the fire. Clare had to wonder at the man's stubbornness: she could see even now that the boy and girl had Brad's genes. They would have his dark skin, his dark hair and dark eyes, his long body. It hardly seemed possible that Jon still hoped these children were his own, even if he had agreed to claim them.

"I know he forced you," Jon was saying carefully. "You had no choice, not in any of this. You didn't leave me by choice."

"Jon," Clare put out a hand, reaching for her son.

"And so I am going to take you back into my tent and I am going to explain to the Council and to the elders what I saw here."

Again the hunter's voice rose in pitch. He clenched the arm holding the infant against his chest. As Clare watched, the boy arched his back.

Jon continued talking, ignoring her outstretched hand. He had something to say. This speech had been planned. "You stayed with these people because you were alone. You were pregnant. You were frightened. You had no choice." Suddenly, the hunter fairly spat at her, "What they did to Elise! It's unspeakable."

In the dim light under the tree, Clare strained to study Jon more closely. He had always kept the skin on his face shaved clean, what many men did to show their skill with a knife. But now the hunter's beard sprouted in patches, uneven and untrimmed. His eyes were puffy, darkened underneath. He held her son but didn't look at him.

"Yes," Clare said softly. "That's right. You're right."

Jon wrinkled his nose as if the smell of the birthing bed was becoming too much.

"Where's Lucia?" Clare repeated the question.

The hunter shifted his eyes. "She went to get water. She'll be back soon. We leave tomorrow."

"I just gave birth," Clare explained the obvious, thinking to give Brad more time to plan, "and the babies . . ."

Unexpectedly, it was the girl who stopped nursing and began to fuss, which tipped her brother into a wail, his small fists coming up in the air, his small legs kicking out at Jon's chest. Jon jerked as if a stick of firewood had come alive in his hands. Instinctively he gave the screaming baby to Clare, who enfolded her son and found him a nipple. The boy was abruptly quiet, but the girl began to cry more seriously.

The hunter passed a hand over his eyes. "I'm here to take you away," Jon repeated. He seemed to grit his teeth. "You and the children. We need to get you away from here. This place is . . . haunted."

He means Elise, Clare thought. That's how he thinks of her.

Clare slept again but only for a little, not nearly long enough. Then Jon was back, grabbing her sandals and Lucia's bag of medicine, picking up the sling with its half image of a swallow and pulling Clare out of the grassy bed so that she barely caught the twins before they tumbled to the ground. She thought he was going to strike her, and she bent over the babies to protect them. But he was dragging her outside.

"No!" she screamed.

"Fire!" Jon shouted. "Put on your shoes."

The sun was so bright. Clare squinted at the horizon.

"Can't you smell it?" Jon sounded excited.

Clare could barely smell anything but herself. She clutched the whimpering babies more firmly. She squinted and sniffed. She steadied her trembling arms and legs and sniffed again. Yes, there it was. Yes, she couldn't not smell it. Smoke.

Another Confession,
submitted by Carlos Salas

I love you. You have been my teacher for five years now, ever since I was a boy. I've only seen a picture of you on the screen of my solarcomp, the one where you are smiling right into the camera on your own solarcomp and your hair is down and not in a braid, the one where anyone can see that you are smiling but still sad about something. I love you and it doesn't matter anymore if you know this since you have disappeared and probably won't ever read what I send you. You will never know how I feel. In a way this has given me the freedom to write it down.

Another Assignment,
submitted by Alice Featherstone

I hate to keep complaining, but I really think it is wrong that you've gone off without a word. I suppose I should be honest and admit that I was getting to like your assignments, and I was looking forward to the next one. It seems to me that I think better when writing and that I hardly know what I think until I am writing what I think.

Life is getting a little dull here in the Great Nation of Colorado. Of course, we don't call ourselves a nation. Maybe we do feel superior to all of you farther south, where you never see snow, where you talk funny and don't enunciate your p's and q's, so to speak, but we are still very much part of the North American tribes. We admire the Council although my father says we should have more representation on it since we have so many more people; it's only fair, he says, and gets quite passionate. My father is a wordy person to begin with, and when he gets quite passionate you really don't want to be there having to listen to all those words.

But that's not what I wanted to write about, and this is one reason I miss your assignments; they helped me focus. They gave me "structure," a word I know you would use in one of your comments, and in that structure I feel more free than just walking the trails here on my own.

Lately I have been thinking a lot about China. Let's say that I leave Colorado and cross North America and get to New York Harbor Two and take a boat to Africa. There I venture into the dark interior and discover an amazing culture of great spirituality and tenderness. These people spend entire days making up songs which they sing to each other for entire nights. They have very few material possessions, not even spears, for they live only by gathering plants and catching fish with nets in the great lake that dominates their world. They love their children above everything else and are always asking them about their dreams. The children explain their dreams very carefully because these people believe that all dreams come true. They sleep with the animals they do not hunt. Yes, although this sounds like a tall tale or myth, these people actually cuddle right next to the gazelle and the zebra. Of course they no longer scavenge or go into the cities. When I try to show them my solarcomp, they simply look away; they live in peace and harmony without any thought of the future or the past. Although I am impressed by this beautiful and astonishing culture, I know I cannot stay here, for I will never truly be one of them. I do not have their purity of heart but must keep traveling. Like "a rolling stone," I have to move on.

One day I find myself in China. Let's say that my days were eventful between leaving the coast of Africa in my trusty boat and walking the quiet streets of Beijing. Because I am a mute, I don't feel the sadness. And I have to wonder if these streets are as empty as they seem; can it really be that all the people of China are gone, every last one?

I think not. From my reading, I know that the Chinese were very advanced technologically; their computers and computer scientists were among the best in the world. They believed in technology with all their hearts. If it seems unbelievable that no one at all survived the supervirus in China, it seems equally unbelievable that whoever did survive would give up on the worldwide web. Personally, I doubt that very much. Instead I think they gave up on us. After all, the Chinese had good reason to be suspicious of Russia and America (although not, I guess, of Costa Rica) and maybe they thought that we had started the supervirus. Maybe they thought we were tricking them with our talk of The Return and the Great Compromise and ecological harmony. Or maybe they just weren't interested in all that. Maybe they didn't respond to our emails because they didn't want to, and they just listened to our conversations instead and kept careful note of what we were doing. While we gave up our guns and our ships and our airplanes, they kept theirs and fixed them, one by one, and all the while they had children who had more children who fixed more machines. Maybe they have plans to visit us now? Maybe they have evil scientists working away on planes to fly over here and enslave us all.

I think you would stop me at this point from being "too creative, perhaps" and losing the thread of my plot.

"Weren't you last on the streets of Beijing?" you might ask. "And while I think it's good to speculate about what might have happened in China, you don't want to let your imagination run completely wild."

Of course, I do want to let my imagination run completely wild; that's exactly what I want to do. But I also have to agree with some of what you say, and I don't really think the Chinese are coming to get us in their airplanes. I just wonder what's happening in the rest of the world. Outside Colorado! What else is happening! Don't you wonder, too?

CHAPTER TWENTY-THREE

DOG

The golden animals came together over food and found that ironic, especially the two cats, who seemed disposed to irony. Sharing food, the deer and the bears and the mice and the cats and the horses and the camel and Dog entered into each other's lives, feasting on those physical memories—nibbling sweet grass, chewing cud. Dog was especially intrigued by the rumen, with its stages of digestion and dense populations of bacteria and protozoa breaking down cellulose, the rich community within the stomachs of the ungulates like nested Russian dolls. (What were Russian dolls?) How extraordinary. The microorganisms breeding and giving life to the larger organism. The synergy, the symbiosis. Many different species side by side, dependent on each other, inside each other, combined into one thing.

Sharing food, they shared everything. They entered into each other's thoughts, and Dog added new parts to his composite personality—the subtlety of deer and caution of mice and selfishness of cats. In turn, the other animals gained his experiences and those experiences he had from Brad and Luke/Lucia and the giant short-faced bear, absorbing this new knowledge almost effortlessly. They were a unique form of consciousness, after all, no longer constrained by brain size or lack of neural networks. Wheelboarding through the lab. Albert Einstein. Email.

Email! Words that traveled over great distance. All the non-Paleos were impressed by that, but it meant even more to the saber-toothed cat. "I've always felt limited," she said, "by what I could and could not explain to the other cats." Already, Dog noted, she was speaking differently.

For all the golden animals, Dog included, merging with Elise was particularly dramatic. The human cortex. The pathways of language. Syntax and meaning. Dog had entangled with humans before but not like this, not briefly becoming one consciousness.

When that happened, when they briefly became one consciousness—after they had eaten together and entered into each other's lives and entered into each other's thoughts and become full to the point of bursting—a part of Dog panicked.

He wanted to keep to the habit of himself. This was another way of dissolving, if not into the larger universal consciousness, then into a group of diverse beings that could, it seemed to Dog, swamp his own unique beingness. He wasn't ready to be a four-year-old girl, loving Clare more than he loved Luke. He didn't want to be a colt or a grumpy camel. He didn't want to be a feline.

When that happened, when the experience of being one became too overwhelming, Dog withdrew.

And they were all thrown back into their slightly separate selves, somewhat less separate than before.

"That scared you," the saber-toothed cat said.

The scavenger gene, Dog thought. We're built to run away.

"A little," he admitted. "I know you can know what I am thinking now. I know I don't have to speak to you like this in words and sentences. But I prefer it."

"There's some advantage," a deer offered, "to the different voices."

"Yes, that's what I mean." Dog was grateful. "There's a certain exchange of ideas when we are all different or pretend to be."

"A kind of energy," a second deer said. "Things bouncing off things."

"Maybe that's why unconscious consciousness became consciousness. And why consciousness itself split into parts." This from a bear.

"I want my mother." The contrary camel.

"We all keep wanting different things when we are separate." Elise.

"I want two things that seem to oppose each other. I want to enter the larger consciousness, to dissolve, and then I want to come back to myself, my unique consciousness." The calico cat.

"That doesn't seem possible." A mouse.

"But could it be possible? Someday?" Another mouse.

"We've done something like it just now, among ourselves." Dog.

"Perhaps we need to practice. Let's try that again?" The saber-toothed cat.

The question turned into assent, and they merged again and then withdrew into their separate, slightly less separate selves. This time, Dog felt more in control. All the animals were encouraged and pleased. They could do this as a group, merge and withdraw. What else could they do?

"I think we need more of us," the mice said together.

The golden animals walked on, talking among themselves, walking through fire and burned grassland that reminded Dog of walking long ago with Luke through the burn of another fire—charred earth dotted with charred animals caught by surprise. The air had been hazy with smoke, the smoke burning Dog's eyes, the ground burning his paws. That fire, too, had been started by an evening lightning storm, slowed at first by rain and the cooler temperatures of night, then spreading fast in the next day's heat and wind.

"We've walked a circle," Elise said to Dog when at one point they walked through the fire again, the flames high on each side.

"We're going back to your mother now and your new sister and brother."

"But that's where the fire is going, too," Elise said.

Dog thought that maybe he should have thought about this before, and he began to run, and they all followed him until they came to the juniper tree, where Elise taught them the trick of standing still and becoming invisible.

They saw Jon drag Clare from beneath the juniper branches, the babies crying and struggling in her arms. Holding Clare's wrist, the hunter hurried in the direction of the pools by the ephemeral stream. This is good, Dog thought. Perhaps the streambed would provide a firebreak. Perhaps the pools would give them some protection. Jon and Brad might need to do some clearing of grasses and shrubs. But with Lucia and Clare helping, the work would go quickly. They had just enough time. The fire was moving fast.

"Dog?" He heard Lucia in his mind and swung his holo-body around to search for her, breaking the illusion of invisibility.

"Here," she called, and Dog padded toward the source.

Déjà vu. Dog knew the phrase from Luke, who knew it from the reading he had done as a boy and who had experienced the feeling himself. A feeling of repeating something from the past. I've been here before. I've done this already. Lucia was tied up again. Crazy bushkies.

Maybe that's what humans really are, Dog thought. A species of bushkie. What was wrong with people? What was wrong with his master, his mistress? Why was she always getting tied up and dumped somewhere to die?

This time Brad was tied up beside her, both of them half-hidden in a shallow pit or caved-in animal burrow. Brad was unconscious and Lucia gagged with a rabbit skin. Dog knew who had done this, who had dragged them here, hoping they would die from heat and dehydration and save him the trouble.

Dog shivered although he wasn't cold. Dog whined and growled and couldn't help himself. Luke! he shouted in warning. Lucia! He howled. The fire was coming. He felt bad, bad, bad. He couldn't bite through the yucca rope. He couldn't drag Lucia out of the fire's path. He couldn't do anything in the physical world. He was built to be useless. The habit that was Dog felt distraught.

He felt a weariness, like Marcus Aurelius, the Roman emperor on the plains of battle fighting the barbarians. "Evil," the emperor wrote over two thousand years ago, "the same old thing. No matter what happens, keep this in mind. It's the same old thing, from one end of the world to the other. It fills the history books, ancient and modern, and the cities, and the houses too. Nothing new at all. Familiar, transient."

That was Brad, Dog knew—Brad dreaming or hallucinating. Dog whimpered. You want different things when you are separate. Dog didn't want Lucia to die in the fire. (What was the point of all this birthing and dying?) The golden animals surrounded him. Elise pretended to pat his shoulder. They tried to think of ways to help, but none of them had a physical body.

"Let's tell my mother," Elise suggested, and so Dog did that.

But Clare was also helpless, with the babies in her arms, although she started yelling at Jon and tried to turn back. Jon only grabbed her with bruising strength and kept moving forward.

"You said the boy was a mute," the calico cat said.

The habit of Dog felt distraught and annoyed. Yes, yes. What did that matter? No matter.

"But he is not a mute now," the cat insisted, and the golden animal was right.

"You changed him somehow," the camel said, "when you were here before."

"Do that trick with time," a horse urged. "We could use five minutes."

The cat had a plan. Dog's visit into the womb had shifted the boy from mute to receiver and that apparently was not a hard thing to do. Mutes were so close, almost there—a bit of consciousness away. The problem wasn't physical. This was about thought that could travel in waves. And waves weren't always or only physical. A little proximity . . . a direwolf in the brainpan. Newborns were so plastic.

Jon would be different, of course. His mind and brain had hardened. He would be less plastic. But he was still human, the calico cat said, and humans and cats had a special relationship. Before the supervirus, before all the beloved pets were suddenly freed to go extinct or feral, the cat's ancestors had learned how to rub up against humans and lie down against humans and purr for humans and drowse and harmonize. The cat's ancestors understood humans— the cat preened a little—and if he were to creep into Jon's mind now, if he were to lie down next to certain neural networks, if he were to stretch and purr, drowse and shut his eyes in contentment . . . they would harmonize. The proximity. A subtle shift. A little extra consciousness. Mute to receiver.

Then the Paleos could talk to Jon as they talked to Clare and Brad and Lucia. Maybe they could convince him to let Clare go. Or untie the other humans. The cat said this would work. His genes told him so.

The question became an assent. They only had a few minutes left, but the cat went off and accomplished his task with seconds to spare. It all happened on the quantum level.

Then Dog went forward alone to speak to Jon as soon as they were back in normal time. And when Jon understood, when he heard the voice of the direwolf in his mind, he was overjoyed—as the golden animals had hoped he would be. Jon had always wanted to be a receiver. Jon had always felt left out. All his life, he had watched other hunters know things he did not know. Even small children could tell when a teratorn had found something dead or warn the tribe that a glyptodont had lumbered too close to the hot springs.

Then someone would be assigned to tell Jon—don't go over to the hot springs. There's a glyptodont.

He had compensated, of course. His work with ravens and crows, intelligent corvids, was praised by the elders. But Jon had never felt satisfied. Yes, he could *ka-ka-ka* and *kroack* and *thonk* and gurgle and hunch his shoulders. Still, how could he ever really know if the conversation had been a success, if he had really been communicating? *This, this,* he said to Dog, is what he had always wanted. Jon felt enlarged. He felt freed. "I can hear you," he marveled.

"You'll hear all of us," Dog assured him.

"The glyptodont? Teratorns?"

"Humans and Paleos have this ability. Now you have it."

Jon took a moment to pause and say thank you to the earth and sky. To the precious world surrounding him.

Clare took this as an opportunity to break away, while Jon was standing still and preoccupied, talking to Dog. She wrenched her arm free and started back for Brad and Lucia. The twins continued to cry and complain. Dog noticed how the air was getting smokier.

"No!" Jon grabbed Clare again.

"Listen to me," Dog said.

"Later," Jon said, "there will be time for this later." And he shut down his mind and went back to dragging Clare in the direction of water.

The saber-toothed cat stood behind Dog, her holo-tongue lolling between her curved teeth. "Let me try now."

"To talk with him?" The habit of Dog despaired.

"No, not to talk with him," the big cat said.

CHAPTER TWENTY-FOUR

BRAD

Brad was coughing, and that woke him up. Also Luke was slapping his face and shaking him by the shoulders, trying to pull him out of the pit. Brad's arms were untied, and perhaps it was the pain of returning circulation that caused his eyes to snap open. His shoulders and arms and feet were loose, and he could stretch, and he did, and the cramps in his muscles started, and he almost screamed. But then there was water on his mouth and down his throat, and this was the most important thing although his stomach protested and he threw up, his entire body hurting now.

Somewhere a baby cried. Clare was holding Brad, giving him more water, making him get up despite the cramps and pain. Clare was here, and that must be his baby. Brad felt weak with relief and dehydration.

"Get up, get up!" Clare shook him.

How could she be so cruel?

"Brad! The smoke! You smell that, don't you?"

"There's a fire," Dog whined.

Brad pushed up on his wooden legs. Clare helped lift him, one arm gripping his shoulder and back. When she tried to pull him forward, however, they tripped, almost caught themselves, and then fell to the ground.

"Just give me some time!" Brad hissed.

"There's no time," Clare said.

"Let me take him," Luke shouted. "You take the babies."

Brad suddenly felt a little more awake. Babies? And smoke? A grass fire?

"Where's Jon?" he asked as they stumbled forward. No one answered. Nothing mattered but moving as quickly as they could. Luke urged Clare to go ahead but she only muttered, "I can't go any faster." And she really did look awful, Brad thought, her face gaunt, blood running down her legs. Despite the need to hurry, despite everything, he tried to get a glimpse of the baby crammed into a sling against her breasts. Babies? Yes, he heard them crying and whimpering, two voices.

Brad tried to remember where they should be going—back to the stream where he had gone before to fill up their gourds and water bottles. That seemed such a long time ago. The smoke was making everything look dim. Worse, he had lost his eyeglasses. Half-blind, he stumbled next to Luke, who seemed to be following Dog and the golden animals. Brad tried to think of what they needed to do.

"No," he said when they came to the streambed, and Dog and the golden animals turned right toward the pools of water. They were very small pools in a curve against the grassy bank. "The pools aren't deep enough," he told Dog since that was easier than speaking out loud, "and they are on the wrong side, right against the bank where the fire will be. Flames kill people in a grass fire, but so does radiant heat, and standing in shallow water won't protect us if we can't keep the fire at a distance."

He tried to say some of this to Luke and Clare, but his mouth was too dry.

"Just to the left," he explained to Dog, "the stream dries out completely and gets wider. There's another arroyo coming in at that point, another gravel bed, so that's another firebreak. We are better off there if we have enough cleared space around us. If we can get in the center of that, equidistant from the flames."

"Trust me," Brad mouthed to Clare, and she nodded and turned left.

This was Newtonian physics, nothing more or less, and Brad thought of slopes, the speed of flames, radiant heat in a straight line. How much protection did the arroyo give them? Were five meters of cleared gravel and sand enough? What vegetation should they rip up first? Grass fires didn't shoot out many embers, but there would be a few. How many? Should they stand or huddle, the baby in the center? The babies. There wasn't much time. There really wasn't that much to think about. Still, Brad felt that if he could get the math just right . . .

He pointed to a spot where the arroyo met the streambed, and Clare put down the sling, and then the three adults spread out like hyper-insects, their adrenaline high, moving more quickly than they would have thought possible, pulling up plants and shrubs that had grown up since spring, scuffing over clumps of grass.

A wall of fire makes a particular sound, like nothing Brad had ever heard before, yet something he recognized almost immediately. He yelled at everyone to stop. Stop and huddle around the babies, faces inward! Clare had to be urged away from the patch of grass she was uprooting. "Leave it!" Brad yelled, which made his throat hurt even more. Luke stumbled over, the last to join them, his hands held awkwardly against his chest. Brad noticed that his own fingers were torn and bloodied, too.

Then the fire roared down on them, a broken circle, the mouth of the arroyo a gap, the two ends of the streambed a gap, the fire leaping to the other bank of the arroyo. The golden animals moved in and out of the flames, Elise and the bears and the deer and the horses and the mice and a camel and a small cat, the direwolf and the saber-toothed cat with her blocky head. There was nothing they could do, but they wove in and out of the fire like a wreath, and then when the heat became most intense, they came to stand around the humans, a circle of golden consciousness that couldn't and didn't block the waves of overheated electrons. Still it was a gesture Brad appreciated. It was a comfort, and much more comforting than that, within minutes, as the fire whispered and roared, Brad knew it was not going to kill them. This was the worst it would do, blistering their exposed skin. They would survive.

All the adults wore shoes made of leather and yucca rope, and they were grateful for this as they walked back upstream to the pools, the sand and gravel still hot, the pools also hot and steaming. They found a place to sit nearby, gingerly, in the sand and sun without shade for their burns since all the trees and shrubs were black sticks stabbing the sky. They were alive. They felt euphoric. They felt like talking. They counted their blessings. Brad had a daughter! And a son! Clare sat here beside him! She nursed his children. Clare laughed at his pleasure and beckoned to Elise. "Come here, sweetheart, meet your siblings." The little girl floated over, acting shy.

The babies, impossibly, fell asleep. The adults told their stories. Brad went first, the details boring to him since he already knew them and had spent most of his time in a badger's hole, dreaming about a horse's tail. Clare also described the birth quickly. That was over. She felt chagrined she had never guessed that Brad was tied up all the while, and Lucia, too, thrown in the pit next to Brad. Clare described Jon and his dark eyes in the birthing shelter, the way he held the boy without warmth or kindness, the way he stared at the girl as though she were food.

Clare was most concerned about what Jon had told Brad about the Council and elders. They knew everything. They had Brad's notes on his computer. Had they really sent Jon to take her and Brad back to the lab? Or had Jon come on his own, without permission?

"He thought Elise was . . . a ghost." Clare worried this piece of information. Jon had obviously been shaken by Elise. He thought her unnatural, the unique consciousness of a human reanchored, reassembled, without the physical biohologram. A new kind of being in the world. Perhaps he was having a religious crisis?

"That's a nice way of putting it," Brad said. "He tried to kill me, and he tried to kill Luke, to get us out of the way."

Clare corrected, "He didn't kill you, although he could have. He tied you up."

"He left us to burn!"

"Later, yes, when the fire came." Clare shook her head. She had known Jon all her life. He had always been a good hunter, singing sweetly by the fire. Brad had seen that himself at the summer camp: Everyone liked Jon. "I just can't believe . . . someone could change that much."

No one spoke for a moment. Then Luke said dryly, "I guess we've all changed."

Clare seemed happy to drop the subject. "He was taking me to the pools," she went on. "And then he suddenly stopped. He stopped, and I broke away so I could come back and find you, untie you, and then he grabbed me again. And then . . ." Clare looked around for Dog. But Elise, Dog, and the golden animals had gone wandering off some time ago. "The saber-toothed cat was there, jumping into Jon. *She jumped into him*. She disappeared. And Jon slumped over and fell down."

Brad had a lot of questions about that. But he asked only, "Was Jon dead?"

Clare didn't think so. She didn't know.

Brad shifted in his burned skin, his neck and arms painful. None of them wanted to think about what had happened to Jon when the fire swept over him. Certainly, they needed to have a talk with Dog. The golden animals had some explaining to do.

"If Jon didn't come on his own," Clare obsessed, "that means the Council does want to see us. He said they were angry, and that sounds true. What will they do about Elise? What if they take the babies away from us?" She looked down at the infants shaded by her body.

Brad wanted to hold her but couldn't make himself move. "We'll never let that happen," he said.

Now Luke told his version, how Jon had attacked him late in the night when Clare was sleeping and Lucia relieving herself under the glittering stars, enjoying this rare moment alone—the river of stars, the open plain after the cramped birthing tree. Lucia had breathed in deeply. To the west, she could see lightning flashes in the sky. She could hear thunder and feel the heat of the day still rising from the ground. Perhaps the fire had started then. She had suddenly felt so tired. It had been a long birth. Before she could even shake herself dry, Jon had her in a chokehold on the ground and trussed like a javelina for roasting.

"We treat javelinas better," Brad said, watching Clare. Perhaps she would always feel sorry for her former student and lover. "We don't roast them alive."

"Well," Luke shrugged. "The man is dead now. You can be sure of that."

And Brad was sure, poking Jon's body with his foot. Perhaps that was disrespectful, but he felt he had earned a little revenge. Then he felt guilty. He would not have wished this death on anyone. Then he felt vengeful again. The hunter had left him and Lucia to the same death.

Dog and Luke watched him kick the blackened flesh. The three of them were on their way back to the birthing tree where Brad hoped to salvage his solarcomp, maybe his eyeglasses, anything of use spared by the flames. Brad noted that Jon's body was fairly close to the streambed, a good distance from where the hunter had stood with Clare when the saber-toothed cat jumped into his brain and put him to sleep. At least, that was Dog's story. The hunter had only been put to sleep.

"He must have woken up," Brad murmured to himself. "Tried to run."

"We could bring him back," Dog urged suddenly, speaking to Luke, too. "If you took something now, some DNA . . ."

Luke made a sound of disgust.

"No," Brad said firmly. This was finally the right decision. He had promised Clare and Luke both. He thought of Clare, waiting by the pools. With two babies. This was still a surprise. "No," Brad repeated. "That's not going to happen. That's never going to happen again."

"Muck-a-luck, it's never going to happen," Luke said and pointed his finger aggressively at Dog. "One of yours killed a human being. Have you forgotten that?"

Dog lowered his head and nosed his flank as if biting for a tick. He shook himself like someone finished with grooming, sat on his haunches, and went through his explanation again. Brad only half listened. They had already heard Dog make this speech, with Clare and Brad and Luke asking questions, with the saber-toothed cat standing nearby but not speaking herself.

Yes, the saber-toothed cat had leapt into Jon's mind and body, lying next to a certain neural network. She had—to use a metaphor—begun to eat, like chewing the gristle on a bone. Chew, chew, chew. Gnaw, gnaw, gnaw. The saber-toothed cat used the memory of her jaw muscles, the strength of those muscles, to bite down, tear down, tear apart. She only had to cut through one connection between sleep and wakefulness, a little bit of gristle connecting one thing to another.

"But it was a physical connection in the brain," Luke said now, again.

Dog admitted that.

"I thought you couldn't affect the physical world?"

Dog had thought so, too. But not all parts of the brain were purely physical. Sleep was a transitional time, consciousness deliberately becoming unconscious. Sleep wasn't about death or physical injury, a lack of blood to the brain or an absence of oxygen. Sleep was a kind of choice. And saber-toothed cats had a special relationship with humans. They loved humans.

"She didn't hurt him," Dog insisted. "She only put him to sleep. That's all she can do. She put him to sleep just that one time. You were in trouble! It was an emergency."

"What about you?" Luke pressed. "Can *you* jump into our brains and eat them?"

This question had also been asked before, and Brad understood that Luke simply needed the reassurance. He needed to hear Dog say it again.

"No," Dog said. "Only the saber-toothed cat."

Brad watched as Luke sighed and let his shoulders loosen. Saber-toothed cats had always been drawn to the flesh of humans, their favorite food. That was normal. That was familiar. Dog was clearly telling the truth. Surprisingly, Brad also felt better now. The direwolf twined around Luke's legs before moving forward and pretending to sniff at Jon's corpse, the clothes and skin burned away. Then he looked back meaningfully at the two men. They got the message. This could have been them, not Jon.

"What's done is done," Brad said out loud, and he meant all of it—all they had done, and Luke understood that, too. Without speaking, they walked on to the charred juniper tree where Brad's melted solarcomp lay with the other debris, ash and lumps of nothing useful. There was nothing to bring back to Clare. All their supplies were gone but the clothes and shoes they wore and the sling with the image of a swallow. They didn't have any spears. They didn't have any water bottles or gourds. They didn't have a bone awl. They didn't have any medicine. They didn't have a way to communicate with the lab or Clare's tribe or any tribe. They didn't have any maps to pull up on the solarcomp they didn't have. Brad didn't have any eyeglasses. They were all in some pain, with first-degree burns. Only the babies had escaped injury.

Brad thought of what they did have. Water and the skills to get food. Water and the skills to make what they needed. Water and the option of scavenging in the abandoned cites for what they couldn't make. Back to Los Alamos, Brad thought reluctantly. He knew the store where the eyeglasses would be kept in a bottom drawer. He remembered bursting into tears at the children's playground, the waves of sadness.

"Hey," Luke rummaged at the base of the blackened tree. "Oh, well, no." Luke sounded disappointed. "Never mind."

For no reason at all, Brad thought of Jon's biohologram deflating. He imagined that moment when Jon's unique consciousness dissolved into the larger consciousness, knowing everything now, part of everything.

No one wanted a campfire that night. They stretched on the sand by the pools, eating the cooked meat Clare had stripped from the rabbits and mice caught unaware by the flames. Luke had also gathered yucca root, already half-baked, and mesquite beans from a stand of trees downstream, inexplicably untouched. Tomorrow, Luke promised, he would find what he needed to make a paste for their injured skin. The coolness of the night refreshed them, and Brad thought he smelled rain.

"Rain?" Clare looked up at a cloudless sky, the stars appearing in small groups. "Tomorrow," Brad predicted, "I think it will rain."

Clare was dubious but willing to believe. "That would be nice," she said amiably. Soon she fell asleep, the babies asleep, at least for a few hours.

Elise and the golden animals wandered away. Dog stayed by Luke.

The old man lay on his back staring up at darkness, stars shimmering and a sliver of moon. "What were you thinking?" Luke murmured. The refrain was a joke that had never been funny and now was just annoying.

"You know the story of George Fox," Dog said, as though he had grown up all his life a Quaker in Costa Rica. The voice of the direwolf sounded clearly in Brad's thoughts and, Brad knew, in Luke's as well. "When George Fox's wife went to her husband and asked him to prove the existence of God's love, he said he could not. Only she could prove the existence of God's love. 'How can God prove the existence of His love?' George Fox asked his wife. 'Can He speak to us through the trees? Through the animals? Through the sky? No, He speaks to us through you. He proves His love through you. How can He prove His love? He has only Thee.'"

"So He has Thee now, Dog?" Luke asked.

"Yes, we exist now," Dog said. "Because of you."

The old man muttered, "I was a crazy bushkie. Brad should have never listened to me. You should have never . . ."

Brad half listened to them quarrel, the same old quarrel, and then he didn't listen, thinking instead about the future of his children. He felt fierce. Focused. They would have a future. His children would live in abundance, the best of times, the best of worlds.

CHAPTER TWENTY-FIVE

CLARE

In a landscape billowing soot, the remains of trees and bushes looked like corpses. The pools were a barren difficult place without shade, the wind whirling ash into Clare's eyes. Even so, they stayed almost another week, eating the actual corpses left behind by the fire, building a ramada out of mesquite, and resting as much as possible. They needed something to carry water in, and Brad went back to Jon to discover that his fallen body had protected the gourds tied at his waist. (Clare thought of Jon, whom she would leave here soon. His bones would not be gathered now or mourned by the tribe but picked up casually by coyotes and ravens and carried away.) Luke made a spear, showing unexpected flair at knapping stone. Brad made rabbit snares that were less elegant but perfectly usable. Clare nursed the babies and sent her strength flowing into them and back into her. They prepared to journey on, even though they had no idea yet what direction they would take.

Luke argued for the south. The peyote fields had a bad reputation, but for that very reason they were a good place to hide. Surviving where less grass grew and fewer animals ate the grass would be difficult. The south was hotter, drier, thornier, unpredictable. But they were a functional group, not a lone bushkie sent out to die. Importantly, the elders might accept this as a kind of self-exile. If Clare and Brad and Luke willingly chose to remove themselves, the Council might not feel the need to come after them. The peyote fields would be their punishment. They would be left alone.

Brad was adamantly opposed to the idea. The south was too dangerous, not just a difficult place to survive—as barren and bleak as this, Brad gestured at the dead trees and black soil surrounding them, using the burnt legacy of the grass fire to bolster his argument—but potentially full of murderous bushkies. Surely Luke remembered being kidnapped by bushkies, tied up, and almost sacrificed in a stone circle? Apparently bushkies could also form groups, bands of delusional schizophrenics. Brad had no intention of sending his family into that kind of danger. And he objected to the assumption that he and Luke and Clare needed to be punished—to go into exile. Instead they should go back to the lab, where he would plead their case. He had important friends at the lab. He had influence.

Luke shot back that it was Brad who was being delusional if he thought he could talk the Council and elders into ignoring what had happened with Dog. With Elise. With the golden animals. Rules central to their culture had been dangerously ignored. Defied. Overthrown. Thanks to the Round River people, this was no secret either. By now everyone in the world had heard some kind of rumor that was becoming a story bigger and more imaginative every day. Luke remembered well the self-preserving politics of the Council. With all the North American tribes watching them, *and* the Russians *and* the Costa Rican Quakers, the elders would *not* pat Brad on the head and tell him to go off and be a good boy next time. At the least, they would take away the babies and give them to proper parents to raise. At the least, they would ban Elise and the golden animals from the lab and the camps. At the least, or at least likely, they would imprison one or more of the three adults. At the most—who knew what they would do?

Clare let the men talk out their ideas, arguing in the ramada, arguing while they made their hunting weapons. She listened to both sides, her mind so much clearer now, more and more back to her old self. (Only sometimes she felt her stomach drop at the enormity of what she had done. She looked at Elise and could hardly believe this was her daughter, this shimmering creature. Her life made whole.) Finally one night she called for a decision as they ate dinner, billowing clouds in the west lit with pink and orange like a grass fire in the sky. Clare listened again as the two men repeated their main points. When Brad's voice rose to a certain level, she intervened.

"Of course, you're both right," Clare said from behind the babies. "We have to hide from the Council. We have to find a safe place to live. And we have to think about the future as well, for our children and for ourselves. We want to flourish, not just survive. So there has to be a third alternative. There has to be . . . somewhere the Council and the elders won't find us, at least not for a certain amount of time. There has to be somewhere close by the lab but not too close where we can hide but still negotiate with the tribes."

"North, still?" Luke protested.

"North, but where no one goes. Where no one has a reason to go," Clare said. "Maybe the hunting is bad. Maybe there's a bad feeling. Something we can live with. A place they won't think about. Meanwhile we'll keep in contact. We'll arrange meetings—on our own terms."

"Not a city, not a town," Brad objected. "They are too sad."

Luke looked at Dog.

"What?" Clare prompted.

"Yes, that might work," Dog said to everyone.

Luke and Dog had been to this place a long time ago, south of the lab, east of Albuquerque. They had climbed to the top of a high mesa rimmed with rock where the Acoma Pueblo had stood for over a thousand years. For hundreds of years, only one trail snaked up to the village, with a rope ladder for the last treacherous feet. Inaccessibility was the pueblo's defense, since few enemies wanted to make an attack huffing and climbing a steep slope. Later in the twentieth century, people had built a road, also winding dizzily upward. That road was the main access now, the trail lost and overgrown.

Brad had never heard of the Acoma Pueblo.

Luke pointed out that this was a good sign.

"There'd be no water on the mesa," Brad countered.

"Rain catchments, nano catchments," Luke replied. "People lived there before."

"We'd go elsewhere for hunting then."

"That's mostly what they did. They grew food, too."

Clare could see that Luke was conceding. Perhaps Brad's reminders had convinced him, how the bushkies had thrown stones, rocking him backward. And how Clare had saved him, her spear in the crazy bushkie's chest—although that seemed a thousand years ago, too. The old man shrugged at her. Was this what she wanted? Would this make her happy? She nodded back, and after a time, after more questions, Brad also nodded, conceding as well. Clare knew he was thinking they could shelter on the mesa temporarily, while he emailed and cajoled his friends at the lab, using his charms to talk them back home.

Clare nursed the boy. The girl was asleep. Clare didn't think they could ever go home. She remembered Jon's reaction to Elise. Other people would feel the same way. Her children would never be accepted in the lab or in the tribes. Clare felt the grief of that. She felt regret for her lost family and friends. But she felt the pull at her breast more. She remembered how much babies anchored you to them.

Brad and Luke began to plan. For their first months, maybe through winter, the mesa was big enough to provide food, with plenty of mice and rabbits, probably even a resident deer herd. And Luke hadn't felt any sadness from the pueblo. Probably not many people had lived there at the time of the supervirus. Luke only had good memories of his stay there, chanting to the sun, killing a bear with Dog, eating bear fat.

In the dimming light of day, Brad drew a route in the sand. He wanted to stop at Los Alamos for a pair of eyeglasses and the things he needed to build a solarcomp. But—Brad reconsidered and redrew his map—Los Alamos took them too far north. So it would have to be Albuquerque, and that wasn't good. Albuquerque was one of the big places that receivers avoided.

"What will we do about fire?" Luke wondered. "That's what brought in the Round River people."

"Right," Brad thought. "We'll have to come up with new ways of preparing meat, baking roots. We can make solar ovens . . ."

We will have to come up with rules, Clare thought, as she put the babies down beside her in their nest of rabbit fur. If they were going to build a new community, they had to make agreements, contracts of behavior among the humans and between the humans and the golden animals. She had already talked to Dog and the saber-toothed cat. She knew what the big cat had done, leaping into Jon's mind, putting him to sleep. She had already warned Dog and the cat both: This could never happen again. They would have to agree never again to interfere with the physical world, the world of humans.

"I promise," Dog had said.

"I promise," said the saber-toothed cat.

Clare had never known a Paleo to lie or be able to lie.

"No, we can't," Dog told her. "We can't lie to you."

There would have to be rules, Clare thought, for the people who would eventually come to the mesa to see the golden animals and to see Elise. Because, Clare knew, once the Council and elders had been pacified, these people *would* come. They couldn't be stopped. Like Brad, they would want to know. They would be curious. They would be eager. Unlike Jon, they wouldn't be afraid of Elise as a ghost or spirit. She was something new. A door had opened. A wind was blowing through the open door. Eventually, some of these people would want to join their community, and that would be a good thing as the babies grew up and needed children to play with and marriage partners, too. This would be the start of a new tribe, different from any other tribe in the world, any other in the history of the world.

Clare understood that she, herself, would have to change. She would have to accept the golden animals as part of her family. They shouldn't have to hide from her or follow behind. There shouldn't be any more secrets.

And she would have to be more firm with Elise. People would be coming to meet the little girl, and Elise would need to make these people comfortable, to comb and braid her hair, to walk on the ground. Clare thought she had already seen a difference in her oldest daughter. Now she was a big sister with responsibilities. She was already maturing, speaking more seriously, not so flighty or self-absorbed.

There would have to be rules. You shouldn't do something just because you could. There would have to be new agreements. They were moving now beyond The Return, and that thought made Clare open her eyes in the darkness, where she lay next to the babies. They would have to be careful. Thoughtful. Clare let the two men plan out food and water and cooking and eyeglasses while the moon rose and the stars appeared and the babies murmured. The boy gave a big yawn. The girl sighed as though in the middle of a dream.

Clare had to watch where she put her feet. In the last hundred fifty years, the asphalt road had cracked and heaved, and grass and shrubs now covered these holes. It would be easy to turn an ankle or trip and spill the babies from their sling. Clare watched her feet and tried to look only at the view when she and Brad and Luke stopped to catch their breath as they climbed up, up, and up the steep road, the plain of yellow grass spreading below, the mesas and buttes spreading into the distance. In their travels here, stopping at a small town outside Albuquerque, getting their supplies, and then walking quickly east, Clare had noted these pillars of rock standing like sentinels, red rock layered with white. All the mountains in this area were bare boned, without trees, sculptures of wind. There would be less game here in this vast desert bowl and fewer people looking for game, and that suited Clare just fine.

They switchbacked to the top of the mesa, the blue space below getting bigger and bigger, more and more space everywhere. Clare's rib cage seemed to expand. Her heart ached with a longing to fly, and her limbs felt lighter, her bones weightless—as if she really *could* fly: jump up, flap her wings, and be gone. Oh, yes, she thought, she would like living here. She would like all this space and sky.

"*A Stairway to Heaven*," Brad said.

Clare smiled back. "I don't know that quote."

"It's the title of an old book from the twenty-first century, a biography of Albert Einstein. *A Stairway to Heaven*."

"I've never heard of it."

"When we get the solarcomp working," Brad promised, "when we have the web again, you can read it." Brad was also in high spirits, wearing a new pair of eyeglasses, with a second pair in his pack along with the motherboard and computer supplies they had scavenged.

Clare nodded, although she doubted she would have time in the immediate future to read a book. Once they reached the pueblo, there was so much work to do and so few people to do that work. Still . . . she let her mind drift a bit, with Luke and Brad right beside her watching for animals or signs of danger, with Dog and the golden animals looking after them, too.

She thought of her students. She would make time for a long email. She owed them an explanation, and she wanted to write it all out from beginning to end, not holding anything back. At least, not anything important. She would start with Brad's quest and how they had met Luke. What Brad and Luke had done to bring back Dog's unique consciousness. What she had done. She'd tell them about Elise. That would be shocking, she knew. But she'd be honest about everything. (Except, perhaps, about Jon. What he had done. You could draw boundaries when you wrote. Jon had behaved badly. She didn't need to tell the world.)

She'd introduce the golden animals. The bears, the horses (the darling colt), the deer, the mice, the camel, the calico cat. She'd describe the two Paleos, Dog and the saber-toothed cat, and the long talks they sometimes had now that these animals spoke in sentences.

"Dear Carlos," Clare imagined writing. Yes, she would send each one an individual letter, something personal. "When I read your last email to me, I was touched. It's natural to feel that way about a teacher, especially one with whom you have shared the intimacy of writing but never knew physically. You never saw me sneeze or act grouchy in the morning. You felt liberated at how easily and powerfully you could express your feelings and thoughts when you wrote, and you projected some of that good feeling—that love and joy of creative expression—onto me. I became your confidante and we have, indeed, had many good collaborative moments in your papers . . ."

Brad spoke suddenly, "Have you ever grown food?"

"Oh, you know," Clare brought herself back. "It's not exactly against The Return. It just never seemed necessary. We throw out seeds of plants we like to eat. We don't tend them but we plant them, I guess, where we know they'll get more water than usual."

"I think we had a garden at the lab. I can't believe I never paid any attention."

"Hmm," Clare said.

Brad began to plan a garden.

Dear Alice, I'm so sorry I stopped responding to your assignments. In truth, I didn't know what to say. My life and plans were very uncertain then, and I didn't want to upset you with possibilities and ideas that I didn't yet understand myself. Now things seem a little more settled, and I want you to know that I very much enjoyed reading about your "adventures" in China. I was also pleased to see how you acted as your own editor when you pretended to know and respond to what I would say. Yes, you wandered off topic and lost the thread of your plot. But sometimes that can be fruitful, when we are trying to discover what is really most important to us, when we are trying, still, to find our real themes—the heart of the story.

As for the Chinese coming to get us in airplanes, I think you are right again—that's not going to happen. On the other hand, other surprises may . . .

Dear Dimitri, I know that change can be difficult. It's upsetting that someone in your tribe wants to start using guns to protect yourselves from the tigers that are growing more numerous in your area. Of course, I agree with you. I also think that relying on guns for this problem would be a bad idea. Like you, I believe your tribe can come up with more creative solutions.

Do try to remember, though, that the person who is trying to make this happen had a son who died and that he or she is still grieving that loss. It may not be easy for you to understand the feelings that come with the death of a child, the sense of disharmony and disconnect, but I have experienced them myself, and I know these feelings sometimes make us do things we wouldn't do otherwise. I will explain more about that later in this email.

First I want to talk with you about The Return, which we cannot think of as something that will always remain the same. Our ancestors lived this kind of life for tens of thousands of years, but eventually, inevitably, something happened and things changed. Paleos like the mammoth and saber-toothed cat disappeared, and for a long time that affected how we saw physics and the relationship of consciousness to matter. The cloning of the Paleos was another change. And global warming. And the supervirus. As with many processes—think in terms of the metamorphosis within the moth's cocoon—change triggers more change and then change can start happening ever more quickly. The Return now is part of the accelerating nature of human and cultural evolution. The Quakers remind us, "All is flux." In that flux and chaos, many things happen that are outside our control. What we are able to control is our own acceptance and response . . .

Dear María, I am so proud of you for your long quest, your quinceañera! I know your parents must be proud, too. You'll be taking your place as an adult now in your tribe. You'll start to make decisions with the others, and perhaps someday you will even be an elder yourself and certain important decisions will be yours to make . . .

CHAPTER TWENTY-SIX

DOG

Dog sat and admired the view. A thunderstorm built in the west, billows of white and gray and dark-gray cumulonimbus forming into massive towers, warm air rising through rapidly dropping temperatures until the condensed water and ice became heavy enough to fall, the electrical energy building as more water and ice particles were repeatedly split and separated. Here and there shafts of sun pierced through the cloudscape illuminating a red rock butte or patch of yellow grass. The world glowed, bathed in color, saturated with red and orange and yellow. The plain of grass and desert scrub and rock formations stretched to the horizon, bounded by bony mountains in the far distance. Some of the mountains looked like sleeping animals, some like the parts of human giants—a resting head, a shoulder and arm. Dog knew the old myths, what Clare told Elise at her pretend bedtime, what she whispered to the babies as they fell asleep. Spider Woman. The Warrior Twins. Lucy the Staunch Standard Poodle.

Humans loved stories just as Dog loved stories.

Now the golden animals surrounded him. They couldn't stay away for long. The golden animals admired the view. A small puffy cloud scuttled in front of the thunderstorm like a white-tailed deer. A dazzling spear of lightning cracked open the sky. The earth boomed.

Elise was singing. Then she interrupted herself, "My mother needs me back home." As she practiced keeping her holo-feet on the ground, the child teetered on the edge of rimrock, the drop below her straight down, heart-stopping if any of them had a heart. Lately Elise had taken on the task of entertaining her brother and sister while Clare prepared animal skins and finished the winter garden that Brad had started and soon abandoned. The four-year-old was also letting Clare braid and fuss over her hair. She had a little bit of the horse in her now, compliant and willing to please, and she had Dog's voice whispering in her ear about what love meant, what it meant to make the people you love happy. She loved her mother. And she loved the babies, their contagious smiles when she made funny faces and told them jokes.

"You have time," the saber-toothed cat said. "They'll nap a little longer."

The saber-toothed cat also liked to help Clare, nudging the babies to sleep when they were fussy, when they got tired of pruning their neural networks and learning language and mastering the movements of their arms and legs. The twins were working hard, and they were hard work, too, for everyone else. No one had foreseen how hard it would be raising up human twins.

Dog thought of Brad, who was also working doubly hard, taking his turn with the babies, hunting rabbits, gathering roots, thinking up new inventions like solar ovens that cooked their food without smoke—and then, at night, spending hours at his computer. His stream of tedious emails to the Council. His secret emails to the blonde-haired woman and other allies. His theories and explanations broadcast to the tribes around the world, with math equations at the end.

Like Clare, Dog believed Brad was naive when he insisted that someday the Council would let them come back to the lab. That all would be forgiven. This was not Dog's own experience. He remembered his mother's teeth on his neck.

"Look," Elise spoke, and Dog let her voice surprise him. "Something beautiful."

Thirteen sunflowers of varying size from one to three meters floated in the air just past the rimrock ledge. Each one had its composite disk of flowers, each ray flower adding to the circle's edge with a long curling yellow petal, each flower in the center containing an ovule fertilized and becoming a seed. The composite disk, the thick stalk, the large healthy leaves glowed, luminous, like a pillar of light.

Dog was so happy he pretended to drool although there was no one like Luke or Brad to see him. He was so happy he did a whirl, a dance, his front legs held stiffly in front. He was so happy he wagged his tail, which was not something direwolves normally did. He had so hoped the sunflowers would return to them after finding each other in the past, after gathering together as a group.

"Beautiful!" the golden animals spoke together. The golden sunflowers lined up like musical notes on the score of a song. Or now, as they shifted, like the strokes of a Chinese ideogram. These images, the golden animals knew, came from Brad and Dog's long delicious afternoon with the peyote plant and the musically flowing stream and Brad's TOE. Dog had seen then: Sunflowers had a good relationship with Brad. Who could explain it? They simply liked him.

"Come closer," Dog suggested. Did they need to be coaxed?

The sunflowers drifted back and forward. They waited. They were mute.

Merge and separate. "Shall we?" Dog asked the group.

But the question did not immediately become assent.

Surprisingly, the saber-toothed cat hesitated.

Dog understood. The saber-toothed cat had a little bit of the dire-wolf in her now. Just a little bit, she wanted to run away. Because plants were so different. Their consciousness was so different. Their experience of time was on the quantum level. Look at how they had traveled backward—to that long-ago afternoon before Dog and Luke had ever met Brad, before Brad had turned on his radios. Plants were different in the way rocks were different with their crystalline structure.

Dog felt a quiver in the land as though a red rock butte had suddenly startled, as though the bony hills had opened their eyes. His own haunches quivered with sympathy, the muscles that were not really there. Where would it end? The water rushing in. The barriers breached. Many different species side by side, dependent on each other, inside each other, combined into one thing.

Dog and Luke were on an adventure together in a cave overlooking a slickrock canyon, waiting out a violent rain. Although Brad and Clare seemed content on the mesa, Luke more often went exploring, going down to the plain for bigger game, watching for signs of other tribes. In truth, Luke was often restless and needed to be away from the domesticity of camp. Usually Dog went with him, half the golden animals staying with the babies and the others trailing discreetly behind.

Dog couldn't help but worry on these trips. He often annoyed Luke by urging their return to the mesa, where it was safe. The high crumbling pueblo was not only remote and free of large predators but also defensible against other people. The winding road remained the only access to the top, and this narrowed the area the golden animals had to patrol. Dog always kept someone at the entrance to that road, most often one of the five mice. In an emergency, a golden animal would send out the alarm. In an emergency, the saber-toothed cat would put their enemies to sleep. No one would be allowed to hurt Dog's humans. No one would take the twins away.

Just thinking about it, the habit of Dog growled.

Of course, he couldn't protect Luke or Brad or Clare or the twins from other enemies. Not from disease or old age or accident. Dog thought of Jon and felt regret. The hunter's sweetness. The hunter's darkness. Jon would have been a good addition to their group. Dog rested his muzzle on his paws, watching the rain fall and fill the newly running creek below. "This rain will loosen the soil," he said to Luke. "You should be careful of rock slides. And flooding."

"You're as bad as a ground sloth," Luke grumped. He was in one of his moods.

"Watch out," a sunflower whispered in Dog's ear. Dog felt the scruff of his neck being grabbed and, forewarned, he lifted his head as though in response.

"Listen to me, Dog. I'm serious about this." Luke shook Dog lightly. "When it's my time, just let me dissolve. I'm not coming back."

Showing his teeth, Dog broke away and snapped at the crazy old bushkie before settling back into a lump of slightly damp fur, nose to tail, curled at Luke's side and staring morosely at the rain.

Someday, years in the future, Luke would be a good addition to their group. Someday, many years past that, Brad and Clare would be a good addition to their group, as would their children and grandchildren. Other golden animals had found a way. Like the sunflowers, other golden animals were coming toward the mesa, slowly, not in a hurry, but ineluctably drawn. They no longer needed Brad's radios. They no longer needed Dog's numbers—sine and cosine. Slowly the group would grow and gather strength, merge and separate, merge and separate, become something new. Slowly the group would become bigger and bigger until someday, many many years from now, the entire planet would be a ball of light.

"Just let me go," the old man muttered.

Lovingly, Dog licked Luke's hand. As if he would ever let that happen.